APPALACHIAN DAUGHTER

MARY JANE SALYERS

DEDICATION

To all the daughters,
who like me,
grew up in Appalachia.

ACKNOWLEDGMENTS

Many thanks to the writers group who met at my house and were my first readers, especially Nancy Flinchbaugh, whose encouragement helped keep me going. I am indebted to the teachers and participants at the Green Lake Writers Conference, the Appalachian Writers Workshop, and the Antioch Writers' Workshop for their instruction, advice, and critiques–especially Barbara Smith, who copy edited an early version of the manuscript. Dozens of family and friends read the manuscript at various stages and gave me helpful feedback. I have neither space nor memory to name all of you– but your interest and suggestions were invaluable. I'll mention two: Fran Randall, whose enthusiasm gave me the impetus to begin the publishing process; and Marjorie Dolbeer, who proofread the final copy. Special thanks to my husband, Bill Salyers. I couldn't have done it without his help, advice, and encouragement, not to mention his computer skills. Finally, I must thank my Tennessee family and neighbors whose lives and experiences were the inspiration for Maggie's story.

Campbell Holler–October 7, 1895   Harvey has tore my heart out. Johnny and Jimmy are gone. May never see them again. Will his rage never end?

(Diary of Mary Louise Campbell)

CHAPTER 1

Harlan, Ky–May 20, 1875   Wedding day. Harvey arrived yesterday. Has wagon and team to haul our goods. Says cabin and barn built. Leave tomorrow for the property in Tenn. So proud to be his wife.
(Diary of Mary Louise Campbell)

May 1949

Kneeling beside her locker in the elementary wing of the school building, Maggie Martin listened with a sinking heart as her eighth grade classmates discussed their summer plans.   Visualizing her own summer as three months of drudgery and tedium cooped up in Campbell Holler like a caged bird, she shook her head as if she could throw off the dread of isolation and loneliness.

Maggie and her best friend, Mary Ann Collins, had emptied their locker, stacking their books on the floor and sorting the various odds and ends they had accumulated. Maggie shot the last piece of scrap into a trash can like a basketball through the hoop. "We better hurry. Time for the last bell, and everyone else has gone back to the classroom."

As Maggie bent to lift the stack of books, someone slammed into her knocking her down, scattering her books in all directions. Lying on the floor, arms and legs flailing wildly, she focused on the face above hers– Walter Spinks, a senior. "Hey, you big ox, get off me!"

"Sorry, Maggie, I tripped." Walter's big ears and wide grin reminded her of a monkey–a monkey who made no attempt to get up, but purposely ran his hand under her blouse.

1

Maggie shoved at him and screamed, "Get your hands off me, you big ape!" Struggling frantically and kicking the trash can over, scattering papers over the hallway, she grabbed a book and swung as hard as she could from her awkward position, catching his temple with a satisfying thwack.

"Why, you little bitch!" Walter rolled over and sat up holding his head with both hands.

Maggie leaped up, raised the book high, and whammed it down hard on the top of his head. "Don't you ever touch me again or I'll kill you!"

Mary Ann, almost to the classroom door, turned as soon as she heard the commotion and hurried to Maggie. "Are you hurt?"

"I'm not hurt! But I'm mad as a riled up hornet!" She shook her history book menacingly at Walter. "Get up, you big lunkhead, and get out of here, or I'll hit you again!"

Groaning and holding his head, Walter got slowly to his feet just as Mrs. Weldon, the eighth grade teacher, stepped into the hallway. "What's going on here?" she demanded, twisting her head on her long skinny neck like a suspicious vulture.

"I accidently tripped and bumped Maggie," Walter, still holding his head, said innocently while backing toward the door to the parking lot. "I apologized, but she hit me with her book." He pushed the door open and rushed out a second before the bell.

"Maggie, that temper of yours will get you into a peck of trouble if you're not careful. Now get this mess cleaned up." Mrs. Weldon pointed to the trash scattered over the hallway then turned back to the classroom.

Maggie glared daggers at Mrs. Weldon's back. *I hate you, you old hag!* Gathering her books, she joined her classmates exiting the building, leaving the trash on the floor. Fighting tears, she walked toward her bus hardly responding to her friends. "Bye Maggie." "Have a good summer." "See you in ninth grade." She slammed her books onto her favorite seat in the back of the school bus, and opened the window, her face flushed and contorted. *When did it get so hot? Not at all like May weather.* Sweat ran into her eyes. After wiping at the sweat with the back of her hand, she straightened her clothes, tucking her blouse into her skirt, and flopped onto the seat.

She held her honey-brown braids on top of her head while she fanned the back of her neck with her report card. She crossed her legs and jiggled her foot, restless as a mother hen sighting a circling hawk. She brushed her disheveled hair away from her face. *I hate Walter Spinks. I wish he was dead!* She took a deep breath, but the air felt heavy in her lungs like breathing mist. Her side hurt where Walter had crashed into her, and she felt bedraggled like her grandmother's old red hen after a raccoon tried to carry her away.

She smoothed the skirt her mother had made from feed sacks over her knees. Her mother had complained this morning when Maggie had worn it, saying she should save it for her Sunday best. *Seems like Mama and me is always having our differences these days. We didn't used to have so many disagreements, but here lately, she finds fault with everything I do. She probably won't even look at my report card—much less notice I made all A's. She thinks I should forget school.*

Maggie knew her mother agreed with most of their mountain neighbors who said too much education corrupted the young. Maggie's mother, Corie Mae, quit school before she was as old as Maggie. She would like Maggie to stay home and help with the difficult work required to provide for the large family. Thankful her father wanted her to go on to high school and took pride in the good grades she made, she sighed and closed her burning eyes. Now thinking of the long summer ahead of her, she already felt lonesome for her friends. *I feel like the little lost sheep in the Bible.*

"Move your books Maggie Martin."

Snapping out of her reverie, she lifted the books onto her lap to make room for her cousin, JD Campbell, who slouched into the seat, a big grin on his face, his dark, curly hair falling over his forehead. "Wake me when we get to the holler," he murmured, folding his arms over his chest and closing his eyes. She looked at JD's long, dark eyelashes curled up from his closed eyelids. *I see why all the girls go crazy about him.* Although nearer in age to JD's younger brother Kenny, she felt closer to JD, who seemed more like an older brother than a cousin. Having grown up together in Campbell Hollow in houses only one hundred yards apart, they had spent countless hours playing and working side by side since their toddler days.

With disheartened spirit, Maggie stared out the window at the students scurrying for their busses. When the bus driver started the motor, Maggie shook JD's arm. "Quick, JD, check if all the kids got on. Mama'll kill me if one of them misses the bus!"

Slowly getting to his feet, JD counted them off. "One, two three, four, five—yep, everybody's here." He slid down, resting his head against the back of the seat, and closed his big brown eyes again. He had rolled the sleeves of his plaid shirt almost to his shoulders, exposing his bulging biceps. She noticed the lump in the pocket made by a pack of cigarettes. His jeans, though faded, held a sharp crease.

Suddenly Maggie slumped down and hid her face behind a book. "Please don't let Walter Spinks see me."

JD opened his eyes and sat up. "What's he done now?"

"Right before the last bell, while I stooped down cleaning out my locker, he pretended to trip and fell down on top of me. My books went flying like an explosion. Then he put his hand under my blouse. I had to hit him with my history book to get him off. And then old witch Weldon yelled at me for hitting him."

3

JD stood, slapped his fist into his open palm, and stepped into the aisle. "That no count dog! I'm going to give him what he's got coming."

Maggie jumped up, spilling her books onto the floor, and pulled him back into his seat. "No, JD. Don't do it. Please. He's bigger than you. He'll kill you." Maggie held tightly to his arm. "Besides, I fight my own battles. I hit him so hard he's going to see stars for a week. Please, stay out of this."

JD jerked his arm loose and stood up again glaring at Walter, who had taken a seat behind Johnny Ray, Maggie's little brother. "I don't care. It's time somebody taught him a lesson."

"Please, JD," Maggie begged, dragging him back to his seat again. "Here, help me pick up my books. Mama has a fit if our books get so banged up she can't sell them for the best price. You don't want her taking a switch to me, do you?"

JD sighed and reluctantly stooped to pick up the books, placing them back in Maggie's lap. He slumped into the seat once more. "I'll get him yet, just wait and see."

Maggie punched his arm with her elbow. "Forget about Walter. I don't think he'll have nerve enough to look at me after this, much less touch me. I hope I gave him a concussion that lasts for a week."

"At least you won't have to worry about him after today. I heard he's joining the Marines." JD rubbed his hands together. "Just think. We've got three whole months with no school. I'm going to have one great summer."

"I hate summers. So much work. We plow, we plant, we hoe, we pick, we can, we wash, we iron every day from sunup to dark. I never get to go anywhere or see my friends. I'd rather go to school any day." Maggie slumped under the weight of the dreary prospects for her summer. She understood the necessity of the hard work, and she willingly did her part with a competence beyond her fourteen years. But she chaffed under the isolation and loneliness. A blanket of sadness settled over her, and she took deep breaths to keep from suffocating.

JD sat up a little straighter. "I'm aiming to get me a job and buy a car. Then I won't be stuck in that holler working my tail off."

"Where can you get a job at?"

"I don't know, but I'll think of something. I'm sick of Mama treating me like a six-year-old. Getting out the first chance I get." He closed his eyes again.

She sighed. Without JD she looked forward to a totally intolerable summer—like losing an arm or a leg. She wished she could get a job. Then she could buy clothes for high school next year. *I hate wearing feed sack dresses. But Mama'd never let me go to work even if I could get a job.* She swallowed, trying to hold back tears that stung her eyelids.

4

JD opened one eye and looked sideways at Maggie. "What's the matter, Cuz? You look about as happy as a hound dog with the mange."

Maggie turned toward him. "On top of being attacked by that big ape, I found out today we have to buy uniforms for gym next year. Mama'll never agree for me to wear shorts. She won't even let me wear jeans or pants unless I'm picking berries. She says it's a sin for a woman to dress like a man. But ever'body'll make fun of me if I have to take gym in a dress!" Maggie looked out the window so JD wouldn't see the tears in her eyes.

JD grinned. "Easy. You don't tell her. I do all kinds of stuff Mama would beat me black and blue if she knew. I just don't tell her."

"I can't keep her from knowing. I'll have to buy the gym suit somehow, and I'll have to take it home to wash."

"Maggie, Aunt Corie Mae's too hard on you. She has tied you to her apron strings so tight you'll never get away unless you put your foot down and tell her what you aim to do."

"But you know what a bad temper Mama's got. She don't tolerate backtalk. She'd thrash me like whipping a copperhead if I did that."

JD shook his head and closed his eyes again. The bus had three more stops before reaching the stop for Campbell Holler. Maggie settled back in her seat. *If this is the way the summer will go, I'll never live through it.* She had barely shut her eyes, when Johnny Ray screamed. Both Maggie and JD leaped up, and Maggie's books slid onto the floor.

When they saw Johnny Ray holding his head and crying, they knew immediately what had happened. Walter Spinks liked to turn his class ring upside down and whack people on their heads as he went down the aisle to get off the bus.

"That does it! Going to get that sucker." JD rushed down the aisle after Walter, who had exited the bus.

"You'll get in trouble," Maggie yelled, but JD leaped out the door. The driver, ignoring the ruckus, closed the door and continued down the road. Maggie watched out the back window as JD and Walter slugged each other like mad drunks on a Saturday night.

"Hit him, JD! Beat the stuffing out of him." One of JD's classmates stood beside Maggie in the aisle looking out the rear window until the bus went around a curve.

That's really my fight. I should have got off with JD. But as the oldest, Maggie had the responsibility of seeing all the children home safely. "I hope he beats that bully to a pulp," she said under her breath, as she crawled around on the floor trying to retrieve her books. More likely Walter, a much larger boy, will whip JD, and then Aunt Opal will give him a worse thrashing.

Seated once more, sweat trickled down her back, and her blouse stuck to the back of the seat. The oppressive heat of the unseasonably warm weather added to Maggie's depression. She put her face closer to the open window to get some cooler air and stretched out her long legs. She noticed dark clouds in the west. *Maybe it will rain and cool things off.*

Maggie and Kenny made sure all the children crossed the highway safely after the bus dropped them at the road going up Campbell Hollow. Usually Johnny Ray complained constantly and wanted to stop in the shade, but today he skipped along with the neighbor children, kicking rocks in the dirt road and chanting, "School's out! School's out!"

The six families who lived in the hollow had a total of twelve school-age children. For the Martin and Campbell children, it meant a one-mile walk from the bus stop to their homes at the head of the holler. As they passed the unpainted houses of the neighbors, Maggie marveled at the contrast between those who worked hard to survive on a few hilly acres and those who lazed in careless squalor.

After a quarter mile, the road rose to the top of a hill where a large beech tree made a canopy creating a cool resting spot. They stood in the shade and waited for Johnny Ray, who lagged behind. "Johnny Ray, you better hurry and catch up," Maggie called. "Audie Lee Johnson's house is just ahead." Actually, the Johnsons' house was back a long lane hidden by a grove of pines, so that it was not visible from the road..

"I ain't afraid of Audie Lee Johnson," Johnny Ray called, but he hurried to catch up.

"Is Audie Lee deaf?" Jeannie, the youngest of the three Martin daughters, asked.

"I think he can hear okay, he just can't talk." Kenny kicked a rock from the roadway into the small stream that ran nearby.

"I think he's scary looking. I wouldn't want to meet up with him by myself." Jeannie hugged her stack of books tighter to her chest. "He staggers around like a drunk and always has that tow sack slung over his shoulder. I'd be scared to know what's in it." Jeannie moved to the other side of the road.

"He won't hurt you," Kenny said. "Mama says he's tetched in the head, but he don't hurt nobody."

Johnny Ray, out of breath from hurrying to catch up, argued , "That's not what Charlie Haskins told me. His mother told him if Audie Lee caught him after dark, he'd throw that sack over him and carry him away."

Kenny laughed, "Naw, that ain't so. His mother's just scaring him to make him come inside after dark. In all the years the Johnsons have lived in this holler, I ain't never heard tell of Audie Lee hurting a thing."

In newly planted fields, tiny corn plants made neat green rows stretching away from the road. The ridges forming the holler reached out like two arms hugging the valley between them. By the time they reached land belonging to the Campbells and Martins, the holler had narrowed considerably and the fields rose more steeply toward the sides of the ridges.

As they came over a small rise in the road, Maggie saw the roof of her house. The Martins lived in the old house her great-grandfather Campbell had built when he bought fifty acres at the head of the holler a few years after the Civil War. He originally built a two-room log cabin, but during the years he had added a second story, a lean-to kitchen, and front and back porches. Now the Martins filled it to overflowing with the family of seven children.

Maggie huddled the kids in the middle of the narrow, dirt road. "Don't none of you say a word about JD getting off the bus. Don't want him getting in trouble."

Kenny lifted Johnny Ray's chin, looking directly into his eyes. "That means you, Tattle Tale!" Then he turned toward his own home farther up the hollow.

* * *

An hour later Maggie sat on a low stool with the milk pail between her knees. The crown of her head pressed against Big Red's flank as she bent forward to reach the milk-swollen udders. During her tenth summer, her father had taught her to milk, and it became her job to milk their two cows every evening while her father did the morning milking.

Now that her father did not have to be home in the evening in time to milk, he often got an extra hour or two working as a laborer for other farmers in the area. For the last two years, he also had raised corn and hay on Mrs. Robinson's farm for half the produce. Maggie admired the way her father worked so hard to make things better for the family. He finally had saved enough to hire a well digger. They no longer had to carry water from the spring up the road, but they did have to draw up the water and carry it into the house. If they could get through the summer with no setbacks and have a good harvest, maybe by winter they could have the pump installed and bring the water into the kitchen.

Maggie thought about the many differences between her parents. Her father's calm demeanor, his sense of fairness, his delight in the accomplishments of the children, and his optimistic outlook contrasted sharply with her mother's approach to life. "Like day and night," she said aloud. However, she had to admit her mother was no slacker. Feeding and clothing a large family with their meager resources—a never ending job—Corie Mae managed with great competence, ingenuity, and resourcefulness. In that respect her parents were alike—both working from before daylight until after dark day after day.

Maggie lifted her head to wipe the sweat from her eyes with her sleeve.

She extended her lower lip and blew her breath up over her face. Earlier she had pinned her heavy braids on top of her head. Now she repositioned the bobby pins, which had worked loose. *Wonder how JD made out. Hope he didn't get beat up too bad.* Maggie rubbed her face with her other sleeve before she rested her head against Big Red's side and resumed milking. The cow's body had collected all the heat of the day, and now it radiated out stifling her breath and making her feel faint.

When she finished, she stood, carefully lifting the pail of milk brimming with white foam. With her free hand, she pulled her sweat-soaked tee shirt away from her homemade bra, letting in some air, then picked up the three-legged stool and turned toward the door. Maggie carried the pail to the small feed room and carefully covered it with the lid. She took the lead strap from the nail near the door and turned to get Curly, Big Red's calf, from his pen on the east side of the barn.

Back toward the highway, the sky swirled with coal-black clouds, and the air felt cooler *Probably means a hail storm's on the way. Better get Curley and Bossy into the barn right quick before the storm hits.* Once she finished milking Bossy, Maggie grabbed both pails of milk, rushing to get inside before the rain came. About halfway to the house, Maggie felt the first drops. The strong wind flattened her skirt against her legs, and she bent forward as the wind pushed against her. Running as fast as she could without spilling the milk, she reached the kitchen door just as the hail began to rat-a-tat-tat on the tin roof.

In the kitchen, Maggie strained the milk through a muslin cloth into four half-gallon canning jars and tightened the lids. Since the Martins had no refrigerator, Stuart, her nine-year-old brother, would take the milk to Aunt Opal's refrigerator when the rain stopped.

The rain and hail hammered the roof, and the fierce wind howled like a banshee. Maggie could barely hear her mother and her younger brothers and sisters in the front room. Through the kitchen doorway Maggie could see her mother sitting in her rocking chair holding six-month-old Jay hugged tightly to her thin, petite body, her brown eyes full of fear. The children knelt or sat on the floor around her. When a clap of thunder sounded, Corie Mae put her hands over her ears and scrunched down as if dodging an attacker. Jay began to cry.

From all her agitation, Corie Mae's dark braids, which she usually wore wrapped around her head, drooped below her ears. "Sing, you all, and pray," she yelled. "God deliver us from this storm!" Then she began singing "Rock of Ages," rocking in time to the music and motioning for the children to join in. Maggie glanced out the kitchen window and saw the trees bending in the wind, while the hail continued to pelt the roof. *Wow! I hope that wind doesn't blow a tree over on the house. We don't often have a storm this bad. No wonder Mama's so afraid.*

Maggie had heard her mother tell many times about getting struck by lightning as a teenager. Corie Mae had stood beside the stove stirring a pot of soup beans, when the electric current from the lightning had moved down the chimney, knocking Corie Mae back against the kitchen cabinet. *Guess if it had happened to me, I'd panic too.* Maggie frowned, feeling a twinge of guilt for judging her mother.

Maggie had finished washing the milk pails when a sudden flash of lightning crackled, and thunder shook the house. The dogs, huddling under the porch, yipped and whined, and the single light bulb hanging from the ceiling went out. "Margaret Frances, get in here right now!" Corie Mae ordered.

* * *

The wind and fury of the storm passed after a half hour, but the rain continued to fall in torrents. After finishing the supper dishes by the light of a kerosene lamp, Maggie pointed to the milk jars. "Mama. I guess it doesn't make sense to take the milk to Aunt Opal's since the power's off. Should I take it down to the spring?"

"Yes, Maggie, you should. This rain's probably flooded the spring house, so make sure the water ain't over the tops of the jars. You can carry the jars in the bushel basket that's on the back porch." As Maggie went out the back door, Corie Mae called, "Come right back. We got a lot of work to do tomorrow. I want you in bed early."

Fortunately, the rain had slowed to a light drizzle. Once on the dirt road, Maggie saw water swirling in the ditches, overflowing the road in places. A tree had blown across the fence, and in the near dark, Maggie noticed the rain had washed a gully down the middle of the cornfield. A muddy lake stood in the low place opposite the house. Maggie dodged the puddles as best she could in the dim light, but so much mud stuck to her shoes, she could hardly lift her feet.

"Hey, Mag. Wait up."

Maggie turned and saw JD coming down the road, his wet shirt sticking to him like an extra skin. "You okay?"

When JD reached her, he took one handle of the basket. "Yeah, I guess I'll live."

"You look like death warmed over. How'd the fight turn out? Last I saw from the bus, you two really laid into each other."

"I gave old Walter as good as he gave me. He got in a few good licks, but he quit the fight. I bet both his eyes'll be black by morning. I know I knocked a tooth or two loose cause he spit out blood, and my hand hurts like hell."

Until a couple of years earlier when the Rural Electric Co-op finally brought electric lines up the holler, the spring, a few yards off the road between their two houses, had served both families. It not only had kept their milk and other foods cool, it had also provided all their water. JD helped Maggie position the jars of milk on a ledge where the spring water flowed around them.

"Do you think Aunt Opal'll be mad?" Maggie knew Opal had a violent temper and would beat the boys over the smallest infractions.

"She'll probably take a belt to me."

"I'm going with you. I'll tell Aunt Opal Walter Spinks started it."

"Thanks, Cuz, but I don't think you can talk her out of it."

"At least I can try."

They went to the back of JD's house, stepped up onto the porch, and slipped off their muddy shoes before going into the lamp-lit kitchen.

"Oh my God! Where have you been? I been worried sick." Aunt Opal dried her hands and stepped away from the dishpan. "How come you didn't come home on the bus?"

"I got off at Spinks. Had some business with Walter."

"What sort of business?"

JD ignored her question. "I had got almost up to the holler when the storm started. I sat on Wilson's porch until the worst passed."

Aunt Opal grabbed JD's arm. "Answer my question!"

JD shook his arm loose, pulled a chair from the kitchen table, and sat down. He reached for a piece of cornbread which sat on the table. "Something personal. Nothing for you to worry about."

"Don't you talk to me like that!" She jerked JD's face toward the light of the kerosene lamp on the kitchen table. "You've been in a fight, ain't you? Here I been worrying my head off, afraid you was hit by lightning or something and you're picking a fight." She reached for the belt that hung on the kitchen wall. "You know I don't allow no fighting."

"He didn't start it, Aunt Opal." Maggie stepped between them. "Walter Spinks hit Johnny Ray and made him cry."

"Nobody asked you. Now get yourself back home and mind your own business. This don't concern you." Aunt Opal pointed toward the door.

Maggie took a few steps toward the door. "Please, don't whip him, Aunt Opal."

"I said go!" Aunt Opal gave Maggie a push out the back door.

Maggie dallied putting on her muddy shoes, trying to listen. She stepped off the porch and stood in the shadows.

After two or three licks, JD yelled, "That's enough, Mama!"

Whack. "I'll decide when it's enough!" Whack.

With each lash, JD yelled louder. Maggie watched their shadows dancing about the room and heard the crash of a chair turning over. Finally

JD dashed out the door with Aunt Opal still thrashing him. As he jumped off the porch, he scooped up his shoes and ran around the corner of the house. Maggie, on the opposite side of the porch, slowly backed deeper into the shadows.

"You come back here or I'll beat the tar out of you." Aunt Opal yelled into the night, but JD didn't answer, and Aunt Opal finally went back into the house. Slipping and sliding in the mud, Maggie ran down the road hoping to catch up with JD, but she couldn't see him. When she reached her home, she gave up. *I can't imagine where he could have gone.* Since she saw no lamplight in her house, Maggie thought everyone had gone to bed. She sat on the back porch taking off her shoes when the screen door suddenly flung open. She jumped up quickly.

Corie Mae grabbed Maggie's arm. "I thought I told you to come straight back. Where you been all this time?"

"JD got caught in the storm. I went to see if he got home." Maggie pulled her arm out of Corie Mae's grip.

"Don't be giving me any sass, young lady."

"I'm not, Mama. I just answered your question." Maggie walked around her mother and opened the screen door.

"Don't you walk away when I'm talking to you."

"Mama, I'm all muddy. I need to light a lamp and wash up so I can go to bed."

"Just because you got all A's on your grade card, don't think you're too smart to do as you're told." Corie Mae followed Maggie into the house and watched as she lit a lamp. "You might have more education than me, but that don't mean you can do as you please. I'll not have you disobeying."

"You don't need to yell at me, Mama. I took the milk to the spring house and went to check on JD." She washed her face and scrubbed the mud off her ankles and legs. "I don't know why you're so mad. I didn't do anything wrong."

"Looks to me like you's getting above your raising." Corie Mae turned her back and went through the front room to her bedroom.

Puzzled by the strength of her mother's animosity, Maggie blew out the lamp and carefully felt her way to the narrow steep stairs leading to her bedroom on the second floor. Surprised to find both her sisters already asleep, she stripped off her clothes and put on her nightgown. Lying in bed in the pitch-black darkness, she felt much too agitated for sleep. *Why does she think I'll disobey her just because I have more education than she does? What's she afraid of? I don't understand.* She fluffed her pillow and turned on her side. *At least she looked at my grades.*

* * *

The next morning Maggie opened her eyes and lay quietly listening to the birds. The sunlight streamed through the little window beside the bed, which she shared with Betty Lou, her twelve-year-old sister. Ten-year-old Jeannie slept across the small room on a makeshift bed her father had built into the wall. Through the open doorway, she could see into the other small bedroom on the second floor where her father had built bunk beds for nine-year-old Stuart and seven-year-old Johnny Ray. All of them slept on mattresses filled with corn husks. Four-year-old Junior and six-month-old Jay shared the downstairs bedroom with her parents.

Being careful so she wouldn't disturb the sleeping children, she dressed and went down the stairs into the front room. The sun made a puddle of light on the braided rug Maggie's mother had made using strips of cloth from worn out sheets and old clothes. Near the front door stood the grandfather clock great-grandma had brought with her from Kentucky when she had married Great-grandpa Campbell. It no longer worked, but her mother valued it as one of the "nice" things in her home. The hand-carved rocking chair, which her mother prized, also had belonged to Great-grandma Campbell.

Through the window, Maggie saw her father sitting in the porch swing smoking his pipe. She walked out, making sure the screen door didn't slam.

"Good morning, Sunshine."

"Hi, Daddy. We worried when you hadn't got home by dark last night." Maggie sat beside him.

"I think that was the worst storm I ever seen. I stayed at Mrs. Robinson's until the worst of it passed over. They's a big ditch washed all the way across the road before you get to Johnsons. It's so deep a car or a wagon can't cross it. Me and the preacher'll have to repair the road soon as it dries up a little."

"Do you want me to do the morning milking now that school's out?"

"Yes, that will help a lot, but I already done the milking this morning. I'm glad you left the cows in the barn last night. Trees have blowed over in a couple places and tore down the fences. We'll have to fix them before we let the cows back in the lower pasture." Ray smoked in silence for a few moments. "I guess the 'lectric's out everywhere cause all the houses was dark when I come home. We're lucky that the crops ain't very high yet, but the hard rain washed some fields out, so I reckon we'll have to replant them."

Maggie watched her father lift his head to blow the smoke toward the porch ceiling. She noticed his clean-shaven face. Grandma Campbell often commented that Ray Martin was the only man she knew who shaved every day before working in the fields. Maggie liked the way his deep blue eyes often twinkled with humor. She felt fortunate to have inherited his tall build and fair complexion. His hard work through the years, mostly outside, had given him a rugged, seasoned look, somewhat older than his thirty-six years.

"Soon as I finish this coffee, I'm fixing to check on your grandma and grandpa. After you eat, I want you to take the cows to the pasture behind the cornfield where none of the fences is down. If the preacher's able, I aim to work with him and the boys to cut up the trees that blowed over."

It always amused her when her daddy called his father-in-law "the preacher." Grandpa Campbell had only a fourth-grade education, and he had never had a church, but he did call himself a preacher. Sometimes a Pentecostal church invited him to preach. His religion, taken mostly from his Kentucky relatives, included snake-handling and speaking-in-tongues. Occasionally he got a ride to a church near Newport where he knew some people would take up the serpents. When Ray had married Corie Mae and come to live in the old home place, he made clear to his father-in-law that his family would not go to a Pentecostal church. He would take his new wife to the Baptist church a couple of miles down the road.

After knocking out the ashes, Ray put his pipe in the pocket of his bib overalls. He handed Maggie his coffee cup, pulled on his muddy boots, and gave her a good-bye salute.

As she made her way to the barn, Maggie detoured from the path in several places to avoid deep mud. Even so, with each step her father's old shoes, which she always wore to the barn, slurped like sucking the last of a Coca-Cola through a straw. When she opened the feed room door to get the lead straps for the cows, she gasped. JD sat behind the big wooden barrel that held the cow feed. "You scared me! What you doing here?"

JD stood up. Now Maggie could see his black eye and a bad bruise on his left jaw. "Wow! Spinks did leave some marks on you."

"Yeah, but that's not half as bad as what Mama done." He turned his back and dropped his jeans. Maggie gasped again when she saw the bruises and welts. Blood had dried in streaks down his legs. He pulled up his pants and turned toward Maggie.

"I'm sorry, JD. I wish you had just let it go and stayed on the bus. Then you wouldn't be in this trouble."

"Heck, it was worth it, Mag. I told old Walter if he ever put a hand on you again, I'd knock the rest of his teeth out."

"Now, that really makes me feel bad."

"It's not your fault. He's had it coming. I should of jumped that bully a long time ago."

Maggie kicked a corncob. "What're you going to do now?"

"I'm leaving. I ain't never going to let her beat me again. I knew she'd be mad, but there wasn't no call to do this to me. When I finally got away from her, I came here and spent the night in your barn."

"Where're you going?"

"Hitchhike to Detroit and stay with Daddy. If I show up, I reckon he'll have to take me in. Maybe I can just live with him till I graduate from high school. I'll wait to leave till after dark tonight so nobody'll see me leaving. Right now I'm starving. I didn't have no supper. Do you think you can help me?"

"You better hide up in the hay loft till dark cause they'll come looking for you. Daddy's gone to check on Grandpa and Grandma. Then he planned to get you and Kenny to help repair fences and stuff. I'll try to get down with some food as soon as I can. First, I have to take the cows to the back pasture."

"You're a good cuz!" JD put his arm around her shoulders and gave her a quick hug. "I hate to ask you this, but have you got any money?"

"Sorry, I don't have one red cent." She looked at him with wide eyes. "I got an idea. Joe Clark's been your best friend for a long time. Why don't you see if he'll loan you some money?"

"Good idea." JD nodded, patted Maggie's arm, and turned toward the ladder to the loft. Maggie took the lead straps and headed for the cows standing near the barnyard gate. *What am I going to do without JD?* The tears ran down her cheeks and fell to the ground in spite of her best efforts to staunch them.

* * *

The week after JD left turned really crazy. Aunt Opal had pretended she didn't know what could have made JD leave. Maggie had no sympathy for her tearful worry about where he might have gone or why he would do such a thing. Finally, Reverend Lewis had come to tell Aunt Opal about the phone call from Uncle Thomas saying JD was in Detroit with him. The Lewises had the only telephone for miles around, and they often delivered messages for people in the community.

The morning after Uncle Thomas' message, Maggie had almost finished milking when her father had appeared at the stable door. He remained silent until she had turned the cows into the pasture. Then he had looked intently at her. "Did you know JD was running away?"

She could not lie to her father, so she had confessed everything. "Daddy, you should of seen how Aunt Opal bruised his legs where she beat him. He made me promise not to tell." She hung her head, no longer able to look at her father. "I'm sorry."

Ray had put his hand under her chin, lifted her face, and looked into her blue eyes for several seconds before finally saying, "I think you probably done the right thing, Sunshine."

Now, she sat on a big rock near the spring. She faced the house, so she could see anyone coming in her direction. At church this morning

Reverend Lewis had slipped her an envelope addressed to her in care of the Lewises. On the back of the envelope JD had written, "Don't let no one else see this!"

"I guess you and JD have some secrets," Reverend Lewis had said.

Maggie had smiled without saying anything and slipped the letter into her Bible. She had been antsy all through Sunday dinner and until the girls had washed and put away the dishes. Then she had taken the Grace Livingston Hill novel Mrs. Lewis had lent her and told her mother she was going down by the spring to read. After checking carefully to see that the coast was clear, Maggie took out the letter and ripped it open.

> Dear Cuz,
>
> Thanks so much for helping me make my getaway. I hope you didn't get in no trouble for it. I spent the first night at Joe Clark's house. Like you said, he loaned me some money & helped me get some medicine for my cuts and bruises. You & Joe was the only ones who knowed I was headed for Michigan.
>
> Daddy was mad as hell when I showed up. But he calmed down a little when he saw how bad Mama had beat me up. He says I can stay here until his vacation in July, but then I have to come back home.
>
> Here's the part that you can't let nobody else know about.

Maggie scanned the path to the house and the roadway making sure no one approached. She opened her book and placed the letter inside to appear as if she were reading the novel.

> Daddy is living with a woman here. They have been together for nearly three years and they have a little girl. I can't believe I have a little sister! She is really cute & seems to like me. Here's the part you won't never believe. Daddy's woman is colored!

She gasped. Her mouth gaping, she quickly looked around again before rereading the last few sentences. *I don't believe this! Aunt Opal will just die.* Shaking her head from side to side, she returned to the letter.

> Stella's real nice, & she's been good to me. She said she's going to fatten me up before she lets me come back to Tenn. It's hard for me to imagine being fat, but her cooking beats the heck out of Mama's. My black eye is

pretty well gone, & my legs don't look too bad neither. I
can't say I'm looking forward to coming back home, but I
guess I won't have much choice.

Maggie tried to picture Stella, but since she had never actually seen a
Negro, her mental image lacked clarity. She took several deep breaths to
calm her pounding heart before she started reading again.

Thanks again, Cuz, for your help. I guess I'll see you in
about six weeks. I promise after I get home we'll have
some good times. Now, take this letter & burn it & keep
this news to yourself. DON'T TELL A SOUL! Daddy
told me the beating I got from Mama was nothing
compared to what he would do if I ever let Mama know
about Stella & the baby. I just had to tell someone, & I
knowed I could trust you to keep it to yourself.

Your cuz, JD

Maggie hadn't realized she had held her breath until it suddenly
escaped with a whoosh, like somebody had stuck a knife in a tire. Still not
convinced she had understood, she read the letter once more before tearing
it into small pieces and stuffing them into her pocket. She would put them
in the stove later.

*So... this is our little secret. Uncle Thomas will come home in July pretending to be
Aunt Opal's faithful husband, thinking she'll never know the difference.* She
wondered how long he thought he could get away with this double life. *I
guess he's already managed to fool everybody for three years.*

"How could Uncle Thomas do such a thing?" she said aloud. She
sucked in a sudden breath when she thought of the trouble ahead if
Grandpa found out. Maggie remembered one Sunday last summer, during
a dinner at Grandpa's house, she'd heard him brag, "No niggers ever eat or
spend the night in this county. We let them buy gas but tell them to keep
moving after they pay for the gas." She also remembered later her daddy
had made it clear that they were never to say the word "nigger." Instead
they should say "colored" or "Negro." But Maggie had had no problem
with that since no Negroes lived in her county.

She looked toward the house and sighed. *If this news gets out, it won't be
me who tells.* She finally stood to walk to the house. Time to do chores. She
thought of all the work they would have to get done before JD and his
father came in July. Six more weeks of drudgery, but at least JD was
coming back. With that encouraging thought, she quickened her steps and
managed a crooked smile. *Maybe my summer won't be so bad after all.*

CHAPTER 2

Campbell Holler–July 12,1880   Picked blackberries–
made jam. Beans ready to pick next week. Soon have
apples. Must get preserving finished before baby
comes in September.
(Diary of Mary Louise Campbell)

July 1949

Maggie, Betty Lou and Jeannie finished placing fifty half gallons of
freshly canned green beans on the shelves of the root cellar. Jeannie
rubbed the sweat off her forehead. "Mama says we'll need fifty more
cans of beans to get us through the winter."

"I hate canning beans. Those vines give my arms a rash." Betty
Lou flipped her dark braids over her shoulders, and scratched her
irritated forearms.

"Oh, don't be such a baby! Do like Grandma and make a paste
by mashing up cucumbers and rub it over your arms." Maggie began
to close the heavy wooden doors to the root cellar. "At least it don't
take as much time as stringing them up with a needle and thread for
leather breeches like Grandma does."

"Ugh!" Jeannie wrinkled her nose. "Grandma told me yesterday
her beans would be ready by the end of next week, and she wants me
to help her. Last year me and her had strings of green beans hung to
dry all across the back porch. They looked like a green curtain."

"But I like Grandma's leather breeches," protested four-year-old Junior, who liked to watch his big sisters and listen to their talk. He padded on bare feet covered in yellow mud from wading in the little brook that ran along the dirt road to join the creek farther down the hollow.

Maggie smiled at him and roughed his hair like swishing the suds in the dishpan. "Wish Mama had a pressure canner so we didn't have to boil the cans in a big tub over the fire in the backyard. Takes a lot of wood to keep that tub boiling for three hours."

"Lucky for us, no beans is going to be ready this week while Uncle Thomas and Uncle WC are here." Betty Lou rubbed her rash-covered arms. Shortly after returning from serving in World War II, their two uncles had taken jobs in an automobile factory in Detroit. Each month they sent money to support their families and came home for a short visit once or twice each year. The children enjoyed the attention and special treats their uncles heaped on them during their visits, especially Uncle Thomas. Maggie stopped in the shade of the apple tree. *Now that I know about his other woman, I probably won't even be able to look at Uncle Thomas. But I'll have JD around again.* That thought made her mouth curl up in a satisfied grin.

Suddenly a shrill scream pierced the air. "The rooster's chasing Johnny Ray again!" Junior yelled. Corie Mae rushed out the back door just as Johnny Ray raced around the side of the house with the rooster only a step behind him. When Betty Lou swung a stick at him, the rooster skidded to a stop and ran the other way. Johnny Ray leaped into Maggie's arms, gripping her around the waist with his legs and holding tightly to her neck, like a drowning man clutching his rescuer.

"You okay, Buddy?" Johnny Ray sniffed and nodded his head. Maggie could feel his trembling arms and pounding heart, and she tried not to laugh, knowing the rooster really could hurt him. For some strange reason, the rooster never attacked anyone else. And it made a funny sight to see them—Johnny Ray galloping as fast as his skinny legs could go, screaming his head off, and the rooster flapping his wings and batting at him with each step. Sometimes the rooster stalked him or hid behind the smokehouse or the woodshed to ambush Johnny Ray.

"Maggie, can you catch that rooster?" Corie Mae stood on the stone porch steps, arms akimbo. "If you can catch him and wring his neck, we'll make chicken and dumplings for dinner tomorrow. Thomas, JD, and WC should get here sometime tonight, and after church we'll all go to Grandma's house for dinner." Then she reached to take Johnny Ray from Maggie's arms. "That's the last time that old rooster'll chase you, Honey."

Maggie had watched her mother wring a chicken's neck many times. It seemed fairly simple. Mama held the chicken by its head, swung it around in a small circle a couple of times with a little jerk to break its neck. Then she tied its legs to the clothesline and cut off its head with a butcher knife. Maggie knew she could do it.

Jeannie, Betty Lou and Junior helped Maggie herd the rooster into the chicken house where Maggie caught him. Squawking, he flapped his wings, and pecked at her, as she carried him out by his feet. While the children watched, she grabbed him by the head and began to swing him around at arm's length. Because he weighed more than she expected, she couldn't quite give his neck that jerk the way her mother did. Thinking his neck should surely be broken after about ten circles, she turned him loose. He went up about a dozen feet into the air and came down flapping his wings, hit the ground, and staggered off. The children hooted and shouted.

"Catch him!" Maggie screamed. The poor rooster, still addled after his aborted execution, lurched like a drunk toward the hen house. Betty Lou had him in an instant. "This time I'm going to cut off his head with the ax." Maggie headed for the woodshed.

* * *

Maggie loved Sundays—the only day they did not work, except to prepare meals and care for the animals. Best of all, she could see Mary Ann at church. But today her eagerness to see JD occupied all her thoughts. The difficulty of keeping quiet about JD's letter had required much restraint. A dozen times she had caught herself just before blabbing some comment. *Guess I won't see him until after church when we go to Grandma's for dinner. Don't think I can act normal around Uncle Thomas. Hope he won't guess I know his big secret.*

After Sunday School, Mary Ann and Maggie chose their usual seats a few rows back on the left side where she could watch as Betty Lou played the offertory. After Betty Lou had taken piano lessons from Mrs. Lewis for several months and learned a simple hymn,

Reverend Lewis had asked her to play the offertory each Sunday. Maggie liked to watch her father while Betty Lou played. He leaned forward with his arms folded across his chest watching with intense concentration, his eyes shiny.

As Betty Lou finished, Grandpa Campbell surprised Maggie by walking down the aisle and taking a seat in the second pew. *Oh, no.* Every time Grandpa Campbell came, Preacher Lewis called on him to "say a few words," which always turned into a sermon. Grandpa only showed up when he had something to say, and usually what he said embarrassed her. *He'll get up there and preach and preach, and church will last till way past noon.*

Just as Maggie feared, Reverend Lewis came to the pulpit. "We're glad to have Preacher Campbell visiting with us today." He nodded to Grandpa. "I'm wondering if you would be so kind as to share a few words."

Grandpa Campbell stood and walked to the platform carrying his well-worn Bible. A short, slightly-built man with thin gray hair and sharp features, he wore blue overalls under his old brown suit coat. As usual his plaid shirt was buttoned to the collar, but he never wore a tie. "Thank ye, Brother Lewis. You're always so gracious to me when I come here to give ye a word from the Lord."

Maggie could hardly believe her eyes when Grandpa removed a paper from his Bible. Grandpa never wrote out or read his sermon. He believed the Holy Ghost filled his mouth with the words of the Lord as he spoke, as did most Pentecostal preachers.

"This here's a article from the newspaper gived to me by Brother Hicks down to Maple Grove. The Holy Ghost laid it on my heart to give ye a warning from the Lord today. It says here that they's making a new Bible." He held up the article. "They's already printed the New Testament, and they's working on the Old. It says here the whole Bible'll be ready by 1952. It's called the Revised Standard Version." He folded the paper and replaced it in his Bible. Then he hit the pulpit with his hand, making Maggie jump, and she and Mary Ann got the giggles.

"This is the work of the Devil!" he shouted. "The Devil and the Communists. The Communists are taking over the world. Just read the news. They've done took over China and closed the churches and killed the Christians. Now they're coming after us. I'm warning ye today, Brothers." Grandpa was getting wound up. Maggie scooted lower in her seat as if she could disappear.

Maggie knew his religious beliefs had come from Great-grandpa Campbell's family, which had a long history of ecstatic religious practices. But she didn't understand why Grandpa believed the Bible taught so many restrictions. He believed a woman should never cut her hair or wear makeup or jewelry. Women should wear long skirts and keep their arms covered. A woman must obey her husband, and if she disobeyed, the husband should beat her into submission. Children must be disciplined into total obedience by whatever means necessary. He could quote a scripture to support every opinion. To Maggie those rules did not sound like what a loving God would expect.

Maggie looked at her father, who sat in his usual place in the second pew with his good friend Larry Collins, Mary Ann's dad. Her father also wore overalls, his plaid shirt buttoned up to the collar, and though midsummer, a gray suit coat. She wondered what he thought about this tirade.

Fortunately her father did not agree with Grandpa on the discipline. Ray hardly ever raised his voice, and Maggie had never seen him hit any of the children and certainly not Corie Mae. A different story for her mother, who frequently raised her voice and also wielded a mean switch when one of the children disobeyed. She had learned the hard way that it did not take much to get her mother riled. Maggie looked across the sanctuary where her mother sat holding sleeping Jay in her lap. Corie Mae sat with closed eyes, lips firmly pressed together, her head nodding in agreement as she listened.

Grandpa, red faced from all his shouting, preached in the customary way of the mountain preachers. "I tell ye, brothers, huh! I'm giving ye a warning from the Lord today, huh! The Bible says, huh! Not one jot or tit, huh! Will be added or changed from the Word, huh! This is the work of Satan, huh! The Communists are trying to tear down our country, huh! We must fight against this great evil, huh! Don't let this new Bible into your church, huh! Don't let your children read it, huh! God will bring down HELLLL fire, huh! To burn up all those who bring this evil among us, huh! OHHHHHHHHHHHHHHH hear me today, huh! My dear friends."

Maggie sighed with relief when Grandpa began to wind down. He finished by again thanking Reverend Lewis for inviting him to deliver the "words from the Lord." He turned, shook hands with the pastor, who sat on the platform behind him, and, picking up his Bible, walked straight down the aisle and out the door. Maggie slid further down in the pew, folded her arms across her chest, and rolled her eyes at Mary Ann.

* * *

Whenever the family shared a meal, they always went to Grandma and Grandpa Campbell's house. After a short courtship, Grandma and Grandpa had married when Grandma was eighteen. Great-grandpa had helped them build a house at the head of the holler. They used timber from the land, which they cut themselves and hauled to the sawmill. Great-Grandpa had insisted they build a big house because he knew the difficulty of raising a family in only four rooms. So the house had four rooms on the first floor and two rooms upstairs. Maggie thought her mother lucky to have had a room all to herself.

Like Maggie's house, it remained unpainted inside and out. Grandpa had made much of the furniture himself, mostly cane-bottomed straight chairs with ladder backs. Grandpa had dug a well, but the house had no running water. The family often met in the large dining room for Sunday dinner, where everyone sat around the large table except Grandma Campbell and Corie Mae, who hovered nearby ready to refill glasses and wait on the table. Maggie wondered if anyone would mention Grandpa's denunciation of the "new Bible," but everyone seemed interested in the big dinner the women had prepared.

"Pass me some more of them dumplings," Grandpa said.

JD picked up the large bowl and looked into it. "Sorry, Grandpa, but they's all gone."

"You mean we've et all them chicken and dumplings already? Them was real good dumplings–light as a feather–best chicken and dumplings I ever tasted, wasn't they Johnny Ray?"

Johnny Ray smiled and then gave a forlorn look at his own plate, still full of green beans and new potatoes.

"Clean up your plate, Johnny Ray, so you can have some of Aunt Lillian's banana pudding." Corie Mae carried a stack of small dishes to the table.

"I'm too full." Johnny Ray pushed his lower lip out in a pout.

"Guess you can sit there till your plate's clean, then," Corie Mae said, and began dishing up banana pudding for everyone else. While Corie Mae left to carry some dirty plates into the kitchen, Uncle Thomas took Johnny Ray's plate, raked most of the beans and potatoes into his own plate, and motioned for Johnny Ray to begin eating what little remained.

A few minutes later when Johnny Ray asked if he could have his banana pudding, Corie Mae snapped, "I told you to clean up your plate."

"I did, Mama," Johnny Ray bragged, and Corie Mae stared at his empty plate with a puzzled look. No one said a word, but Maggie saw Uncle Thomas punch Johnny Ray under the table. She had not thought about it before, but she suddenly realized that Uncle Thomas was often guilty of deceit and now he was teaching it to Johnny Ray.

The girls helped their aunts wash the dishes and then joined the rest of the family on the front porch where most of the men smoked. Grandma Campbell had a dip of snuff in her lower lip. Corie Mae had taken Junior and Jay home for a nap.

Grandma sat beside Grandpa in the porch swing, a flyswatter in her right hand and her spit can on the floor to her left. The other adults sat in straight-backed chairs while the kids sat on the porch steps or on the floor. "Tell us a story, Uncle Thomas," Johnny Ray begged.

Uncle Thomas leaned his chair against the porch rail on its two back legs. Maggie never knew whether to believe his stories or not. Even though she now thought him a big hypocrite, she had to admit that Uncle Thomas told wonderful stories. Johnny Ray and Jeannie moved closer, looking up at Uncle Thomas with shining, eager eyes. Maggie sat beside JD on the steps facing the yard where she could hear but wouldn't make eye contact with Uncle Thomas.

"See, right before I joined the army, old man McCann come down here one day and asked me to help him load up a steer he wanted to take to the sale barn. So I went up there where the Johnsons live now to see if I could help. He'd put a cattle bed on his wagon and backed it up to the stable door and made a ramp. He wanted to run the steer up the ramp and into the wagon, but the steer would balk. Ain't no way he was going up that ramp.

"We'd get him started toward the ramp, and ever' time just as he was almost there, he'd jump sideways and run to the other side of the stall." Uncle Thomas gestured so forcefully he lost his balance and the front legs of his chair slammed down like a sudden clap of thunder. "He stepped on my foot and about broke my big toe when I tried to head him off, and then he butted old man McCann back against the wall and knocked the breath clean out of him." At this point JD got up and quietly walked away.

Uncle Thomas lit the cigarette he had taken from the pack of Lucky Strikes lying on the porch rail, and tilted his head back to blow a cloud of smoke toward the ceiling. "First, I didn't know what to do–old man McCann was laying over in the corner, looking like he wasn't breathing at all, and that stupid steer was looking at him all walleyed, pawing the hay-covered stall with his front hoof. I was standing over McCann trying to figure out what to do when he finally opened his eyes and drew in a breath.

"Now, when that old man got back on his feet, he was real mad. He picked up a piece of two-by-four that was laying in the hay manger. This time when that old steer got up to the ramp, McCann yelled real loud, 'You god damn son of a bitching bull!' and whacked him on the be-hind as hard as he could with that board."

Grandma gasped. "Now watch your language, Thomas Duncan Campbell. You know I don't allow no swearing in my house."

"I'm sorry, Mama, but I'm just telling it like it happened. That's exactly what old man McCann said, 'You son of a bitching bull' and whacked the daylights out of that steer's be-hind."

"Humph!" Grandma spit ambeer into her tin can.

"Well, when McCann hit him, that steer jumped so high he was in the wagon all in one leap. I guess he thought McCann was going to hit again cause he tried to climb right over the top of the cattle bed. Somehow, he got both his front feet caught, and there he stood on his hind legs with his front feet wedged between the two top slats and his head hanging over the top. He bellowed, stomped, and jerked every which way. I thought he would tear that cattle bed right off the wagon."

"How'd you get him down?" Kenny asked.

"Well, I'll tell you. I said, 'Mr. McCann, what you going to do now?' And he said, 'Oh, I reckon he'll hang there all right till I get him to town.' So he put the tail gate up, got on his old tractor, and pulled the wagon out into the lane. "Then he said to me, 'Sonny.'

He always called me 'Sonny.' 'Sonny,' he said, 'I want you to stand here on the drawbar so's you can watch him while I drive.' I tell you, it was a sight to see. Here we was driving down the road with that steer hung up by his front legs, his head hanging over the rails and him looking at me with his walleyes and bellering like a pig stuck in the fence. And old man McCann just grinning and waving to everybody we passed like it was the way everybody took a steer to the sale barn.

"And when we got to the sale barn, nobody could believe their eyes." Uncle Thomas puffed out another cloud of smoke. "Mr. Justice come out and took a look. 'Well, hell, McCann, what you got him hanging up like that for?'"

"'Don't you be helling me, Justice. It just seemed like a good way to bring him in.'

"'How you going to get him down?' Justice wanted to know.

"'I sold him to you. You get him down.'

"'Damn it, man. You probably already broke his legs.'

"'I never done no such thing. He got hisself up there. Let him get hisself down.'"

Uncle Thomas flicked his cigarette butt into the yard. "Those two old men stood there yelling and cussing each other for a good fifteen minutes. Finally Jeff Holmes come out, and the two of us prized the slats apart enough so's the steer could get loose. Lucky for old man McCann his legs wasn't broke, cause Justice allowed as how he'd not pay a dime for no damn steer with two broke feet." Uncle Thomas scratched his head. "I reckon that was the last time McCann ever asked me to help him." He roughed up Johnny Ray's hair. "What do you think, Buddy? Was that a good enough story for you?"

"Oh, that was a wonderful story, Uncle Thomas. Can you tell us another one?"

"Maybe later." Uncle Thomas stood. "Hey, kids, let's go shoot some baskets. Johnny Ray, you can play on my side."

Ray also stood. "Maggie, you girls go shoot baskets, and I'll do the milking. Come home for supper in about an hour."

On the way over to Uncle Thomas's barn, Maggie passed the two cars parked beside the house. JD, sitting behind the wheel of the black car smoking a cigarette, motioned her to come over. "How do you like my car?"

Maggie's mouth dropped open. "How'd you get a car?"

JD looked around to be sure no one could hear him. "Daddy bought it for me. It's to bribe me to stay here and keep my mouth shut."

Maggie went around to the passenger side and got in. "This is nice!" She ran her hands over the dashboard and the green plaid seat covers. "I never dreamed you'd actually have a car. What is this ? A Ford?"

"No, a Chevrolet. Daddy says I have to help make the payments, so I've got to get a job right quick."

"When can I have a ride?"

"Tomorrow." JD opened his door and got out. "Now, we better get our butts over to the barn."

JD and Kenny had nailed an old peach basket above their barn door for a hoop. Lots of Sunday afternoons, all the kids played with the basketball Kenny had gotten for Christmas a couple of years earlier. Uncle Thomas, Johnny Ray, Kenny, and Betty Lou made up one team; JD, Maggie, Stuart, and Jeannie the other. After half an hour, JD's team led by 30 to 15, and Maggie had made 20 of those points.

"How'd you get so good?" Uncle Thomas asked her.

She suppressed the urge to smirk at him. "I don't know. Just luck, I guess."

"Going to go out for the team at school?" Uncle Thomas threw the ball to Kenny.

"Oh, you know Mama'd never let me do that. She really don't even want us girls to come over here to shoot baskets."

"Maybe she'll change her mind," Uncle Thomas suggested.

Maggie shook her head. "Kids, time to go home for supper."

* * *

After a busy week, Maggie and JD finally had a few minutes alone on Friday evening when he came over to the barn while she milked. Maggie asked him about Stella's baby.

"Meeka's fourteen months old and toddles all around. Stella's sister, who lives in the other side of the double house, takes care of her while Stella goes to work."

"Can she talk?"

"Says a few words. She calls me 'Hayde.'"

"What does she call Uncle Thomas?"

"Dada."

"Uncle Thomas pay attention to her?"

"Every night when he gets home from work, he plays with her until Stella gets supper ready. He gives her lots more attention than he ever gave me or Kenny."

"What will happen when your mother finds out about Stella?"

"Let's just hope she never finds out because she'll be mad enough to chew nails and spit rivets. Anything in her way she'll bust like kindling. I sure hope I'm not around if it happens."

"I'm worried about what Grandpa will do when he hears about Stella. You know how he can't stand colored people, calls them "niggers," and always badmouths them."

"Listen, Maggie, nobody knows except you and me, and we ain't telling. So if we keep our mouths shut, Mama and Grandpa won't never know. That's the way it's got to be." Maggie nodded. JD also had told her he and Aunt Opal hadn't spoken since he got home. "I'm not speaking to her till she apologizes for beating me up. Daddy told me I should just stay away from her, and she wouldn't bother me no more. They had a big argument about it last night. Probably good he's gone most of the time working in Detroit. They'd be fighting like cats and dogs if he stayed here much." He helped Maggie put the cows into the pasture.

"Daddy said I should spend more time helping Grandpa," JD said, "cause he's not able to work like he used to. But Grandpa's worse than Mama. I can't do nothing right. He yelled at me yesterday when I helped him hoe corn. Said I worked on the wrong side of the row. Like I hadn't been hoeing corn since I was six years old. What the hell difference does it make what side of the row you're on? He threatened to hit me with his hoe if I didn't get on the other side."

The week after Uncle Thomas and Uncle WC went back to Detroit, JD got a job pumping gas and doing work at a filling station. Maggie seldom saw him except when he roared down the road. Ray told Corie Mae if JD was not careful, he was going to skid on some gravel and wreck his precious car. Maggie worried her mother would forbid her to ride with JD. *Why did I think I'd have a better summer when JD came home?*

* * *

Early in July Maggie saw an opportunity to make some money selling blackberries. Wearing a long-sleeved flannel shirt under a pair of her father's bib overalls, she carried two large pails onto the front porch. Corie Mae followed her through the screen door, carrying seven-month-old Jay on her hip. "Now, where's Johnny Ray?"

"Do I have to take him with me?" Maggie pleaded. "He won't pick berries; he'll just complain the whole time."

"Now, Maggie, I ain't too set on you going berry picking anyway. So iffin you don't want to go, that's just fine." Corie Mae's compressed lips made a line across her face. "But if you're going, you ain't going by yourself. You know I don't allow my girls out in the woods alone."

"Okay, Mama." Maggie noticed the edge in her mother's voice. *I've tried so hard not to upset her. Wonder what she's mad about now.*

"Johnny Ray," Corie Mae called, "get yourself out here right now." She shifted Jay to her other hip. "Want me to get a switch?"

"No, Mama," Johnny Ray whined as he came through the screen door. He also wore a long-sleeved shirt and overalls that had once belonged to his cousin JD. The many patches on the knees indicated they had passed on to JD's younger brother Kenny and then to Stuart before they had become Johnny Ray's.

Corie Mae put her hand under Johnny Ray's chin and turned his face toward her. "Now, you listen to me. You stay where you can see Maggie all the time, and you mind her too. Do you hear me?"

"Yes, ma'am."

"Take Sadie with you. She'll sniff out any snakes. If you get these two buckets full, that'll be the four gallons you promised Mrs. Kaiser." She shifted Jay again to the other hip. "Now, if the prison whistle blows, come straight home. Sometimes when convicts escape, they come right up this holler."

Maggie walked down the porch steps to the yard and called, "Here, Sadie." The beagle promptly came out of her dog house to join them as they went down the stone steps to the dirt road.

"I want you'ns back by dinnertime," Corie Mae called after them.

They walked a few yards down the road in silence. Maggie

28

noticed the Queen Anne's lace along the dirt road was beginning to bloom and wild daisies polka dotted the hillside. She took a deep breath to take in the fragrance of the sweet honeysuckle growing on the fence. Then Johnny Ray got that mischievous twinkle in his eye. "I know why you want to pick blackberries and sell them. It's cause you want to buy store-bought underwear so's the girls at school won't laugh at your flour-sack bloomers when you take gym class."

"Why, Johnny Ray Martin, whoever told you such a thing?"

"Nobody. When I was sick last week and slept downstairs in Junior's bed, I heard Mama and Daddy talking. Mama sounded all mad. She said you was getting too highfalutin' just because you was going to be in high school next year. She said you was thinking you's too good to wear the clothes she made for you. But Daddy said to let you do it. It couldn't hurt nothing. Besides it's no fun to be laughed at. Mama said okay, but she still didn't like it none."

"Well, don't you go blabbing it, you hear?"

Johnny Ray grinned. "On the first day of school soon as we get on the bus, I'm going to yell real loud. 'Hey, everybody, Maggie's got on store-bought bloomers!'"

"You do, and I'll..."

"You'll do what?"

"Tell you what I'll do, Johnny Ray Martin." Maggie gave him a coy look from the corner of her eye.. "If you pick that bucket half full of blackberries today, I'll give you a dime."

"Really?" Johnny Ray's eyes widened. "You promise?"

"Cross my heart."

So that explains why Mama's mad. Daddy took my side and overruled her. She appreciated when her father often intervened when she and her mother were at odds. Over the last year, the friction between Maggie and her mother had become more frequent. She couldn't help grinning.

"Where're we going to pick at anyway?" Johnny Ray asked.

"When Mama did the wash for Johnsons last week, Mr. Johnson told Mama we could pick in the field behind their barn. He said nobody else would pick them, and they'd just rot on the vine."

Johnny Ray stopped dead in his tracks. "I ain't going."

"Don't be silly. Mama said you had to go."

"But we might see Audie Lee."

"What if we do? He won't do nothing."

"JD told me he catches birds and bites their heads off. He said if you meet up with Audie Lee Johnson, he'll open up his sack and make you eat a dead bird." Johnny Ray turned and started walking toward the house.

"Mama'll whip you if you go back. Besides, I won't give you a dime."

Johnny Ray turned to face her. "But I'm afraid of him!"

"JD just tells you stuff like that cause he knows you're a scaredy cat. Audie Lee can't talk, but he don't hurt nobody. He just roams around picking up odds and ends. Grandpa Campbell saves his tobacco sacks for him, and Audie Lee finds pretty rocks in the creek to put in the little sacks. He likes marbles and buttons, too."

"I'm still afraid of him." But he began to walk slowly back toward her.

"Besides," Maggie argued, "we won't pick near the house. We probably won't even see him." She wished she felt as confident as she sounded. For years, she had heard tales about all the weird things Audie Lee Johnson did. She knew most of it was not true, but he did give her the creeps. She hoped she would never meet him when she was alone.

They had walked a quarter mile down the road toward the state highway. Maggie stopped and pointed to the hillside beside the road. "Johnny Ray, look how deep this gully is where that bad storm washed out the road." The water had come down the hillside like a river leaving a gorge six feet wide and three or four feet deep, completely washing out the road.

"If Daddy and Grandpa hadn't fixed it, we still couldn't get across."

As they stared at the ugly gully dissecting the hillside, Maggie saw a glint of sunlight on something about six feet up the trench. She jumped into the ditch and climbed on all fours up the steep crevice. Whatever it was, it had been buried in the hillside for a very long time. "Throw me that stick over there, Johnny Ray, so I can dig this out."

Maggie used the sharp, pointed end of the stick to work the object loose. She jumped back down to the bottom of the ditch beside the road and reached for Johnny Ray's hand to pull her back up to the roadway. She held out her hand so Johnny Ray could see the flat, heart-shaped object somewhat smaller than her palm. It to look at Johnny Ray's berries. "Do you have your bucket full?" S... called.

When he didn't answer, she called louder. "Johnny Ray?" *What's he up to now?* She walked around the clump of berry bushes and saw his bucket, but he was nowhere in sight. Thinking maybe he had stepped back into the woods to pee, she walked to the other side of a bushy white pine a few paces into the woods. She knew he would be afraid to go far alone. Alarmed, she called again and a movement several yards away in the woods caught her eye.

She drew a sharp breath when she saw a man in prison clothes clutching Johnny Ray against him with one hand over his mouth. The man leaned back against a fallen tree and held Johnny Ray between his legs. Her heart pounded so loud she could hear it, and her knees felt weak.

"What are you doing?" she demanded and took a few steps toward them.

"Stay right there, or I'll slit his throat."

Maggie saw the small pocket knife he held at Johnny Ray's throat. She could see Johnny Ray's eyes, huge and full of fear. "What do you want? Turn my brother loose."

"Listen, girl, you do just like I tell you, and your brother won't get hurt." Maggie nodded. "You see them clothes hanging on that line down the hill there? Well, you go down there and get me a shirt and a pair of pants. Don't tell no one. I'll give you five minutes, and then if you ain't back with those clothes, I'll start cutting off his ears, and then his nose before I slit his throat."

Johnny Ray's body stiffened, and he tried to twist his head, but the man held him tight. Maggie could hear his muffled cries.

"Don't be afraid, Johnny Ray. Do just like he says. I'll be back in no time." She looked at the man. "You hurt my brother, my daddy'll kill you." Maggie turned and ran like a scared rabbit through the pasture toward the Johnsons' backyard. She had never been so fraid.

I wonder why the prison whistle didn't blow. Please, God, don't let him urt Johnny Ray. She opened the gate and cautiously walked toward the othesline. She took the clothespins from a shirttail and clipped em back on the line. Then she moved to take a pair of pants. Just she gripped the clothespin, a dirty hand covered hers and another nd pulled down the line so she stared right into Audie Lee's eyes.

seemed to be some sort of jewelry. A short piece of a chain was still attached. On one side red, white, and crystal stones circled a center of gold colored filigree. Maggie rubbed it with her fingers to get the clay mud off.

"What is it?" Johnny Ray asked.

"Reckon it's a necklace of some kind. Must be real gold cause it shines here where I rubbed it."

"Can I have it?"

"Maybe. I'll ask Daddy if he knows what it is." She stuck it in her pocket "We need to get on down the road, or we'll never get these berries picked."

They soon reached the fence marking the beginning of the Johnsons' farm. Maggie climbed through the strands of barbed wire and held the wires up so Johnny Ray could crawl through. "Come on, Sadie," Maggie called to the beagle, who had trotted on down the road ahead of them. "We'll have to keep an eye on Sadie, or she'll be off chasing a rabbit stead of sniffing out the snakes."

"But if it's a blue racer, it might chase us!"

"Snakes don't chase people, silly."

"Yes, they do. JD told me a blue racer chased him from Grandpa's barn all the way home."

"Johnny Ray, how many times do I have to tell you that JD's making all that stuff up? Snakes don't chase people."

"Bet you five dollars."

"When are you going to have five dollars? Want to bet your dime?"

"No."

By now they had walked about two hundred yards from the road along the edge of the cornfield that sloped uphill. Just above the field a raised place marked the site of the first house built in the hollow. Only a pile of rocks that had once formed the chimney remained.

"Is that where we're going?" Johnny Ray pointed.

"No, that pile of rocks makes a perfect place for a nest of rattlesnakes. We'll go around those trees and up through the pasture towards the woods." She pointed to the right a few hundred feet farther up the hillside where the cleared ground ended and the woods began.

"Does Mr. Johnson own all this land?"

"Yes."

"But I thought he worked at the prison. How can he do that and all this farming, too?

"He is a prison guard, but he does his farm work evenings and weekends."

"Does Audie Lee help him?"

"I doubt if Audie Lee does much farm work, but Mama says he helps cook and clean house."

"Is Mr. Johnson his daddy?"

"No, he's an older brother. Their parents are dead, so Mr. Johnson takes care of Audie Lee."

"How old is Audie Lee, anyway?"

Maggie tried to keep the irritation out of her voice. "Mama says he's probably in his late twenties."

From the hillside above the barn they could easily see the backyard and the back of the Johnson house. "Why, it's painted white!" Johnny Ray seemed surprised. "I wish our house was white instead of that old ugly gray." Except for June Wilson's house on the highway and the Johnsons' house, none of the houses in the holler had ever been painted.

"Someday I'll get a job and make a lot of money. I'll buy the paint and you can paint our house," Maggie suggested.

"I wonder why they have clothes on the line. Mama didn't do no wash for them today."

"Sometimes Mr. Johnson washes some clothes on the week that Mama don't do it. I guess he must have done some before he left for work this morning."

They had reached the briars that had grown into large clumps of canes hanging full of dark, ripe fruit. "Okay, little brother, look at all these berries. Here, Sadie, check out these bushes and make sure there's no snakes." When it seemed safe, Maggie pointed out several long briars loaded with berries at the edge of the woods. "Now, you pick here. Just pick the black ones. The red ones are sour. I'll go over there to that bunch of briars. Remember," she reminded him, "have to get half a bucket full to get a dime."

Soon she had the bottom of her bucket covered. She whistled when she noticed Sadie was out of sight, and shortly the dog came trotting out of the woods. "Here girl, you stay with us. We didn't bring you to hunt rabbits. You're supposed to hunt snakes." After a

few minutes, Maggie walked over to check on Johnny Ray. He had about a cup of berries in his bucket. "Hey, little man, you're doing real good. You're going to get that dime, all right."

Johnny Ray smiled at her praise, revealing a purple mouth. He rubbed his sleeve over his forehead. "I'm so hot."

"Well, hurry and get your berries picked so we can go home and eat dinner." Maggie began to walk back to her spot. Suddenly a blood curdling scream made her heart stand still. Maggie raced to Johnny Ray's side and knelt beside him. "What happened?" Johnny Ray, standing several steps back from the briars with his hands over his face, had dropped his bucket, spilling his berries. "What's the matter?" Maggie pulled his hands away and saw his eyes full of tears.

"A big bee! Hit me right on the head."

"Did it sting you?"

"No," he reluctantly admitted.

She put the bucket back in his hand and began to pick more berries to cover the bottom of his bucket again. "You know how Stuart catches June bugs and puts a string on their legs so they fl[y] around in a circle?" Johnny Ray nodded. "That wasn't a bee th[at] flew out at you. It was a June bug. They like to eat berries. Y[ou] scared the bug more than it scared you. It only tried to fly a[way] before it got hurt. One flew out at me a minute ago, and I al[most] yelled and dropped my bucket too." She gently pushed him to[ward] the briars and encouraged him to resume his picking.

"Just keep your eyes open. Maybe you'll see the next one [before] it surprises you." She returned to her bucket and resumed p[icking.] Sadie barked in the distance chasing a rabbit far down the [holler.] *Oh well, that's what a rabbit dog's really supposed to do.*

Maggie had picked more than half her bucket full, sh[e said,] "Johnny Ray, I'm going around to the other side of these bri[ars.] stay right there."

He nodded to let her know he had heard her. "I have [mine] almost half full."

"Good boy. I'll be over to see in a minute." She wal[ked around] the bush and grinned to see so much ripe fruit like t[his] hanging in great bunches from the graceful briars. She c[ould fill a] bucket in no time. Visualizing the panties and bras in t[he Sears] Roebuck catalog, she planned to come back every day fo[r a week to] pick buckets of berries. For a moment she forgot she [ ]

He shook his head from side to side and tried to make her take her hand away.

She had never seen him so close before. The old hat shaded his face, but Maggie could see that his small beady eyes, too close together, made him appear slightly cross-eyed. His long nose and receding chin surrounded by unshaved stubble reminded Maggie of a groundhog. He angrily pried at her hand and shook his head while he made strange grunting noises.

"Audie Lee, I've got to borrow these for a little while." Her voice shook. "My brother's in trouble, and if I don't take these clothes, something bad'll happen to him." She couldn't tell if he understood what she said. The angry expression on his face didn't change, but he gripped her hand more insistently.

"Please, Audie Lee," she pleaded. But he only shook his head.

Suddenly, she remembered the piece of jewelry she had found in the gully. With her free hand, she pulled it from her pocket and held it out where Audie Lee could see it. He looked at it with interest. "Go on, take it."

Audie Lee looked at her and grinned. He released her hand and took the shiny thing, turning it over and studying it closely.

When Maggie reached the woods, she hurried toward the man holding Johnny Ray and threw the clothes at his feet. The man released Johnny Ray, and she dropped to her knees, grabbing him in her arms. "Are you okay?" Johnny Ray, trembling from head to toe, nodded. He clung tightly to her and sobbed into her shoulder. "Take those clothes and get out of here," she hissed. She hugged Johnny Ray to her, and they watched the man pour all of Johnny Ray's berries into Maggie's bucket.

"I need some food," he said. "Besides, no one'll be suspicious of a berry picker." Maggie opened her mouth to protest but changed her mind. "Thanks for your help," he said and walked into the woods carrying the clothes under his arm. Maggie watched him go and fought back tears of relief.

Still on her knees holding her brother, Maggie squeezed him tight. "You were so brave. I'm proud of you."

"But he took all our berries," Johnny Ray protested. "Now I won't get my dime."

"I know." She smoothed his hair and hugged him again. "But at least he didn't hurt you. We'll pick some more berries tomorrow.

You'll still get your dime."

From a distance the prison whistle gave a long blast announcing to the countryside that an inmate had escaped. "Let's go home." Maggie stood up and took his hand "Mama'll be worried sick about us."

CHAPTER 3

Campbell Holler–September 15, 1885   Harvey off to
camp meeting again.   Gone 2 weeks.   Boys helped dig
potatoes and onions. Been playing mandolin and teaching
them songs. Harvey ain't here to forbid it.
(Diary of Mary Louise Campbell)

August 1949

Maggie had finished washing the milk pails when she heard a car. After
quickly drying her hands, she rushed to look out the front door and saw Mr.
Johnson handing a package to Corie Mae, who had stepped out onto the
porch.

"June Wilson told me the mailman left this package at her house, and
she asked me to drop it off for you."   He mentioned he had been
concerned when Ray had come to tell him about the escaped convict and to
offer to pay for the clothes the prisoner took. "I found out last week the
man has been recaptured."   He noticed Maggie standing inside the screen
door. "Glad he didn't hurt you." Maggie smiled and nodded.

Corie Mae held the package to her chest. "Kyle, you're very kind to let
us pick the berries. After Ray heard about the convict, he come home early
several afternoons to go with Maggie, and they got lots of berries. They
didn't see no more prisoners, but they did see a few copperheads." Corie
Mae turned to Maggie. "Go get a couple jars of that blackberry jam for Mr.
Johnson for bringing the package."

After Maggie returned with the jam, they stood on the porch chatting.
A car came up the road, a cloud of dust billowing up behind it. They

watched as Reverend Lewis slowed to steer around Mr. Johnson's car and wave before he continued toward the head of the holler. "What's he coming for?" Corie Mae wrinkled her brow. "Hope nothing bad's happened."

"I'll be getting on home." Mr. Johnson took the jars from Maggie. "Thanks for the jam." He hurried down the stone steps to his car and backed up to turn around in the lane to the barn.

Corie Mae handed the package to Maggie. "I guess this is your new underwear."

Maggie studied her mother's face but couldn't interpret its meaning. "Thank you, Mama." Without saying anything, Corie Mae opened the screen door to go finish preparing supper.

* * *

Corie Mae had poured the cornbread batter into the hot iron skillet when Grandpa walked into the kitchen. Corie Mae took one look at her father's troubled face, closed the oven door, and rushed to him. "Papa, what's wrong?"

"Well, Sis, Preacher Lewis brung us some bad news."

Corie Mae led him into the front room, and sat down in her rocking chair. Grandpa pulled over a straight chair and sat beside her while the children huddled in the doorway listening. "Reverend Lewis got a call from your cousin Lottie saying Helen died yesterday."

"Oh, no." Corie Mae began to sob into her apron.

"What's wrong, Mama?" Junior ran across the room and crawled into her lap. Grandpa took out his bandana and blew his nose.

Maggie returned to the kitchen to make sure the supper was not burning. She remembered her mother telling stories about how Aunt Helen, Grandpa's only sister, was her favorite aunt. Maggie felt a special kinship to Aunt Helen because her parents had given her Aunt Helen's middle name, although no one called her "Margaret."

After Great-grandpa died, Great-grandma had asked Corie Mae to move into the house with her. Later Great-grandma and Corie Mae had ridden the Greyhound bus to Kentucky where they spent most of the summer with Aunt Helen, Great-grandma's only daughter. Fifteen-year-old Corie Mae and Lottie, Aunt Helen's daughter, became really close. Lottie was in love with the preacher's son and before the end of the year had married him.

That summer Corie Mae had met Ray, who lived next door to Aunt Helen. Corie Mae had told the children how Lottie and her beau and she and Ray had spent time together going to church, taking long walks, and visiting the soda fountain at the drug store. The next year Ray had come to seemed to be some sort of jewelry. A short piece of a chain was still attached. On one side red, white, and crystal stones circled a center of gold colored filigree. Maggie rubbed it with her fingers to get the clay mud off.

"What is it?" Johnny Ray asked.

"Reckon it's a necklace of some kind. Must be real gold cause it shines here where I rubbed it."

"Can I have it?"

"Maybe. I'll ask Daddy if he knows what it is." She stuck it in her pocket "We need to get on down the road, or we'll never get these berries picked."

They soon reached the fence marking the beginning of the Johnsons' farm. Maggie climbed through the strands of barbed wire and held the wires up so Johnny Ray could crawl through. "Come on, Sadie," Maggie called to the beagle, who had trotted on down the road ahead of them. "We'll have to keep an eye on Sadie, or she'll be off chasing a rabbit stead of sniffing out the snakes."

"But if it's a blue racer, it might chase us!"

"Snakes don't chase people, silly."

"Yes, they do. JD told me a blue racer chased him from Grandpa's barn all the way home."

"Johnny Ray, how many times do I have to tell you that JD's making all that stuff up? Snakes don't chase people."

"Bet you five dollars."

"When are you going to have five dollars? Want to bet your dime?"

"No."

By now they had walked about two hundred yards from the road along the edge of the cornfield that sloped uphill. Just above the field a raised place marked the site of the first house built in the hollow. Only a pile of rocks that had once formed the chimney remained.

"Is that where we're going?" Johnny Ray pointed.

"No, that pile of rocks makes a perfect place for a nest of rattlesnakes. We'll go around those trees and up through the pasture towards the woods." She pointed to the right a few hundred feet farther up the hillside where the cleared ground ended and the woods began.

"Does Mr. Johnson own all this land?"

"Yes."

"But I thought he worked at the prison. How can he do that and all this farming, too?

"He is a prison guard, but he does his farm work evenings and weekends."

"Does Audie Lee help him?"

"I doubt if Audie Lee does much farm work, but Mama says he helps cook and clean house."

"Is Mr. Johnson his daddy?"

"No, he's an older brother. Their parents are dead, so Mr. Johnson takes care of Audie Lee."

"How old is Audie Lee, anyway?"

Maggie tried to keep the irritation out of her voice. "Mama says he's probably in his late twenties."

From the hillside above the barn they could easily see the backyard and the back of the Johnson house. "Why, it's painted white!" Johnny Ray seemed surprised. "I wish our house was white instead of that old ugly gray." Except for June Wilson's house on the highway and the Johnsons' house, none of the houses in the holler had ever been painted.

"Someday I'll get a job and make a lot of money. I'll buy the paint and you can paint our house," Maggie suggested.

"I wonder why they have clothes on the line. Mama didn't do no wash for them today."

"Sometimes Mr. Johnson washes some clothes on the week that Mama don't do it. I guess he must have done some before he left for work this morning."

They had reached the briars that had grown into large clumps of canes hanging full of dark, ripe fruit. "Okay, little brother, look at all these berries. Here, Sadie, check out these bushes and make sure there's no snakes." When it seemed safe, Maggie pointed out several long briars loaded with berries at the edge of the woods. "Now, you pick here. Just pick the black ones. The red ones are sour. I'll go over there to that bunch of briars. Remember," she reminded him, "have to get half a bucket full to get a dime."

Soon she had the bottom of her bucket covered. She whistled when she noticed Sadie was out of sight, and shortly the dog came trotting out of the woods. "Here girl, you stay with us. We didn't bring you to hunt rabbits. You're supposed to hunt snakes." After a few minutes, Maggie walked over to check on Johnny Ray. He had about a cup of berries in his bucket. "Hey, little man, you're doing real good. You're going to get that dime, all right."

Johnny Ray smiled at her praise, revealing a purple mouth. He rubbed his sleeve over his forehead. "I'm so hot."

"Well, hurry and get your berries picked so we can go home and eat dinner." Maggie began to walk back to her spot. Suddenly a blood curdling scream made her heart stand still. Maggie raced to Johnny Ray's side and knelt beside him. "What happened?" Johnny Ray, standing several steps back from the briars with his hands over his face, had dropped his bucket, spilling his berries. "What's the matter?" Maggie pulled his hands away and saw his eyes full of tears.

"A big bee! Hit me right on the head."

"Did it sting you?"

"No," he reluctantly admitted.

She put the bucket back in his hand and began to pick more berries to cover the bottom of his bucket again. "You know how Stuart catches June bugs and puts a string on their legs so they fly around in a circle?" Johnny Ray nodded. "That wasn't a bee that flew out at you. It was a June bug. They like to eat berries. You scared the bug more than it scared you. It only tried to fly away before it got hurt. One flew out at me a minute ago, and I almost yelled and dropped my bucket too." She gently pushed him toward the briars and encouraged him to resume his picking.

"Just keep your eyes open. Maybe you'll see the next one before it surprises you." She returned to her bucket and resumed picking. Sadie barked in the distance chasing a rabbit far down the hollow. *Oh well, that's what a rabbit dog's really supposed to do.*

Maggie had picked more than half her bucket full, she called, "Johnny Ray, I'm going around to the other side of these briars. You stay right there."

He nodded to let her know he had heard her. "I have my bucket almost half full."

"Good boy. I'll be over to see in a minute." She walked around the bush and grinned to see so much ripe fruit like black jewels hanging in great bunches from the graceful briars. She could fill her bucket in no time. Visualizing the panties and bras in the Sears and Roebuck catalog, she planned to come back every day for a week and pick buckets of berries. For a moment she forgot she had promised to look at Johnny Ray's berries. "Do you have your bucket full?" She called.

When he didn't answer, she called louder. "Johnny Ray?" *What's he up to now?* She walked around the clump of berry bushes and saw his bucket, but he was nowhere in sight. Thinking maybe he had stepped back into the woods to pee, she walked to the other side of a bushy white pine a few paces into the woods. She knew he would be afraid to go far alone. Alarmed, she called again and a movement several yards away in the woods caught her eye.

She drew a sharp breath when she saw a man in prison clothes clutching Johnny Ray against him with one hand over his mouth. The man leaned back against a fallen tree and held Johnny Ray between his legs. Her heart pounded so loud she could hear it, and her knees felt weak.

"What are you doing?" she demanded and took a few steps toward them.

"Stay right there, or I'll slit his throat."

Maggie saw the small pocket knife he held at Johnny Ray's throat. She could see Johnny Ray's eyes, huge and full of fear. "What do you want? Turn my brother loose."

"Listen, girl, you do just like I tell you, and your brother won't get hurt." Maggie nodded. "You see them clothes hanging on that line down the hill there? Well, you go down there and get me a shirt and a pair of pants. Don't tell no one. I'll give you five minutes, and then if you ain't back with those clothes, I'll start cutting off his ears, and then his nose before I slit his throat."

Johnny Ray's body stiffened, and he tried to twist his head, but the man held him tight. Maggie could hear his muffled cries.

"Don't be afraid, Johnny Ray. Do just like he says. I'll be back in no time." She looked at the man. "You hurt my brother, my daddy'll kill you." Maggie turned and ran like a scared rabbit through the pasture toward the Johnsons' backyard. She had never been so afraid.

I wonder why the prison whistle didn't blow. Please, God, don't let him hurt Johnny Ray. She opened the gate and cautiously walked toward the clothesline. She took the clothespins from a shirttail and clipped them back on the line. Then she moved to take a pair of pants. Just as she gripped the clothespin, a dirty hand covered hers and another hand pulled down the line so she stared right into Audie Lee's eyes.

34

He shook his head from side to side and tried to make her take her hand away.

She had never seen him so close before. The old hat shaded his face, but Maggie could see that his small beady eyes, too close together, made him appear slightly cross-eyed. His long nose and receding chin surrounded by unshaved stubble reminded Maggie of a groundhog. He angrily pried at her hand and shook his head while he made strange grunting noises.

"Audie Lee, I've got to borrow these for a little while." Her voice shook. "My brother's in trouble, and if I don't take these clothes, something bad'll happen to him." She couldn't tell if he understood what she said. The angry expression on his face didn't change, but he gripped her hand more insistently.

"Please, Audie Lee," she pleaded. But he only shook his head.

Suddenly, she remembered the piece of jewelry she had found in the gully. With her free hand, she pulled it from her pocket and held it out where Audie Lee could see it. He looked at it with interest. "Go on, take it."

Audie Lee looked at her and grinned. He released her hand and took the shiny thing, turning it over and studying it closely.

When Maggie reached the woods, she hurried toward the man holding Johnny Ray and threw the clothes at his feet. The man released Johnny Ray, and she dropped to her knees, grabbing him in her arms. "Are you okay?" Johnny Ray, trembling from head to toe, nodded. He clung tightly to her and sobbed into her shoulder. "Take those clothes and get out of here," she hissed. She hugged Johnny Ray to her, and they watched the man pour all of Johnny Ray's berries into Maggie's bucket.

"I need some food," he said. "Besides, no one'll be suspicious of a berry picker." Maggie opened her mouth to protest but changed her mind. "Thanks for your help," he said and walked into the woods carrying the clothes under his arm. Maggie watched him go and fought back tears of relief.

Still on her knees holding her brother, Maggie squeezed him tight. "You were so brave. I'm proud of you."

"But he took all our berries," Johnny Ray protested. "Now I won't get my dime."

"I know." She smoothed his hair and hugged him again. "But at least he didn't hurt you. We'll pick some more berries tomorrow.

You'll still get your dime."

From a distance the prison whistle gave a long blast announcing to the countryside that an inmate had escaped. "Let's go home." Maggie stood up and took his hand "Mama'll be worried sick about us."

CHAPTER 3

Campbell Holler–September 15, 1885   Harvey off to
camp meeting again.   Gone 2 weeks.   Boys helped dig
potatoes and onions.   Been playing mandolin and teaching
them songs.   Harvey ain't here to forbid it.
(Diary of Mary Louise Campbell)

August 1949

Maggie had finished washing the milk pails when she heard a car.   After
quickly drying her hands, she rushed to look out the front door and saw Mr.
Johnson handing a package to Corie Mae, who had stepped out onto the
porch.

"June Wilson told me the mailman left this package at her house, and
she asked me to drop it off for you."   He mentioned he had been
concerned when Ray had come to tell him about the escaped convict and to
offer to pay for the clothes the prisoner took.   "I found out last week the
man has been recaptured."   He noticed Maggie standing inside the screen
door.   "Glad he didn't hurt you."   Maggie smiled and nodded.

Corie Mae held the package to her chest.   "Kyle, you're very kind to let
us pick the berries.   After Ray heard about the convict, he come home early
several afternoons to go with Maggie, and they got lots of berries.   They
didn't see no more prisoners, but they did see a few copperheads."   Corie
Mae turned to Maggie.   "Go get a couple jars of that blackberry jam for Mr.
Johnson for bringing the package."

After Maggie returned with the jam, they stood on the porch chatting.
A car came up the road, a cloud of dust billowing up behind it.   They

watched as Reverend Lewis slowed to steer around Mr. Johnson's car and wave before he continued toward the head of the holler. "What's he coming for?" Corie Mae wrinkled her brow. "Hope nothing bad's happened."

"I'll be getting on home." Mr. Johnson took the jars from Maggie. "Thanks for the jam." He hurried down the stone steps to his car and backed up to turn around in the lane to the barn.

Corie Mae handed the package to Maggie. "I guess this is your new underwear."

Maggie studied her mother's face but couldn't interpret its meaning. "Thank you, Mama." Without saying anything, Corie Mae opened the screen door to go finish preparing supper.

* * *

Corie Mae had poured the cornbread batter into the hot iron skillet when Grandpa walked into the kitchen. Corie Mae took one look at her father's troubled face, closed the oven door, and rushed to him. "Papa, what's wrong?"

"Well, Sis, Preacher Lewis brung us some bad news."

Corie Mae led him into the front room, and sat down in her rocking chair. Grandpa pulled over a straight chair and sat beside her while the children huddled in the doorway listening. "Reverend Lewis got a call from your cousin Lottie saying Helen died yesterday."

"Oh, no." Corie Mae began to sob into her apron.

"What's wrong, Mama?" Junior ran across the room and crawled into her lap. Grandpa took out his bandana and blew his nose.

Maggie returned to the kitchen to make sure the supper was not burning. She remembered her mother telling stories about how Aunt Helen, Grandpa's only sister, was her favorite aunt. Maggie felt a special kinship to Aunt Helen because her parents had given her Aunt Helen's middle name, although no one called her "Margaret."

After Great-grandpa died, Great-grandma had asked Corie Mae to move into the house with her. Later Great-grandma and Corie Mae had ridden the Greyhound bus to Kentucky where they spent most of the summer with Aunt Helen, Great-grandma's only daughter. Fifteen-year-old Corie Mae and Lottie, Aunt Helen's daughter, became really close. Lottie was in love with the preacher's son and before the end of the year had married him.

That summer Corie Mae had met Ray, who lived next door to Aunt Helen. Corie Mae had told the children how Lottie and her beau and she and Ray had spent time together going to church, taking long walks, and visiting the soda fountain at the drug store. The next year Ray had come to

Tennessee and married Corie Mae, and the two of them had lived with Great-grandma and cared for her in this very house until she died shortly before Maggie's birth.

When Maggie returned to the front room, she heard Grandpa explain that he told Reverend Lewis he would send JD over later to call Lottie and tell her what the family had decided to do about going to the funeral.

"I just can't believe it." Corie Mae began crying again.

Junior patted her on the cheek. "Don't cry, Mama."

Grandpa took Junior into his lap and patted Cora Mae's arm. "It was her time, I guess. The good Lord knows best. We just have to accept these things. Everything happens for a reason, you know."

Maggie returned to the kitchen and checked the oven, but the cornbread had not browned. The potatoes and beans were done, so she pulled the pot to the back of the stove and went out on the back porch. *This makes me think about last Christmas Eve when Elsie Mae was so sick.* Maggie recalled how she had awakened late that night by what had sounded like a baby kitten mewing. Finally, Maggie recognized the cries of her baby sister. Elsie Mae had been sick for a week with a bad cold. But Grandma Campbell's poultices of onions fried in bacon grease had not helped, and Elsie Mae had gotten worse. Maggie went downstairs where Corie Mae sat near the Warm Morning stove in her rocking chair, holding the toddler to her breast. Elsie Mae's curly red hair framed her face. Maggie had watched with alarm as the baby struggled to breathe.

"Ray's walked up to Johnsons to see if Kyle will take him down to the preacher's house to call the doctor." Corie Mae pointed to the stove. "Would you poke up the fire and put in some more coal? She's hot with fever, but her little body's trembling." When Maggie had built up the fire, Corie Mae pointed toward the stairs. "You go on back to bed. Ain't nothing more you can do for her."

Maggie had held the baby's little hand, but there was no response–her little body limp as a cooked noodle. Maggie had touched the red curls then climbed back up the stairs but could not go to sleep for listening to every rasping breath. After daylight the doctor finally arrived and pressed his stethoscope to her chest shaking his head. He had given her a shot, but it was too late. She had been such a sweet little girl, just barely two.

Daddy was as broke up as Mama. Maggie wiped tears from her eyes with the back of her hand and went inside to check the cornbread, feeling a heavy sadness.

* * *

Later that evening, JD and Aunt Lillian came over, and Maggie, Corie Mae, and Ray joined them at the kitchen table speaking softly so not to disturb the sleeping children. "I told Joe Clark if he'd cover for me the rest of this week at the station, I'd take his shift next week," JD said. "So I guess I'll be driving Grandma and Grandpa up to Kentucky for the funeral."

"I think you and Ray should go too, Corie Mae. I can stay here with the kids. Opal's staying out at Honey Valley taking care of James Scott's mother, but Kenny and the girls'll all help. We can hold things together while you're gone." Aunt Lillian looked first at Corie Mae and then at Ray.

Ray smiled at Aunt Lillian and looked across the table at his wife. "You should go, Corie Mae, but I should stay here to take care of things."

"But, Ray, you ain't seen any of your folks in Kentucky for years. This would give you a chance to visit them." Aunt Lillian lowered her voice. "Besides, Corie Mae needs you."

Ray didn't say anything, but looked down at his hands folded together on the table.

"Go, Daddy." Maggie put her hand on top of Ray's. "With Aunt Lillian here to keep an eye on things, us girls and Kenny can do all of Grandpa's chores and take care of our animals. The world won't come to an end if you're away for a few days."

"It's okay for you to go, Ray." Corie Mae reached across the table. "I'd like you to come with me." When Ray took her hands and gave a slight nod of assent, she said, "Of course, I'll have to take Jay since he's still nursing."

"That's right, Corie Mae." Aunt Lillian laughed. "I can milk cows, slop hogs, cook and clean, but I sure ain't got no milk in these." She placed her hands on her small breasts.

Everyone laughed, and Corie Mae shushed them. "The kids are sleeping."

So they decided that Corie Mae and Ray would go to the funeral with Grandma and Grandpa. As Aunt Lillian and JD rose to leave, Corie Mae hugged her sister-in-law. "This is so good of you, Lillian. I can't thank you enough."

"Don't mention it. You'd do the same for me."

* * *

"Wave good-bye to Mama and Daddy." Maggie held four-year-old Junior on her hip as JD drove away taking the folks to Kentucky.

Junior whimpered, "If Jay gets to go, why can't I go too?"

Maggie hugged him tighter, realizing her mother had never left him before. Aunt Lillian clapped her hands several times. "Okay, kids, we've got stuff to do. Let's go sit around the kitchen table and make our plans." She turned to Maggie. "How many canning jars do you have?"

"Mama told Daddy yesterday we needed to buy some when the rolling store comes."

"This is Thursday, so the rolling store comes today. We need a list." Aunt Lillian motioned to Maggie. "Can you find me some paper and pencil?"

Maggie stood to look for pencil and paper. "We've got four dozen eggs to trade in."

"Good. I have some money too, so we can get sugar, jars and lids, and anything else we need." Aunt Lillian turned to Kenny. "You and Stuart take the little red wagon and go up to Grandma's house and bring back all the canning jars she has. She keeps her empties in the smoke house."

When Kenny and Stuart came back with the jars, she sent them to gather the tomatoes from Grandma's garden. Maggie and Johnny Ray went to pick apples while Betty Lou and Jeannie drew water to heat for washing the canning jars.

Every day Aunt Lillian had them up early and working hard. By mid-afternoon on Saturday, they had canned all the tomatoes, including those from Grandma's garden, canned a bushel of apples, and made a dozen pints of apple butter, in addition to doing all the chores and caring for the animals. Even the rain, falling steadily all day Friday, hadn't kept them from getting the job done. When the children had stowed the last jar on the shelves in the root cellar and taken Grandma's filled jars to her kitchen, Aunt Lillian called everyone together.

"Okay, kids, you've worked really hard. I'm very proud of you all, and I know your mama will be, too."

"Let's not tell her and just have her come to look in the root cellar and see all the new jars. She'll be real surprised."

"That's a good idea, Johnny Ray. After all your hard work, now it's party time." They gathered around Aunt Lillian all talking at once. "When the chores is all done and ever'body's cleaned up, we'll go to Kenny's house and have a party."

Because of the sharp curve in the road and the trees, No one could see Kenny's house from the Martin's front porch, even though it was only a hundred yards away. Uncle Thomas and his father had constructed the house with timber cut from the property–a one story with a large kitchen, a front room, and three bedrooms.

When Maggie's uncles took jobs in Detroit, Uncle WC had offered to pay room and board if Aunt Opal would agree for Aunt Lillian to live there. With this extra money, Aunt Opal had bought much nicer furniture than Maggie's family could afford. She did not like the children to come to her house because they might get her new sofa dirty or track mud on her throw rugs. "Aunt Opal'd have a fit if she could see all of us here on her fancy furniture," Jeannie whispered to Maggie, who grinned and responded, "What she don't know can't hurt her."

After they played several games, Aunt Lillian doled out Milky Way bars as prizes. She led them into the kitchen where they had a feast of pimento cheese sandwiches, made with sliced white bread and fresh tomatoes from the garden, washed down with bottles of cold Coca Cola.

"How'd you get all this?" Stuart wiped the back of his hand across his mouth after a big swig of pop.

"You know when the rolling store was here?" Kenny's eyes twinkled. "After Aunt Lillian bought all the sugar and stuff on her list, she give me another list, and I got all this and brought it over here while you all carried the other stuff to your house."

"You mean you knowed all about this party, and you didn't say a word?"

Kenny just grinned.

* * *

Later Saturday night Maggie sat at the kitchen table brushing the tangles from her freshly shampooed hair while she read her Sunday School lesson. "I think all the little ones is asleep." Aunt Lillian came into the room and sat across the table from Maggie.

"Thank you, Aunt Lillian, for helping us while Mama and Daddy went to the funeral." Maggie smiled at Aunt Lillian. "I think the girls and I could've managed to do the chores and take care of the little ones, but we couldn't have done all that canning. Besides that, you helped us have a really good time. I don't think Stuart and Johnny Ray have said a single cross word since Mama and Daddy left." Maggie paused. "Well, maybe once or twice."

Aunt Lillian laughed. "I've had a good time, too." She watched Maggie brushing her hair for a few minutes. "Would you like me to help you with those tangles in the back?" Aunt Lillian gently brushed out the tangles. "Your hair is really healthy. It's so shiny, and where the sun has bleached it, it has a reddish cast."

"I hate my hair. I wish Mama would let me cut it. I'll be the only girl in high school with pigtails."

"If you'd like, I'll cut it for you. Have you thought how you'd like to wear it?"

They talked about several ways to style Maggie's hair and laughed together at some of the more ridiculous possibilities. When she went to bed, Maggie couldn't stop her busy mind from thinking about starting high school, wishing for new clothes and a haircut, and contemplating the new insights into Aunt Lillian. Amazingly, she had lived next door for years, and yet it seemed Maggie had met her for the first time. *I truly feel I have made a new friend.*

* * *

About time for supper the next day, JD drove up with the folks. Chaos reigned as all the children crowded around the car, talking at once. Aunt Lillian suggested that everyone come in and eat supper. JD took the suitcase out of the trunk and handed it to Maggie. "Got lots to tell you when we get a chance to talk. I don't have to work tomorrow. Maybe we can think of something to do."

"The Intermediate B.Y.P.U. is having a weenie roast tomorrow night at Reverend Lewis's. Maybe we could go to that." Maggie spoke softly so others didn't hear.

"See if Aunt Corie Mae'll let you go, and me and Kenny will pick you up. What time does it start?"

"At church they said 'a little before dark.'"

"Tell Aunt Corie Mae we need to leave about six o'clock, and we'll go to town and hang out at the drug store awhile before it starts." Maggie and JD joined the others on the porch.

"You'ns just make yourselfs at home while me and the girls finish putting supper on the table," Aunt Lillian said. "By the time you get comfortable and wash up, we'll be ready to eat."

During the meal, Corie Mae told about the funeral. "By the time we got there Thursday night, the undertaker had laid out Aunt Helen in the front room at her house. All the family was there. You wouldn't believe all the food the neighbors had brought in."

"I like to split my sides open laughing at that Elmer," Grandpa said. "He's Helen's oldest boy, ye know. Got to telling stories about all the meanness he done when he was growing up. It was so funny to hear him tell it. I got to thinking how bad it was that we was laughing our fool heads off, and there was poor Helen all laid out right in the next room."

"Was the funeral at the church?" Betty Lou asked.

"Yes, and the church house was packed. They was three preachers, and ever one of them preached a long sermon," Corie Mae said. "I was so glad they told ever'body they better get saved so they could go to heaven like Aunt Helen."

Then Grandma spoke up. "I really felt sorry for poor Lottie. She'd stayed there day and night for weeks nursing her mama. It wore her plumb out, and she really took it hard. When the family come up to the casket for the last time, she fainted, and they had to lay her on a bench and fan her to bring her to."

"What'd you all do after the funeral?" Jeannie looked at her mother.

"Me and Ray visited with his sisters. I wish all you kids could of been there. I would like to have Ray's family meet all his kids. They was all real sorry they didn't none of them get to come down for Elsie Mae's funeral last year.

Corie Mae seemed more excited and talkative than Maggie had seen her for a long time. Even though she said the long car ride had tired her out, the circles under her eyes were not as dark as usual. Eager to hear all the family news, Maggie looked across the table at Grandma and Grandpa. "And what did you two do while Mama and Daddy was at Aunt Dar's?"

Grandpa cleared his throat and pushed his empty plate away. "We visited with Helen's kids and grandchildren and..."

Corie Mae interrupted. "Papa, you had JD take you to church on Saturday night." She turned toward the children. "It's the first time he's been to a Pentecostal church in a mighty long time. I guess he had a really good Holy Ghost anointing."

As everyone prepared to leave, Maggie saw Ray had cornered Aunt Lillian in the kitchen to thank her for helping out. "If there's ever a time when you need help, you just let us know. Corie Mae looked so good in the dresses you let her borrow. I wish I had the money to get her teeth fixed. I swan she'd be as pretty as the first time I saw her if she didn't have them rotted teeth."

Aunt Lillian gathered her things. "Well, Ray, just keep working hard. Someday things'll be different." She patted him on the arm as she walked past him.

When the supper dishes were finished, Corie Mae asked if they had finished all the chores. "Yes, Mama, but we have a big surprise for you." Johnny Ray had hovered close to Corie Mae all evening.

"What's that?"

Junior piped up. "Just go look in the root cellar."

"Don't tell. It's a secret." Johnny Ray scowled at Junior and then turned to Corie Mae. "But you'll be surprised when you see what's there."

Corie Mae took the hands of the two boys. "Then let's go see."

* * *

Maggie, frustrated when her mother seemed reluctant to allow her to go with JD and Kenny to the wiener roast for the kids at church, argued her case. "But, Mama, just think. JD and Kenny don't go to church much. Maybe if they went to this youth outing and had a good time, they'd go to church more. At least they want to go to this, but if I don't go, they probably won't neither."

"I don't think it's right for boys and girls to be playing around out in the fields after dark. You never know what might happen."

"But it's going to be at Reverend and Mrs. Lewis's house, and they're both going to be there. It's not like we wouldn't be chaperoned. Seems like you don't want me to do anything except stay here and work."

Corie Mae, pressing her lips together and closing her eyes, didn't reply for a long time. "I still don't like it." But after another moment of silence, she sighed. "Oh, all right, just don't stay out late." She even agreed that Maggie could make a batch of cookies to take.

Only the second time Maggie had gotten to ride in JD's car, she sat in the front seat, feeling she had been freed from jail–with her arm out the window, the wind flowing through her fingers. "You said you had something to tell me about your trip to Kentucky."

JD nodded. "Oh, yeah. I wanted to tell you about taking Grandpa to this little church way out on the side of the mountain where they had a snake-handling service."

"Oh, my gosh. Did Grandpa pick up one?" Maggie's eyes widened, and she held her hand up as if she thought JD would pull out a snake to show her.

"Actually he did. At first, though, he just danced up and down the aisle and said stuff that didn't make no sense. I asked him later what he was saying, and he said he didn't know. It was the Holy Ghost using his voice." JD looked over at her and grinned. "He said it was the most wonderful feeling. Lots of others was speaking in tongues too."

Kenny leaned forward to rest his arms on the back of the front seat. "Well, did they just plunk them down and say 'Come and get them' or what?"

JD grinned bigger and shook his head. "When we first got there, not many people had come. So we went in and sat down close to the back. After a while, a big feller come in carrying a couple wooden boxes with signs on them 'They shall take up serpents.' Grandpa said, 'That's preacher so and so from over at Newport,' and he went up front to talk to him."

"I think I'd have left right then!" Maggie rolled her eyes.

"After Grandpa talked with that preacher for a few minutes, a couple of fellers come in carrying guitars. Another man brought in a set of drums and passed several tambourines to some people. By this time a pretty good crowd had come. Then two more men come in carrying snake boxes. When the musicians started playing, everyone began singing and clapping. They kept on singing one song after another for maybe a half hour."

"What kind of songs did they sing? Did you know them?" Maggie had her arm out the window again.

"The only one I knew was 'Old Time Religion,' but everybody else seemed to know them."

Maggie noticed they passed the funeral home as they drove down Main Street and then stopped at the drug store.

"Hey, there's Bud Summers." JD nodded toward a boy sitting on the steps of the drug store with a couple of girls.

"Who's the girls?" Kenny opened the back door.

"That's Wanda Smith and Juanita Jones. They're in my class at

45

school." They strolled over to JD's friends.

"What you all up to?" asked Bud.

"We're fixing to go to a weenie roast out at Preacher Lewis's house." JD introduced his friends to Maggie and Kenny. "What you all up to?"

"We're trying to think of somebody with a car who could take us to the movie." Wanda smiled at JD and batted her eyes. JD looked at Maggie and raised his eyebrows.

"Don't look at me. I can't go to the movies. I've got no money." Embarrassed, Maggie pushed around some gravel on the sidewalk with the toe of her shoe.

"Me neither." Kenny put his hands into his empty pockets.

"I got enough to get your tickets," JD said.

"But won't we be late getting home if we drive all the way to the theater? It's almost twenty miles." Maggie twisted her hands together. "Besides, Mama thinks we're going to the weenie roast. She'll kill me."

"What's the latest you can get home?" Bud smiled at Maggie.

"About a hour after dark."

"Okay." Bud looked at his watch. "If Maggie's willing, and we leave right now, I think we can make that deadline."

Maggie felt on the spot. She had seen a few films at school but had never gone to a movie theater. Not sure what her father thought about going to the movies, she had no doubt her mother thought it an abomination to the Lord. Torn between wanting to go and being afraid of what her mother would do if she found out, she debated with herself. *She might never let me go out with JD again. On the other hand, I'd really love to see a real movie, and I don't want JD's friends to think I'm a party-pooper.*

She gave JD a help-me-out look, but JD shook his head. "It's up to you."

After an additional moment of hesitation, she shrugged. "What are we standing here for? Let's get started."

"Good sport!" Bud grinned at her, and she noticed his cute dimples.

Maggie watched as JD held the door for Wanda to slide under the steering wheel so she could sit next to him. Bud held the door for Juanita to sit in the back between him and Kenny. Maggie took the only vacant seat in the front next to Wanda. She listened to the talk going back and forth about school starting soon–football practice, new teachers, and most interesting of all, a rumor that girls would not be allowed to wear jeans. Juanita was especially indignant about that. Maggie thought it would make no difference for her. *Mama won't let me wear jeans anyway.*

Wanda asked Maggie what courses she would be taking when school started. "You'll like Miss Erickson, the business teacher. She takes such an interest in all her students, and they always win awards at the County Business Education Fair." Maggie, warmed by Wanda's friendliness, began to feel more comfortable and volunteered a comment or two of her own.

The movie, *Adam's Rib,* starred Spencer Tracy and Katharine Hepburn. Maggie sat spellbound at the action which seemed to happen right in front of her. She found the scenes in the courtroom fascinating, having never actually witnessed a trial. Hepburn's argument in court that women had rights impressed her most. While she did a lot of laughing, she also found a lot to think about. For one thing, it had never occurred to her that a woman could be a lawyer. *I guess there's lots in this world I don't know about.*

When they came out of the theater, the street lights cast shadows on the sidewalk. Bud looked at his watch. "I think we can get you home by your deadline, Maggie, if JD don't fool around too much."

They had a demanding drive over mountainous roads and had to go all the way into town to take the girls and Bud home. JD, wasting no time, whipped around curves with his tires squealing. They laughed together as they shared their impressions of the movie and ate the cookies Maggie had brought for the wiener roast. "Boy, I really like to died when he put that gun in his mouth and then bit the barrel off." Kenny laughed.

"I liked the part where she came into the courtroom wearing his wife's new hat. The look on his face." Wanda put her palms together as if she were about to applaud.

About halfway home, Bud tapped Maggie on the shoulder. "Did you like the movie, Maggie? Glad you came?"

"I enjoyed it a lot, but I may not be so glad tomorrow."

"Don't worry about it, Cuz." JD leaned forward to look at Maggie. "If Aunt Corie Mae gets mad, I'll tell her it was my idea."

As soon as they had dropped Bud and the girls at their homes in town, Maggie turned to JD. "Finish telling about Grandpa and the snakes."

JD nodded. "The snakes came later after they had a lot more singing and shouting and several people got up and gave their testimonies. Finally, one of the preachers got up and read from the Bible where it says people will take up serpents and drink poison."

"That's really in the Bible?" Maggie couldn't believe it.

"Yeah, it also says they can touch fire and it won't burn them."

"I don't believe that. Where does it say that in the Bible?"

"I don't know, Kenny. You'll have to ask Grandpa. Then this preacher got to preaching like Grandpa does, talking real loud and fast and saying 'Huh' at the end of every sentence. He paced around on the platform, sometimes hopped along on one foot. Finally, he come down from the pulpit and opened one of the boxes and took out two big snakes. One was reddish and the other was dark brown. They was both about four foot long."

"Was you scared?" Maggie held her hands in front of her face as if blocking the scene from her sight.

"Not really, but I prepared to get out of there fast if he dropped one on the floor."

"Did he just hold them out at arm's length, or what?" Kenny sat up close with his arms on the back of the front seat.

"He put the snakes around his neck and let them curl around his arms, and all this time, he was still preaching. Then another one of the preachers opened a box and took out a snake so big he could barely reach his fingers around it. Then a whole bunch of people, mostly men, but one or two women, come up and stood in a circle, and they handed the snakes back and forth. That's when Grandpa went up, and somebody handed two snakes to him. Some people would just hold them a minute and pass them on; others would dance around holding them up to their faces, even kissing them."

Maggie shivered. "What'd Grandpa do when he had them?"

"He didn't keep them very long but held them in front of his face like he was talking to them while he was speaking in tongues."

"You'd never catch me picking up a snake, much less dancing around and kissing it." Kenny leaned back in his seat. "Sounds crazy to me."

"To me it makes about as much sense as being at the county fair and calling it church." Maggie was still holding herself stiff, pushed back against the door. "Were all the snakes poison?"

"I asked Grandpa about that, and he said they was. He said some scoffers claim that the handlers have removed their fangs, but that ain't true. He said he had saw one feller get bit once, and later the man died cause he refused to get any medical help. I guess that's why it's against the law in most states to handle snakes."

"Well, it's sure against my law." Maggie shivered again. "Don't want snakes nowhere near me." She turned to JD, "Do all Pentecostal churches practice snake handling?"

"No. Grandpa said they's only a few churches left that do it since it's illegal. He said he only knows of one in Tennessee."

When Maggie walked into the front room, her mother sat at her sewing machine making a dress for Jeannie from some material Lottie had given her when she went to the funeral. She looked up briefly, "Did you have a good time?"

"Yes, ma'am."

"Well, you better get to bed. We got a lotta work to do tomorrow."

"Goodnight, Mama." Maggie leaned over to plant a kiss on the top of her mother's head. "Thanks for letting me go."

"You done a lotta work while I was gone. I 'preciate it."

Maggie climbed the stairs hanging her head in shame. After she got into bed, the scenes from the movie kept running through her mind. She finally drifted off to sleep and dreamed she sat at the defendant's table, accused of lying. When the judge said "Guilty as charged" and slammed down his gavel, Maggie woke with a start. She couldn't go back to sleep. She heard the rooster crowing and knew it was about time to get up anyway.

* * *

In the weeks before school started, they canned more fruits and vegetables and dug white potatoes, sweet potatoes, and carrots. They put apples in the sun to dry, set onions on newspapers to dry in the smokehouse, and made a big crock of kraut. They filled the barn loft with fresh hay, and Ray and the boys had started digging a foundation for the wellhouse where they would eventually install the pump and pressure tank.

On the Friday evening before school started, Maggie decided to approach her parents about the gym suit. Corie Mae sat at the kitchen table making button holes in a shirt for Johnny Ray, and Ray sat in the porch swing smoking his pipe. She joined her father in the swing, enjoying the long twilight of the late summer evening. She breathed in the smoke from his pipe and tasted it in her mouth. The odors of sweat and horse rose from his clothes and mingled with the swirling pipe smoke. They rocked slowly in the swing for several minutes while Ray puffed on his pipe.

"I need you to get the box of last year's books for me. JD's going to take me to town tomorrow to buy books for all you kids. I can sell back any that you kids don't need." Ray took a puff on his pipe. "I heard the state is talking about passing a law to provide all the books for school children. That'd be a big help. Buying books for five students takes a lot a money, especially if I can't buy used ones."

"I wanted to talk to you about that," Maggie said, heart racing and chest tight as a drum. "You know I'll have to take gym class this year, and they expect all us girls to have a gym suit."

"Where do you have to get it at?"

"I think they sell them at Montgomery's Five and Ten where they sell the books."

"Tell me what size to get. Do you have the list of the classes you signed up for?"

She couldn't believe her father would agree to buy the gym suit with no argument. "Me and Mama made out the list yesterday of what grade all the kids is in and what classes I'm taking. It's in the box of books right behind the front door."

Maggie listened to the crickets and the jar flies for a few minutes as a slight breeze cooled her cheeks, and a whippoorwill sang in the distance. In the dimming light she could barely see the fragrant smoke from her father's pipe swirling around his head. She took a deep breath. "Daddy, I was afraid you and Mama wouldn't want me to wear shorts in gym."

Ray took his pipe out of his mouth. "Do you want to wear shorts?"

"I want to wear what everyone else wears. I don't want to take gym in a dress. That'd be real embarrassing."

Ray leaned over and knocked the ashes out of his pipe on the porch rail. "Then I guess we'll just have to buy the gym suit."

"But what'll Mama say? You know she don't let us girls wear jeans or pants, much less shorts."

"I guess we can talk her into it."

Maggie stood, leaned over her father, and kissed him on the forehead. "Thanks, Daddy. I love you."

"Goodnight, Sunshine."

* * *

On Sunday afternoon, Aunt Lillian and Maggie came up the steps onto the porch where Ray and Corie Mae sat in the swing. Maggie had been playing ball at Kenny's barn when Aunt Lillian had come to offer to cut her hair.

Maggie pulled a couple of chairs from the front room so they could all sit on the porch. Maggie saw Corie Mae was still upset. She had objected loudly when she saw the blue gym suit among the books Ray had brought in yesterday afternoon.

"Now, Corie Mae." Ray had spoken gently. "You don't want the kids to make fun of Maggie, do you?"

"I don't believe in women showing their legs like no damn crane!"

Maggie gasped. She had never heard her mother swear. She saw the corners of her father's mouth twitch, and for a moment his eyes twinkled. "Corie Mae, what do you expect Maggie to tell the gym teacher?"

"Tell them her mother won't allow it. If they won't believe her, I'll go tell them myself." Her voice broke, and she seemed on the edge of tears.

"Now, Corie Mae, we ain't going to make trouble." Ray put his hand on Corie Mae's shoulder. "We'll just have to go along. The gym class is all girls, and the teacher's a woman. I asked about that when I bought the books. It's not like she's going to be showing her legs to a bunch of boys." Ray spoke in a calm voice, but when Corie Mae opened her mouth to protest, he held up his hand and shook his head. "This is how it's going to be. Maggie will have the gym suit." And then he had walked out to the wood pile and chopped wood for a long time.

Now Maggie saw her mother's rigid jaw, her lips jammed together tightly. She had refused to go to church, and she hadn't said a word to Maggie.

"Did you get all those taters dug yesterday?" Aunt Lillian asked.

"Sure did." Ray stretched his arms above his head. "I think we've got more food in our root cellar right now than ever before. After that terrible storm back in May washed out so much of the corn, I feared it wouldn't be a good year. But we're really blessed."

"Are you okay, Corie Mae? Maggie said you didn't go to church this morning."

Corie Mae turned angry eyes toward Maggie, then gave her sister-in-law an icy look before nodding. A shudder ran up Maggie's spine. She had a tight feeling in her chest. That look from her mother seemed to cut her like a knife. *No way will she allow me to cut my hair.*

After a few minutes of awkward silence, Ray pointed to the box Aunt Lillian held. "What you got there?"

"Just some hair stuff." She opened the box and held up a pair of scissors and a comb. "I offered to cut Maggie's hair, but she said Corie Mae would have to give her permission." She looked at Corie Mae expectantly.

"No!" Corie Mae turned to Maggie. "You're just trying to find another way to go against me. You've been kicking over the traces all summer long." She stood and walked to Maggie, bending over so her face was inches away. "Nothing's good enough for you, little Miss Smarty Pants. First, it was store-bought underwear cause you're too good to wear what I make for you. Then it was going to a mixed party where boys and girls could do heaven knows what, and you plan to parade around in shorts—all against my will. Now you want to cut your hair like some harlot."

She turned and stood over Ray, her balled up fists on her hips, "And you've took her side against me ever' time. Well, I ain't going to put up with it no more." She stepped back to Maggie, "No, Miss High and Mighty, you ain't cutting your hair!" She slapped Maggie across the face.

Lillian jumped to her feet. "No, Corie Mae! She ain't done nothing wrong. I'm the one suggested it."

Meanwhile, Ray had grabbed Corie Mae's hands and led her back to the swing. She sat down and began sobbing into her apron.

Maggie stood and went inside the house, moving like a zombie. Her mother had whipped her a few times with a switch but had never slapped her. She rubbed her cheek, which still burned, climbed the steps, and fell face down on her bed.

She had doubted her mother would agree for Aunt Lillian to cut her hair, so she couldn't say her mother's refusal surprised her. But all the things her mother had said stung worse than the slap. *What would she do if she knew about the movie?* She lay on her stomach with her head buried in her pillow and cried until, exhausted from the shock and weeping, she finally fell asleep.

Maggie roused when she felt hands on her back. She rolled over and saw Ray sitting on the bed beside her. The dim light made her realize she needed to do chores. She sat up, rubbed her face, and looked at her father.

"You okay?" He touched her cheek.

"I guess." Maggie started to stand, but he put his hand on her shoulder and gently pushed her back down. "I'm sorry, Daddy. I didn't mean to go to sleep. I've got to milk the cows."

"That's okay, Sunshine." He patted her hand. "I done it already."

Maggie's eyes filled with tears again. "I didn't mean to make her so upset."

"I know you didn't." He put his arm around her. "Don't feel too bad about what Corie Mae said. When she calms down, she'll realize you're a good daughter."

"But Daddy, I'm really not such a good daughter." She hung her head. "You recollect a couple weeks ago when I said I went to the weenie roast with JD and Kenny? We didn't go to the Lewises. We met three of JD's friends in town and went to a movie." The tears began trickling down her cheeks again.

Ray sat closer to her and held her while she sobbed. "Sunshine, I'm not glad to hear you deceived your mother, but I still think you're a good daughter. Now's not a good time, so we won't say nothing to Corie Mae about the movie." He squeezed her shoulder again and said, "Come on now, let's see a smile."

"She never hit me like that before." Maggie hiccupped from her sobbing. "And she called me a harlot."

"I'm sorry, honey. I should of stopped her sooner." Ray stood and pulled Maggie to her feet. "Now go down and wash your face. Then go over to Lillian's and get your hair cut."

Maggie looked up to see if he was joking. "Mama won't like it."

"I've worked it out with Corie Mae. She won't stop you. Go on over there if you really want to get your hair cut."

"You're sure?"

"Go. You ain't got all night." Ray grinned and gave her a little push toward the stairs.

Maggie turned and put her arms around him. "Thank you, Daddy. You've been really good to me this summer."

Ray kissed the top of her head. "You deserve to be treated good. You're a good girl. Now get out of here!"

* * *

"Hey, I love your hair cut!" Mary Ann raved when she saw Maggie during lunch hour on the first day of school.

"Thanks. Aunt Lillian cut it last night and pin-curled it. Called it a page boy cut. I've had hair half way down my back so long, I keep reaching up to push my braids over my shoulder."

Mary Ann pointed to the bandage on Maggie's arm. "What happened to your arm?"

"I burnt it taking the biscuits out of the stove this morning."

"Does it hurt much?"

"Yeah, it hurts, but it's not near so bad as the burn Junior got."

"What happened?"

The two girls sat on the steps to the parking lot. They had had no classes together all morning, so this was the first time they could talk. It had been a terrible morning, starting when her father gently shook her awake and told her to get up and cook breakfast. Corie Mae had one of her sick headaches. She hadn't had one all summer, but when she got one, it meant she would stay in bed for three days. No one could slam a door, talk loud, or let light into her room. She would lie in the darkened room with a damp cloth over her eyes.

Ray had told Maggie he would do the milking. "I've made the fire in the cook stove. You make the biscuits and get the oatmeal on, and then roust out the kids."

"So I had the oatmeal all done and had just opened up the oven to take out the biscuits when Johnny Ray come running into the kitchen yelling at Junior." Maggie pushed her hair behind her ear. "I turned to tell him to be quiet and wasn't watching what I was doing. My arm hit the side of the oven, and I dropped the pan of biscuits. The pan landed upside down and I got this burn."

"But how did Junior get burned?"

"Betty Lou was carrying the bowls of hot oatmeal to the table. Junior had Johnny Ray's new pencil, and Johnny Ray wanted to get it back. While running to keep Johnny Ray from catching him, Junior bumped into Betty Lou, and the hot oatmeal spilled across his face and down his chest and arm. It's just lucky it didn't go in his eye. He screamed like a wild panther. Of course, Mama heard him and tried to get up. That made her throw up all over the bed. It was a real madhouse for a while. I'm surprised we got ready in time to catch the bus."

"So how bad a burn did Junior get?"

"Before I could get the oatmeal wiped off him, huge blisters had come up all down the side of his face and on his arm. It even made blisters through his shirt. Daddy had Stuart go get Grandma. She mixed castor oil and egg white together and put that all over his burns and bandaged him up.

The bell rang, and Mary Ann stood up. "I bet you won't never forget your first day of high school!"

Just then Bud Summers came up the steps. "Oh, hi, Maggie. Neat haircut." He held the door for the girls to go inside.

When they had taken a seat in Civics class, Mary Ann leaned over and asked, "Who was that guy, and how does he know you?"

"He's a friend of JD's. I met him a couple of weeks ago when I was out with JD."

"He's cute. Did you see how he looked at you?"

Maggie smiled and ran her hands through her short hair.

CHAPTER 4

Campbell Holler–September 29, 1886 Johnny and
Jimmy–6 and 4–quite a pair. Bought reader and speller
from traveling salesman. No school here. Must teach
them myself.

(Diary of Mary Louise Campbell)

October 1949

Maggie set the cool flatiron on the cook stove and picked up the hot one,
careful to keep the hot handle covered with the thick pad. She licked her
finger and quickly touched the surface of the iron, listening for the sizzle.
Sighing, she returned to the ironing board where she had worked since
finishing the supper dishes but had hardly made a dent in the basket of
clothes her mother had sprinkled earlier.

Betty Lou sat in a nearby chair with a lap full of dried beans. "Hurry
and finish your homework, Jeannie, and you can help me hull these shellies.
I've got homework to do, too."

"Okay, I'm almost finished." Jeannie sat at the kitchen table. "You
can give me my spelling words while we shell beans."

Maggie reached for the list Jeannie had placed on the table. "I'll say
them for you while I iron. Let me know when you're ready."

Everyone worked quietly for several minutes. They could hear Corie
Mae in the front room rocking Jay and singing "We'll Understand It Better
By and By." Then Betty Lou said, "Mrs. Lewis asked me today, when I
practiced piano at her house, if I would play all the hymns for the church
service Sunday after next. She's going to Nashville for a convention. She

felt sure I could play all the music for the whole service."

"Wow, Betty Lou, do you think you can learn them well enough in only a week?" Maggie pressed a crease in the sleeve of Johnny Ray's shirt.

"Actually, I already know all but one. I think I can do it." Betty Lou's brown eyes sparkled. "I'll practice really hard this week." Since the Martins had no piano, every day after school Betty Lou got off the bus at the Lewises to practice before walking home.

While Maggie had the fair complexion and blue eyes of her father, Betty Lou had their mother's dark eyes and hair and petite figure. Her ready smile made dimples in her cheeks. *She's got me beat on looks.* Maggie set the iron down and stretched her shoulders and back.

"Mrs. Lewis also gave me a new piece to learn for the school talent show next month." Betty Lou stifled a sneeze. "These bean hulls give me the sniffles." She pulled a handkerchief from her pocket and blew her nose. "Mrs. Lewis said I can become a music teacher if I work hard."

"You mean like giving piano lessons?" Jeannie chewed her pencil eraser.

"I think she meant a music teacher in school like Mrs. Jones."

"Wouldn't you have to go to college to do that?"

"Probably. She said she thought I could get a scholarship if I keep my grades up and keep practicing. You can get a teaching certificate after only two years at teachers college."

Maggie returned to the ironing board after swapping irons. "Miss Erickson told our class today if we do real good in all our business classes, we could probably get a secretarial job as soon as we finish high school." Maggie unfurled a shirt for Stuart and smoothed it on the ironing board. "She told us about a student who graduated two years ago and got a job in Nashville, and now she's going to college at night. I think that's what I'd like to do."

"Think you can learn that shorthand? Looks awful hard to me."

"Actually I'm making good grades in shorthand, and Miss Erickson gave me extra practice exercises so I can learn faster."

"Now girls." Corie Mae walked into the kitchen with her hands on her hips. "You can't fill your heads with these wild day dreams." Maggie hadn't realized their mother had heard their conversation. "Get this foolishness out of your heads right now." She shook her finger at the girls. "Women don't need college. The Bible says God made woman to be a helpmeet for man. That's what a woman's supposed to do." She pulled up a chair, sat down, and filled her apron with beans from the basket on the floor. "Too much education ain't good for nobody. It makes you think you're better'n others. I quit school in sixth grade, and I've got along just fine. Besides families needs to stay together and help each other." Maggie rolled her eyes at Betty Lou.

Maggie shook the grate on the stove, opened the lid, and put in two sticks of wood. Ever since the brouhaha over getting her hair cut, she had taken great pains to do everything the way her mother wanted. She liked her new look. It took time—pin curls every night and time each morning to comb and style—but the approval from her peers made it worth the effort.

As Maggie returned to the ironing board, Corie Mae looked up. "By the way, Maggie, I'm glad you told me Judy Ryan's mother was sick. This morning I filled the little red wagon with food and spent several hours down there getting the kids cleaned up and straightening up the house. When I got there Leroy had melted lard and poured it over a piece of bread for Judy's breakfast."

"Oooooh Yuk! That makes me want to puke!"

Corie Mae gave Jeannie a warning look. "Not a bite of food in the house."

"Don't they have a root cellar?"

"No, Jeannie. Minnie wasn't able to make garden this year."

"What about Mr. Ryan? Why can't he take care of the kids?" Betty Lou took more beans from the basket.

"I'll tell you why not," Maggie spoke up. "He went down to the sawmill where Mary Ann's daddy works trying to keep the millers from going to work."

"Why?" Jeannie closed her notebook and stacked up her books.

"The miners went on strike several months ago, and Herbert hasn't worked for a long time. That's why his family ain't got no food." Corie Mae reached into the basket for more beans.

"But I don't see why he'd try to keep somebody else from working. That don't make a lick of sense." Jeannie moved her chair closer to the basket, filled her lap, and began shelling beans.

Maggie carefully folded Stuart's shirt. "Mary Ann told me Herbert Ryan and some other miners have picketed the mill every day for weeks, trying to get the sawmillers to form a union. Her daddy's afraid they will hurt somebody, because they try to stop the mill workers from going through the gate." Maggie took another shirt from the clothes basket. "I guess he thinks it's more important to keep honest men from going to work than to take care of his own wife and kids."

"Now, Maggie, "Corie Mae scolded. "Don't be badmouthing our neighbor."

"Mary Ann's really worried her father might get hurt. Herbert Ryan's even threatened Mr. Collins to his face."

"I'd be embarrassed to see my kids going to school as dirty as Judy and Leroy was yesterday. Looked like they hadn't had a bath for weeks." Betty Lou frowned. "I think he should get the kids cleaned up for school instead of keeping other men from going to work."

Corie Mae frowned at Betty Lou, but before she could say anything, Maggie asked, "How was Mrs. Ryan, Mama?"

"Minnie's real bad off. She was so weak she couldn't hardly sit up in bed. I guess she's been in bed for over two weeks and ain't eat nothing hardly. I finally got her to drink a little chicken broth. She told me her sister lives in Hamby, so when Ray come home for dinner, I had him go tell Reverend Lewis to go get her sister." Corie Mae took the last beans from the basket. "Betty Lou, get started on that homework you said you had to do. I'll finish up these beans. Maggie, do a couple more pieces and put the rest on the back porch where they'll stay cool. I'll try to finish up what's left tomorrow."

"Okay, Mama." Maggie sighed with relief. The heavy irons made her shoulders and back ache, and her knees hurt from standing so long. "I have some homework to finish, too." She picked up the spelling list. "Jeannie, ready for your first word?" Jeannie spelled all the words in the list correctly. Although reluctant to admit it, Maggie thought Jeannie the smartest in the whole family. She set the basket of unironed clothes on the back porch. After closing the damper on the stove so the fire would die out, she retrieved her books from the front room and joined Betty Lou at the kitchen table.

Corie Mae worked at the other end of the table picking the pieces of dried bean hulls from the shelled beans. After a bit, she paused and watched Maggie practice her shorthand characters. She said nothing–just shook her head, her lips compressed into a disapproving frown.

Despite her mother's objection, Maggie liked high school. She had made new friends, and she liked most of her teachers. Miss Erickson had encouraged her to do well in the business courses and had given her a tattered copy of the *Harbrace Handbook*. In addition to doing the usual homework for her classes, Maggie tried to find time each day to do extra practices for shorthand and to complete at least one exercise from the handbook. Best of all, most every day Bud Summers made a point of speaking to her when they passed in the hallway.

She had not gone anywhere with JD since school started. He no longer rode the school bus, but drove his car and went directly from school to the filling station where he worked until closing. Any free time he spent with Wanda Smith. But he did make a point of checking in with Maggie at school. He told her Mr. Sexton had taught him how to change spark plugs and oil and do a grease job. He repaired punctured inner tubes and changed tires as well as pumping gas and cleaning windshields. He also had said the lady Aunt Opal took care of in Honey Valley might die. He guessed his mother would move back home soon, much to his disappointment.

By the time Maggie finished her homework, the house was quiet. She got a small jelly glass and filled it with water from the faucet in the kitchen. How wonderful to have water in the house–no more walking to the well and toting it inside. She dipped her comb in the water and combed through each strand of hair before putting it into a pin curl and then tied a cloth around her head to hold the bobby pins in place. She turned out the kitchen light, and as she passed through the dark front room, she saw her father's face illuminated by the flame as he lit his pipe while sitting in the porch swing. She picked up a small quilt her mother had used when she rocked Jay, wrapped it around her shoulders, and slipped out the front door.

"Hi, Daddy."

"What're you doing up so late, Sunshine? It's time you was fast asleep."

"I had homework to do. On my way to bed I saw you out here. Did you have a good day?"

Ray took the pipe out of his mouth. " I helped Bob Jones put up a fence all day. We worked till it got so dark we couldn't see. Then he invited me to eat supper, and after that we worked in his shop making the new gates. I got home just a few minutes ago and thought I'd take a little smoke before I come in to bed."

Maggie pulled the quilt tighter against the chill of the fall night. "Daddy, did you know Mrs. Lewis asked Betty Lou to play all the songs for church on Sunday after next?"

"My little Lou playing the piano for church? I can't believe it." Ray puffed on his pipe. "I love to watch her when she plays. Just seems so natural to her."

"Mrs. Lewis thinks she can be a music teacher someday."

" That'd be so wonderful. I hope all my kids can make something of theirselves. If I'd had the chance, I'd got more schooling myself."

They rocked silently in the swing for a few minutes. "Daddy, did you know the striking miners are picketing the sawmill where Mr. Collins works?"

"Larry talked about it at church Sunday. It's looking bad."

"Mary Ann's real scared. Mr. Ryan and his buddies keep trying to stop the workers at the gate. They even slashed one man's tires, and Mary Ann told me today her father's taking his shotgun to work in his pickup. She's afraid her daddy's going to get hurt, or maybe hurt someone else."

"Well, I think she has a right to be afraid." Ray smoked quietly for a few minutes. Then he tapped his pipe on the porch rail to empty out the ashes. "When I was a kid growing up in Harlan, we had more 'n one man killed during union disputes. That's one reason it's called 'Bloody Harlan.'"

"I don't see why Mr. Ryan is so mean."

"I guess the miners think the union's helped them get better working conditions, and they think if the sawmillers would organize a union, it would help them, too."

"But how is it helping when the miners are out of work because of the strike, and their families don't have enough to eat?"

"Honey, I remember when it was very dangerous to work in the mines. My Uncle Henry died because the exhaust fans was broke, and the mine boss made the men go to work anyway. The gas built up till it exploded, and it took them three days to move all the coal to reach the trapped men. Course, by that time they was all dead. When the union men come in and organized, they was able to force the owners to make the mines safer. So unions ain't all bad."

"If that's true, why do the sawmillers not want a union?"

Ray chuckled. "Well, I guess it's just the stubbornness of mountain people. If you belong to a union, the union bosses can tell you what to do. You have to give some of your paycheck to the union. And if the company is unionized, they won't hire anyone who don't belong to the union. It feels like we don't have any choices, and us mountain men don't like that. That's the main reason I decided to be a farmer." Ray stood up and stretched. "It's really late. We better get ourselves in the bed or we won't get up in the morning." When Maggie stood, he put his arm around her shoulders and gave her a hug. "Don't worry too much about Mr. Collins."

"Okay, Daddy. I hope you sleep well."

"Good night, Sunshine."

Maggie could barely see by the moonlight to find her way to the stairs. As she reached the top and felt her way carefully to her bed, she could hear Johnny Ray coughing in the next room. *I hope he's not getting sick again.*

* * *

Mary Ann met Maggie the next day on the school steps where they often ate their lunches. "Well, it finally happened."

"What's that?" Maggie unwrapped her lunch.

"Herbert Ryan and a bunch of thugs stopped Daddy's pickup on the way home from work yesterday. Before Daddy could get out his shotgun, they pulled him out of the truck, drug him down the bank, and dumped him in the creek. They said they was baptizing him in the name of John L. Lewis."

"Oh my gosh! Did he get hurt?" Maggie took a bite of her biscuit and peanut butter sandwich.

"No, but I never saw him so upset. He told Mama as soon as he got some dry clothes he was going to find those guys and teach them a lesson."

"Do you think he would shoot them?"

"That's what had Mama scared. She told me to jump on my brother's bike and go get Preacher Lewis. When I rode up, Reverend Lewis was fixing to go somewhere in his car. I was so out of breath I couldn't hardly talk, but when I told him, he took off real fast. He got to our house just in time to block our driveway with his car so Daddy couldn't get his pickup out."

"Then what happened?"

"Daddy grabbed his shotgun and took off running down the road, and the preacher went running after him. They was gone for over a hour." Mary Ann stopped to take a bite of her bologna sandwich.

"So, did your daddy go to work today?"

"Yeah, but he let Preacher Lewis take his shotgun. He promised he wouldn't fight back unless they attacked him again. Reverend Lewis planned to talk to the sheriff to see if they can put a deputy at the gate, and Daddy's going to ride to work with Lester Phillips and Tom Lamance so he won't be by hisself anymore." Mary Ann paused for several seconds. "I'm really scared. Daddy's still awful mad. It's untelling what could happen."

Maggie nodded. "Mama went down to Ryan's house yesterday, and Minnie Ryan was real bad sick. The kids had no clean clothes and hadn't had a bath since no telling when." Maggie brushed the crumbs off her lap. "I can't understand how Herbert Ryan would run around the country throwing people in the creek and trying to keep them from going to work when his kids are dirty and hungry and his wife's about to die. And he's supposed to be a Christian and a church member."

"My daddy says he'll never go back to that church again as long as Herbert Ryan's a member. And I don't blame him. Oops, there's the bell."

Maggie took the last bite of her sandwich, folded the newspaper wrapping, and stood to go back inside.

* * *

On Thursday morning, Maggie gathered her stack of books and opened the front door. "Hey, kids, it's time to catch the bus." Betty Lou joined Maggie on the front porch, arms loaded with books. "Come on, Stuart, we'll miss the bus if you don't hurry."

Stuart rushed out the door, pulling on his jacket, and Corie Mae called from the kitchen, "Got your lunch?" As he turned to go back inside, Corie Mae met him and handed him his lunch and math book. "You'd lose your head if it wasn't fastened on."

"I don't see Kenny. Reckon he's already started on?" Jeannie waited at the bottom of the steps.

"He ain't going to school today." Stuart turned up his jacket collar against the cool fall air.

"Why not?"

"When I took the milk to Aunt Opal's this morning, he had his foot propped on the kitchen table with a big bandage on it. He was chopping wood for Grandpa last night, and the ax slipped and cut his foot real bad right through his shoe."

"Did Aunt Opal take him to the doctor?"

"Aunt Opal ain't home, so Grandma doctored it. He said it bled a lot, and it still hurt. That's why he had it on the table. If he kept it raised up, it didn't hurt so much."

The four of them walked rapidly down the dirt road. "It's a good thing Johnny Ray ain't with us, or we'd be late. He's such a slow poke."

"Don't say 'ain't.' It sounds ignorant." Maggie frowned at Jeannie, who stuck out her tongue at her sister. "This makes ten days Johnny Ray's missed already this year. If he keeps this up, he'll fail second grade. But when he coughs all night like he did last night, I guess it's best if he stays home, especially when it looks like rain." Maggie looked at the overcast sky. "He'd really be sick if he got wet."

When they reached the highway, the other children from the holler waited for the bus. Maggie noticed the Ryan children had clean clothes and carried lunches. She barely had time to ask Judy Ryan about her mother before the bus came.

Judy smiled at Maggie. "I think she's doing better. Aunt Lucy's staying with us. She took Mommy to the doctor yesterday, and he gave her some medicine."

Once on the bus, Maggie found a seat, opened her shorthand pad to practice. *I don't care what Mama thinks, I'm going to be a secretary and get a good job. I'm not going to be some man's slave.* She made two more rows of shorthand then gazed out the window. *I hope Bud speaks to me today.*

* * *

On Saturday morning when Maggie returned from milking, Corie Mae had prepared a big breakfast. JD had killed some squirrels and brought them over. They sizzled in a big iron skillet. "What else are we having?" Maggie carefully raised the lid on the other skillet and savored the aroma of fried apples bubbling in the sweet syrup formed by the butter and sugar. "Umm. I do love fried apples."

All the family sat around the large kitchen table enjoying the special breakfast. They ate all the biscuits and gravy and most of the apples. But Johnny Ray had eaten only a few bites. "I can't eat no more." His voice trailed off into a series of hacking coughs. Maggie noticed his cheeks looked red and feverish. Corie Mae had him take a sip of her hot coffee to sooth his throat, but his coughing continued until he finally drew in a breath with a whoop. His eyes filled with tears as the spasm of coughing began again.

Corie Mae sent Stuart to get Grandma Campbell to doctor Johnny Ray's cold. She put Johnny Ray in Junior's bed in the downstairs bedroom and sat with him, wiping his face with a damp washcloth.

Betty Lou and Maggie had finished the breakfast dishes when JD knocked at the front door. He looked troubled as he stepped into the front room. "I'm taking Kenny to the hospital. His foot's swollen twice its size, and there's a big red streak running up his leg almost to his knee. Aunt Lillian thinks he might be getting blood poison."

"Is Aunt Lillian going with you?" Maggie asked.

"That's why I stopped. She's broke out with something on one side of her face. She thinks it's shingles. It's even in her hair." JD looked at Maggie. "I wondered if Aunt Corie Mae would let you go with us. I've got to go to Honey Valley to get Mama because the hospital won't treat him unless a parent's there. I ain't talking to her, so I need you to go explain what's going on."

Corie Mae came from the bedroom. She nodded her consent to Maggie and asked if Lillian seemed very sick. When JD said she had complained for several days about not feeling well, Corie Mae said, "I hope she don't have too much trouble. Sometimes shingles can make a body real sick with a lot of pain. When my Grandma Campbell had them, she complained of pain for over a year."

Maggie looked at her mother, surprised that she asked about Aunt Lillian. The two women hadn't spoken since Maggie got her hair cut. She ran upstairs to change her skirt and blouse and grab a sweater. When she got to the car, Kenny sat sideways in the back with his bandaged foot resting on the seat, fever flushing his cheeks and burning in his eyes. He looked at Maggie and barely nodded.

JD lit a cigarette and started the car. When they got to the highway he turned south toward Honey Valley. "I wish Grandma didn't think she was a doctor. I couldn't believe it when I got home from work the other night, and here was Kenny with his big toe almost cut off, and what does she do? Puts cobwebs and soot on the cut. No wonder he may have blood poison." He blew smoke toward the window which he cracked open. "I can't believe she thought she could treat such a deep cut. I tried to talk her into letting me take him to the doctor, but she insisted her cures always work. Now look what's happened."

"Grandma's cures do work most of the time," Maggie protested. "Junior's burns healed up with no trouble at all."

"Well, they sure didn't work for Elsie Mae, now, did they?"

That idea shocked Maggie into silence. She stared out the window. Bright sunshine lit the mountain sides where the fall leaves made a kaleidoscope of color. Many of the houses they passed had rows of colorful flowers. Blood red dahlias as large as dinner plates grew beside a fence. Another house had a lovely rose garden as pretty as a picture in a magazine. Soon a heavy frost would turn all the wonderful fall colors to various shades of brown and grey. Maggie felt depression weighing heavily.

It never crossed her mind that Elsie Mae had died because Grandma's treatments did not work. Maggie had never been treated by a doctor. Neither had most of the rest of the family. If they got sick, Grandma gave them some home remedy, and they got better. Now she began to wonder if it was a mistake to have Grandma treat Johnny Ray's cold with her onion plasters and various home-made cough syrups. Maybe they should have taken Johnny Ray to the hospital.

Since it was Saturday, no doctor was on duty. It took quite a while to locate Dr. Herman. Maggie watched as a nurse cleaned up Kenny's wound as well as she could. She said, "In all my born days, I've never seen the likes of this!" She gave Kenny some aspirin, and he slept while they waited for the doctor to come.

JD, Opal, and Maggie waited in the area near the emergency room. JD stretched out on a couple of seats and shut his eyes. After a few moments of silence, Maggie turned toward Aunt Opal. "How's Mrs. Scott doing?"

"She's really gone downhill these last two weeks. It won't be long now. Poor thing. She's a real sweet old lady. The doctor give us medicine for the pain. She mostly just lies there with her eyes closed."

"I guess you'll be glad to get back home after being away so long."

"I'd like to be home for a few days, and then I hope I can get another job. Being home right now is hard on my nerves." Aunt Opal raised her eyebrows and nodded her head in JD's direction. JD didn't open his eyes, but Maggie noticed that he shook his right foot as he often did when agitated.

Maggie picked up a magazine and began to page through it. Aunt Opal got up to find a ladies' room. Finally, the nurse called Opal to the examining room. Maggie could hear the doctor's angry voice through the curtains that separated the examining room from the waiting area. She had never heard such cursing.

"Damn it, woman, what the hell were you thinking? Were you trying to kill him?" Aunt Opal protested that she was not home when it happened, but the doctor kept up his tirade.

"Just look what this dad nab quackery has done. I never saw such a mess in my life. He could lose his foot if we can't get this confounded infection stopped, or he could die with lockjaw."

Aunt Opal burst into tears. JD had sat up when the doctor began swearing. Now he locked eyes with Maggie as Aunt Opal rushed through the waiting area on the way to the restroom. They heard the doctor ask Kenny to explain how the injury had happened. Kenny said his grandma had put something on the cut that burned like fire. He thought maybe it was turpentine. Then she had gathered cob webs from the smoke house and scooped up soot from the wood stove in the kitchen. The doctor said the blasted soot was a problem.

"See, it's so discolored from the soot, I can't tell how bad the injury is. It's possible the bone is nicked or even broken. We'll have to x-ray it."

Maggie 's eyes teared when she heard Kenny ask the doctor if he was going to die. The doctor said they would do everything possible to keep that from happening, but it would be touch and go before they got there.

"Boy, he doesn't mince words, does he?" Maggie looked at JD.

"At least he's honest. He ain't promising some miracle he can't pull off. I should of loaded him into the car and took him to the doctor when I got home that night. I knowed it was a real bad cut. Sometimes Grandma can be too bullheaded."

"It's not your fault. You tried."

JD's eyes filled with tears. "Did you hear the doctor say he could lose his foot or even die?"

After what seemed ages, the doctor came into the waiting room and explained he had admitted Kenny. They would not stitch up the wound until they took some x-rays. Meanwhile they would fight the infection with penicillin and soak the foot in disinfectant solutions. Hopefully, we have caught it in time to prevent tetanus. His demeanor was calm and even kind, but he made it clear it would be a few days before they would know whether Kenny was out of the woods.

Aunt Opal said she would stay at the hospital. JD should come back on Sunday afternoon to pick her up. If Kenny seemed better, she would go back to Honey Valley.

They got home in late afternoon. Already late for work, JD dropped Maggie at her house and sped back toward the highway. Maggie checked the kitchen for something to eat, having eaten nothing since the fabulous breakfast. Fortunately, Betty Lou had saved some lunch in the warming closet of the stove. But before she could eat, Maggie went into the bedroom where Johnny Ray rested. Corie Mae said Grandma's onion poultices had broken his fever, and he had slept for several hours. Maggie murmured a "Thank you, Lord" under her breath and sat by the bed holding his hand. He opened his eyes and smiled at her.

"Maggie, 'member that shiny thing we found in the ditch that time?" Maggie nodded. "What happened to it?" Maggie explained how she had given it to Audie Lee.

"Do you think we could get it back?"

"I talked to Daddy about that, and he said to let Audie Lee keep it."

"I wish I had it. I thought it was real pretty. It was a heart, wasn't it?"

Maggie nodded. "You better rest some more." She straightened the covers and patted him on the head.

* * *

Betty Lou had surprised everyone when she played the piano for church. Maggie had chosen a different seat from her usual place so she could watch her father as he focused on Betty Lou. As the service progressed and Betty Lou's accompaniment became even more confident, Ray's eyes filled up, and his Adam's apple bobbed when he swallowed. Maggie could not decide which pleased her more–her sister's excellent performance or her father's obvious pride.

Kenny stayed in the hospital for a week. The infection had gradually cleared up. He would always have a big black scar just behind the joint of his big toe, but fortunately, he had no broken or nicked bones, but he would always have some numbness in his foot due to damaged nerves.

The congestion in Johnny Ray's head and chest had broken up, and his temperature seemed normal most of the time. He continued to complain of a sore throat for a few days, but after a week, Corie Mae decided to let him go back to school. He still looked pale and seemed to have little appetite. Finally, on the Friday before Halloween, Johnny Ray, even more lethargic than usual, ate very little breakfast and dallied about getting dressed for school. When Corie Mae scolded him, he whined, "Mama, I don't feel good." He ran for the back door where he vomited over the edge of the porch. Corie Mae decided he should stay home.

The next Sunday, Larry Collins showed up in his usual place beside Ray on the second pew. He had not attended church for weeks, since Herbert Ryan and his buddies had dumped him in the creek. Maggie had overheard her father telling Corie Mae the pastor and some of the deacons had visited with both Larry and Herbert hoping to reach some sort of reconciliation before Larry's anger turned to revenge. Few people in the congregation that morning realized that Herbert Ryan had also come, as he had slipped into the back pew just before the sermon.

Reverend Lewis gave the usual invitation inviting sinners to give their hearts to Jesus, urging backsliders to rededicate their lives, and encouraging nonmembers to join the church. He added that if people needed to confess their sins and ask for forgiveness, they should come forward. The congregation stood and began singing " Jesus Calls Us."

Maggie watched Mr. Collins, who stood with bowed head, staring at the floor. Finally, on the last verse, Herbert Ryan walked down the aisle. Herbert and the pastor talked quietly for a couple of minutes. Then Reverend Lewis asked if Larry Collins would also come to the front. Larry hesitated for several seconds. Ray laid a hand on his shoulder, and spoke softly to him. Larry finally nodded and went to stand on the opposite side of Reverend Lewis.

The pastor asked the congregation to be seated. "Herbert comes this morning confessing he has committed a wrong against a brother, and he wants to ask for God's forgiveness and for the forgiveness of the church. But most of all he wants the forgiveness of Brother Collins. I want all the deacons to join us in the pastor's study where we can pray with these estranged men. Mr. Worth, lead the congregation in singing and prayers until we come back."

They sang a couple of songs and after a time of silent prayer, two people prayed aloud. Then they sang three more songs and more people prayed. Maggie enjoyed singing hymns, but she began to get antsy as more and more time passed. Mary Ann, sitting beside her, began to weep softly. "What if they get in a fight? Do you think those men can keep them apart."

When the men finally returned, Reverend Lewis explained that Herbert Ryan had given his apology and asked for forgiveness, and after conversation and prayers with the deacons, Larry Collins had received the grace to offer pardon. Someone at the back of the church shouted, "Amen! Thank you, Jesus!"

The pastor asked the congregation to sing "Amazing Grace" and invited everyone to come to the front and shake hands with these two brothers who had taken Jesus' words seriously. Maggie hugged Mary Ann, feeling a heavy load had lifted from her shoulders, as the congregation gathered in the altar, wiping tears from their eyes.

Later that afternoon, Maggie went to the woodshed where Ray gathered kindling to fill the kitchen wood box. "Daddy, what did you think about Herbert Ryan's confession?"

"Glad to see it. The longer it went on, the madder Larry got. You know he comes from Kentucky stock, too. I guess feuding is in our blood. Anyway, I'm glad they could come to a understanding before something really bad happened, and I give the preacher the credit. I know he's worked with both of them for weeks."

Maggie picked up an armload of wood and followed her father into the house. Johnny Ray came into the kitchen where Corie Mae prepared supper. "Mama, my neck hurts, and my knees and elbows hurt."

Corie Mae asked Ray to get an aspirin from the bottle on the chest in the bedroom. When Ray returned with the aspirin, Corie Mae said, "I hate to ask JD to miss school, but I think we should take Johnny Ray to the doctor tomorrow. This aching in his joints seems like a bad sign. Reminds me of how he felt when he got rheumatic fever four years ago."

Corie Mae realized her worst fear when the doctor told them Johnny Ray had rheumatic fever again and sent them home with instructions for two months of bed rest. The doctor emphasized the importance of careful administration of aspirin every four hours, and a penicillin tablet every six hours, adding it would be some time before the extent of damage to his heart could be determined. Within a few days, Johnny Ray began to enjoy having so much attention. He took great delight in ordering Junior to do his bidding. "Bring a drink of water." "Get me a toy." "Tell Mama I'm hungry."

Maggie remembered the conversation she and JD had about Grandma's home remedies, and she wished she had told her mother how seeing Grandma's treatment of Kenney's foot had made the doctor so angry. Maybe she could have persuaded them to take Johnny Ray to the doctor sooner. *It's my fault. Johnny Ray may have permanent heart damage, and now we've got the doctor to pay and we still owe for Elsie May's funeral.* It seemed to her they took one step forward and two steps back.

CHAPTER 5

Campbell Holler–December 18,1886   Excited about
Christmas. Going to town to shop tomorrow. New baby
girl–Helen Margaret. Harvey ready to build 2 upstairs
bedrooms.

(Diary of Mary Louise Campbell)

December 1949

Maggie sat in study hall half asleep when Miss Erickson tapped her
shoulder. "I need to talk to you." She led the way to the conference room
beside the principal's office. Once seated across the table from each other,
Miss Erickson asked Maggie how Thanksgiving vacation had gone.

"Awful!" Maggie propped her chin in her hands.

"What happened?"

"We always kill hogs on Thanksgiving Day. It's a awful lot of work.
I'm just plumb tuckered out, I guess. You caught me half asleep."

"I've never seen a butchering, so I guess I really don't know much
about it. It's easy to think ham comes naturally wrapped in cellophane,
ready to eat. How many hogs did you butcher?"

"We did four–two for us, one for Grandpa, and one for my aunt. We
have this special place fixed up in Grandpa's barnyard where we work, and
I thought my hands would freeze and fall off from the cold."

"I'm sorry to sound so dumb, but like I said, I've never seen animals
butchered."

Maggie smiled and tipped her head to one side. "Maybe next year you
can come out and help us."

"I don't know about that," Miss Erickson laughed. "You do seem tired today. Did it take all weekend to butcher the hogs?"

"The hardest part's cutting it up and canning the meat. We worked on that all weekend. We didn't even go to church yesterday. Actually, Mama, Grandma, and my aunts is–uh, are–still canning meat today."

"You canned the meat?"

"We put the hams, shoulders, and bacon in salt to cure. After they're cured, we'll smoke them, and they'll keep through the winter. But we have to preserve all the rest so it won't spoil, and canning it is the best way we know. We also cut out the fat and rendered it into lard, and my arms ached so bad from turning the sausage grinder I couldn't sleep last night."

"You make sausage too?"

"Yeah," Maggie grinned. "My grandma says we use all the pig but its squeal."

Miss Erickson laughed. "I got so interested I almost forgot why I wanted to talk with you. Mr. Adkins asked me to suggest a student who could help out in the office this period, answering the phone, taking messages, and so on. I wondered if you'd like to do that. It would mean you'd lose this study hall, but I think you'd do a good job. What do you think?"

"Aren't the office helpers juniors or seniors?"

"That's true, but I think you can do all that Mr. Adkins needs. Your typing is accurate, and your speed will get better. Having some office experience will help you get a job after you graduate." Miss Erickson paused for a few seconds. "You don't have to give me an answer right now. Maybe you can think about it and tell me tomorrow."

As they started out the door, Maggie put her hand on Miss Erickson's elbow. "Thank you, Miss Erickson, for asking me. I'd really like to be an office worker."

"Let's go talk with Mr. Adkins now, and you'll be ready to start tomorrow."

After meeting with Mr. Adkins, Maggie met Bud Summers in the hallway.

"Hi, Maggie, what's up?" He wore a blue shirt that made his eyes seem even bluer. Maggie loved his dimples.

"Hi, Bud. On my way back to study hall. What you up to?"

"I'm tardy. Got to get an admit slip from the office."

"Just came from there. Guess starting tomorrow I'll be the office worker this period."

"No kidding? That's great. Say, Maggie, how about going out with me sometime?"

Maggie's eyebrows jumped up to her hair line. "You asking me for a date?"

"You could say that. Would you?"

"Oh, Bud, I'd love to, but Mama says I can't date until I'm sixteen."

"Well, shucks. I'll graduate by that time." He pushed his blond hair off his forehead.

"I'm sorry, Bud, I truly am, but thanks for asking."

"It's okay. Just remember we have a date as soon as you're sixteen." His smile made Maggie's heart skip a beat. "Well, better get my admit slip and get to class. See you around, Maggie."

When she got back to study hall, she almost skipped toward her place at the study table. *I can't believe he asked me for a date!* Bud was one of the most popular students in the junior class–active in sports and other extracurricular activities. His friendly good nature and genuineness made him a favorite of teachers as well as students.

I wish Mama would let me go out with him. She frowned when she remembered how many times she had seen him talking to different girls in the hallway. *What if he's just teasing me?* But she opened her notebook and wrote "Bud Summers" on the inside cover below her name.

When the period ended, Maggie found Mary Ann, Annie Marie, and Ronnie waiting beside her locker.

"Hi, Maggie." They all greeted her.

"Did you get all them hogs killed?" Mary Ann asked.

"Sure did. Had to come back to school to rest up."

"Say, Maggie," Annie Marie asked, "did you read that story for English?"

"I read it on the bus this morning. It seemed pretty dumb to me. Did you read it?"

"I plumb forgot about it until Mary Ann asked me during math class." Annie Marie hung her head in mock regret.

"I didn't read it neither," Ronnie admitted. "In fact, Maggie, we wondered if you'd help us out. Since you always get all the answers right on those silly true-false test she always gives, we thought maybe you could signal the right answers to us. You know, hold your pencil with the eraser up for true and down for false. What you say; will you help your old buddies out?" Maggie didn't say anything. "Please. Just this once. We promise we won't never ask you again."

"Don't you think if we all have the same answers, she might get suspicious?"

"What if we all missed a different question?" Mary Ann suggested.

"That's a smart idea." Ronnie patted Mary Ann's shoulder. "So I'll miss the second one; Annie Marie, you'll miss the forth one; and Mary Ann, you miss the sixth." They all nodded in agreement.

Maggie still looked unhappy. "Oh, all right. But remember, never again."

"Thanks, Maggie, you're a real friend." Mary Ann gave Maggie a hug.

"I've got something important to tell you at lunch," Maggie whispered to Mary Ann.

When the teacher read out the first true-false question, Maggie hesitated. She thought about giving the wrong signal or no signal at all. Finally, she marked her paper with a T and held her pencil with the eraser up. Miss Phillips, her least favorite teacher, never led any interesting discussions. She always read the questions from the teacher's manual without paying any attention to the students. *Serves her right. She should do something besides give us a true-false quiz every day.*

* * *

"Here kids, gather around the stove and warm up." Corie Mae greeted the children as they came in from the bus stop. She moved her rocking chair back to make room for them near the stove. "Your cheeks and noses is red as fire. I knowed soon as we kilt hogs it'd turn winter."

"Did you all get the canning done?" Jeannie asked.

"Most of it. We canned fifty quarts of sausage today. Grandma's making head cheese tomorrow."

"I sure hope she don't give us none. I hate that stuff." Jeannie held her hands closer to the stove.

"I hope she doesn't give us *any*." Maggie corrected. "Use correct English."

"Maggie, leave her alone!" Corie Mae yelled. "She talks just fine. Don't be putting highfalutin notions in her head. You think you are so smart, but you're not one bit better'n the rest of us, so don't go putting on airs." She turned to Jeannie. "Don't listen to her, you hear?"

"Yes, ma'am." Jeannie hung her head. When Corie Mae left the room, Jeannie looked at Maggie and mouthed, "I'm sorry."

Maggie shrugged. She turned to hide the tears that stung her eyelids and fled upstairs, her teeth clinched, her hands balled into fists. She took off her coat and sat on the bed in the unheated room. *Why does she hate me so much?* After a few minutes, she wiped the tears from her eyes with the hem of her skirt. She shivered and draped her coat over her shoulders. Finally, she stood, looked into the small mirror hanging on the wall, and ran her fingers through her hair. She hung her coat on a peg and descended to the warmer front room.

"Mama, can I get up now? I'm so tired of laying here." Johnny Ray called from his bed, which had been set up in the front room where he would be warmer.

"Johnny Ray, you already been up two hours this afternoon," Corie Mae scolded. That's all you're allowed. Now stay in that bed till supper time. The doctor said in two more weeks you can stay up most of the day. So just be patient."

"It ain't fair," Johnny Ray whined. "Maggie, can you read me a story?"

"I will in a minute. I got a book of Christmas stories from the library today. I'll read you one of my favorites." Maggie blew on her cold hands and rubbed them together.

"Can I listen, too?" Junior begged.

"You sure can."

Maggie put her school books away before she led Junior over to Johnny's Ray's bed. She propped herself against the headboard with the boys on either side so they could look at the pictures. She chose "The Gift of the Magi" by O. Henry, which she had read for her English class. Having spent hours looking up the big words as an assignment, she knew the boys wouldn't understand if she read it to them, so she began to tell it in her own words.

"What's a Magi?" Johnny Ray asked.

"You remember in the Bible how the wise men came to bring gifts to baby Jesus? Magi is another word for wise men. This story explains what kind of presents wise people give.

"So is this a story about when Jesus was born?"

"Not really. It is about the true meaning of giving presents."

The boys interrupted her several more times as she told the story. "Did Della and Jim have as much money as us?" "Was Della's hair as long as yours used to be?" "Why didn't you sell your hair for a lot of money?"

"Wait a minute," Johnny Ray cried when Maggie told them that Jim had sold his watch to buy the combs for Della's hair. "Now they've both got stuff that's no good. I don't like this story. I don't think they was very wise. Now they ain't got nothing."

"Let's think about it. What was the most precious thing Jim owned?"

"His watch."

"And what was the most precious thing Della had?"

"Her hair."

"Why would people give up the most precious things they have to buy a gift for someone else?"

After several seconds, Johnny Ray said, "I guess it means you love someone."

"I think you're right. What better gift can anyone have?"

"I want more than love for a Christmas present," Johnny Ray argued. "I want a bicycle."

"I want a cap gun," Junior added.

"Don't get your hopes up. We have to pay Johnny Ray's doctor bill before we can start buying presents."

"Maggie, you know that pretty thing we found that time, that you gave to Audie Lee? Do you think if we still had it we could sell it for a lot of money?"

"I don't know, Buddy, but we don't have it, do we?"

"I think somebody should make Audie Lee give it back. We found it and finders keepers."

"I told you Daddy said we should let Audie Lee keep it. Just forget about it."

Johnny Ray pouted. "I still wish I had it. Maybe someday I'll ask Audie Lee to give it to me."

"Oh, that'll be the day. You're scared to walk past his house by yourself, let alone talk to him."

"I'm not scared anymore." Johnny Ray puffed up his chest and raised his chin like a bantam rooster. "Someday I'm going to tell him to give it back."

When Maggie closed the book and stood, Johnny Ray said, "I didn't like this story. Can you read us a better one?"

"Not right now. I have to do the chores. I'll read you another story later."

As she left the room, Maggie heard Johnny Ray ask Junior, "If you had a watch, would you sell it?"

"Yeah, if I had one, I'd sell it and buy Mama a new bowl cause hers got broke yesterday."

* * *

"Mama, will we have money to buy presents for Christmas?" Maggie sat at the kitchen table doing homework while her mother ironed clothes.

"I don't guess we'll have any. Ray ain't had no work since before Thanksgiving. We even had to use the egg money to pay the electric." After a few minutes, she added, "I ain't in the mood for Christmas nohow. Reminds me too much of how Elsie Mae died on Christmas Day last year."

"I know, Mama. It makes me sad, too. I miss her so much. But, Mama," Maggie said after a bit, " Johnny Ray and Junior are hoping to get something for Christmas. Johnny Ray told me today he wanted a bicycle, and Junior wants a cap gun."

"I can't help it. We ain't got no money. Probably the church'll give out little sacks of candy and fruit after the Christmas program, and I'm trying to make the boys new shirts. I guess that'll be it. They might as well forget bicycles and cap guns."

Maggie finished reading her English assignment. "Mama, Miss Erickson asked me today to be an office worker during my study hall period. Mr. Adkins wants me to start tomorrow." Maggie watched her mother who concentrated on the ironing. She gave a big sigh and pursed her lips, but she didn't say anything. "I'll get good experience that should help me get a job when I finish school."

"Maggie, I ain't expecting you to get no job when you finish school. The Bible says a woman's place is in the home."

"But, Mama." Maggie's voice rang with desperation. "What about all the women who are nurses and teachers? Don't you think it's good when women do work like that?"

"I don't want my girls to be worldly women. I want them to be like the women in the Bible."

"I already told Mr. Adkins I'd be an office worker." After another long period of silence, Maggie sighed loudly. "Mama, seems like you'd be proud that I'm doing well enough in business classes that Mr. Adkins would ask me when I'm only a freshman. All the other office workers are either juniors or seniors."

"The next thing you know, you'll get a job and forget about your family. I'm getting tired of you doing things against my beliefs."

Corie Mae finished the last piece of ironing, put away the ironing board, and left the kitchen without saying "Good night." Maggie stared at her Civics book. She thought her mother probably would get really angry if she knew how she had helped her friends cheat in English class. Maggie regretted she had done that, but at least she had made it clear she would never help them again. When she reached the bottom of the page, she realized she couldn't remember a word she had read. She rested her head on the table. *What do I have to do to please her?*

* * *

Maggie looked up from the desk where she typed a letter for Mr. Adkins when Coach Moore walked into the office and leaned on the counter. "Is there something I can do for you, Mr. Moore?"

"Yes. You're Maggie Martin, right?" Maggie nodded. "I watched you playing basketball in gym class the other day. You're really good. I wondered if you'd join the team?"

Maggie grinned. "I'd like to, Mr. Moore, but my parents would never allow it."

"Have you asked them?"

"My daddy really had to put his foot down just to get my mother to agree for me to take gym. She'd never allow me to be on the team."

"Would you mind if I talked to your parents?"

"I guess it's okay to talk to them, but I can tell you now, it won't do no good, I mean any good."

"I'll try to get out to your house one evening soon. I'd like to have you on the team. We might win some games this year for a change."

"Thanks for asking, Coach."

After the bell rang, Maggie started to her next class at the end of the hallway. About midway, Bud passed her going in the opposite direction. He didn't say anything, but when their eyes met, he winked.

* * *

When the kids got home from school, Mrs. Lewis had finished reading a story to Johnny Ray and Junior and looked up over her glasses to greet the children, who gathered around the stove to warm up.

"Thank you, Mrs. Lewis, for bringing the boys storybooks and reading to them," Corie Mae said when Mrs. Lewis stood. "You've been so nice to visit with the boys since Johnny Ray took sick."

"I love to read to them." Mrs. Lewis reached for her coat and gloves. "Corie Mae, I've a favor to ask of you."

"I'd do anything for you I could. You've always done so much for our family."

"Did I tell you that Ruth Ann and Harold are coming home for Christmas?"

"I reckon you'll be happy to see them. How long they been gone?"

"We haven't seen them for two and a half years."

"I couldn't stand it if one of my kids went away like that, even if they was serving the Lord in a foreign land. I'd never forgive them." She looked at Maggie.

"I'm very excited about their visit. That's why I need to ask a favor."

"I'll sure do my best."

"Actually, I wanted to borrow Maggie and Betty Lou for the next two Saturdays. I want to paint and paper the guest bedroom before Ruth Ann and Harold's visit. If the girls can help me, I think I can get it ready."

"I reckon neither one's ever done any painting or papering."

"I'm sure they can learn quickly, and their help will get the job done in plenty of time–that is, if they'd like to help me." Mrs. Lewis raised her eyebrows in Maggie's direction.

Maggie smiled and nodded her head. "I'd love to help you, and I know Betty Lou would, too." She turned to her mother. "Is it all right with you, Mama?"

Corie Mae hesitated, looking down at the floor. "If Mrs. Lewis thinks you all can do the job, I reckon I can do without you for two Saturdays."

"I'll have James come to pick you up Saturday morning. Is eight o'clock too early?"

"They'll be ready, Mrs. Lewis." Corie Mae walked to the door as Mrs. Lewis buttoned her coat and put on her gloves. "Thanks again for bringing the books."

"Wait, Mrs. Lewis," Junior called as he jumped off Johnny Ray's bed and threw his arms around her. "Thank you for my book. I love it so much."

"I'll tell you, Junior," she said as she smoothed his hair, "that hug made it well worth it."

* * *

After selling a pencil and a pack of notebook paper to a student, Maggie closed the cash drawer and looked up to see Mr. Moore coming through the office door.

"Maggie, I'm so sorry about how my visit with your folks turned out. I'm afraid I may have upset your mother." He leaned on the counter.

"Mr. Moore, I'm not one to say 'I told you so,' so I won't say it." Maggie giggled.

"I hope I didn't make things difficult for you. That certainly wasn't my intention."

"I guess Mama thinks high school's a bad influence. After you left, she threatened to make me drop out of school, but Daddy told her that would never happen."

"I'm so sorry, Maggie. I don't understand why your mother opposes your playing with the team. Certainly I can't understand why she would want you to drop out of school. If I caused that, I'm really sorry."

"It's not anything you did, Mr. Moore. She wants us girls to be what she calls 'Bible women.'"

"What does she mean?"

"Not sure I know exactly, but she thinks the Bible teaches a woman is to be a helper to her husband. She thinks I should get married and start having kids like she did. I don't like to upset my mother, but I plan to get all the business skills I can in school and get a job when I graduate."

"I like your spirit, Maggie. I wish you well with your courses, and I hope that you can carry out your dream without damaging your relationship with your parents."

"Thanks, Mr. Moore. And thanks for asking me to play on the team. I'd really like to play basketball, but I guess it's not going to work out."

"Is your father as set against your playing as your mother?"

"He doesn't believes it's a sin like Mama does, and he lets us girls play with my cousins and brothers at home, even when Mama thinks we shouldn't. But he won't overrule my mother on this."

"Oops, there's the bell. Must go to teach that geography class. You take care, now."

* * *

Maggie took her sausage and biscuit sandwiches to the back corner table in the cafeteria where Mary Ann sat with Annie Marie and Ronnie.

"Hi, you all." She sat across the table from them.

"Are you ready for that big English test we have today?" Mary Ann asked, nodding toward Maggie.

"I studied until Mama made me go to bed last night. I have trouble remembering all those authors' names. You ready?"

"I ain't never going to be ready to pass no English test," Ronnie announced and took a big swig from his milk carton.

Kathy and Billy Ray brought their cafeteria food and joined them. "I think I just flunked my math test," Kathy confessed. "I should of studied last night instead of going to the movies."

"I'm glad you went to the movies," Billy Ray said, and Maggie noticed he had his hand on Kathy's thigh.

"What you doing Saturday, Maggie?" Mary Ann asked. "If Daddy'll bring me over to your house, can we cut a Christmas tree?"

"Yes, Daddy can help you find a tree, so come on over. Betty Lou and I are supposed to help Mrs. Lewis do some painting."

"I thought you did that last Saturday."

"We did, but we didn't get done. You should have seen us. We had more paint on us than we got on the woodwork, I think. We're supposed to finish this Saturday." Maggie turned to Kathy, "How's basketball practice going?"

"Awful. We have our first game tonight. I bet we get beat by twenty points. I wish you could play with us. At least we'd have someone who can hit the basket."

"I wish I could play too, but you know how it is."

"Listen, Maggie. Do you think you could at least practice with the team?

"Yeah, Maggie," Mary Ann said, "if we had a good forward to practice with, we might get better. You know, you wouldn't have to tell your parents since we practice during school hours."

Kathy begged, "It would really help us out. You think you might do that?"

"My mother'd never forgive me if she found out."

The bell rang and everyone stood to carry back trays and throw away trash. "Will you at least think about it?" Kathy said over her shoulder on her way out the door.

* * *

On Saturday morning, Mrs. Lewis came to pick up the girls. Betty Lou opened the door when Mrs. Lewis knocked. "Good Morning, Mrs. Lewis."

Corie Mae came from the kitchen drying her hands on her apron. "Good Morning, Mrs. Lewis. Do you think you all will get the room finished today?"

"That's why I came in to talk with you, Corie Mae. James helped me this week, and we have finished all the painting. I'm quite pleased with it. The girls did a very good job last week. I couldn't have done it without them. I thought today I'd go to Knoxville and get some new curtains and a bedspread. I wondered if Maggie and Betty Lou could go with me. I'll have them back by suppertime."

Corie Mae had a puzzled frown. "But if the room's finished, do you really need them again today?"

"I'd like their help in choosing the curtains and bedspread. I'd really appreciate it if you'd let them go."

"I guess." Corie Mae still seemed confused. "If you really need them, I guess it's okay."

Once in the car, Maggie said, "Thank you, Mrs. Lewis. We never dreamed we'd get a chance like this. We've never gone to Knoxville."

"You're welcome, girls. You did a good job helping me last Saturday. Now today, we're going to have a good time. Here's your pay for working last Saturday." She handed each girl a ten-dollar bill. "You can spend it however you wish."

Maggie looked at the crisp bill. She had never had that much money to spend as she pleased. She folded it carefully and put it in her coat pocket.

"Actually," Mrs. Lewis said as she pulled onto the highway, "I didn't really tell your mother the whole story. Several women from the Women's Missionary Society wanted to do something for your family for Christmas. The women made up some money and said for me to take you girls on a shopping trip for the whole family."

"You mean, we're going to buy presents for everybody?" Betty Lou's eyes seemed big as saucers.

"That's exactly what we're going to do. Maggie, get that tablet and pencil in the seat between us, and let's make a list of what we should buy for everyone."

"Could we get Mama a new dress?" Betty Lou asked from the back seat. "Hers are so shabby."

"Maggie, write down 'dress' for Corie Mae. This is so exciting. I haven't enjoyed the idea of shopping so much in ages."

By the time they reached Knoxville, they had completed the list. The girls found the sights of the big city fascinating, but felt a little apprehensive about the traffic moving so close to their car.

"When we get the shopping done, we'll take all the gifts to my home,"

Mrs. Lewis explained. "James and I will bring them to your house on Christmas Eve. I hope you won't tell your family so we can surprise everyone. I think we'll start here at Sears." She turned into the parking lot. "Then go downtown so you can see all the Christmas decorations."

The girls became impatient when it took so long to find a parking place, and as soon as the car stopped, they jumped out and rushed for the nearest door of the huge store, forgetting to wait for Mrs. Lewis.

* * *

The sun had already set when Mrs. Lewis pulled up to their house. The girls thanked her profusely and got out. As the girls climbed the steps to the house, Maggie reminded Betty Lou to be careful to keep Mrs. Lewis' secret.

"I know that. Do you think I'm stupid?"

"I know how hard it is to keep a secret. When you're excited about something, it's easy to slip."

"If anyone tells the secret, it won't be me."

The family had eaten most of their supper when the girls came into the kitchen. "It's about time you got here." Corie Mae took their plates of food from the warming closet. "We thought you wasn't going to get here, so we went ahead and started eating."

Betty Lou, ignoring her mother, sat down and launched into a detailed account of their day. Her brown eyes shone with excitement, and Maggie noticed her father watched her intently with that twinkle in his eye.

"First, we went to this big Sears and Roebuck store. The parking lot's bigger than our playground at school, and so many people had come, we like to never found a parking place. Mama, it's so big you could buy everything there that's in the catalog. We saw dresses, shoes, clothes for babies, furniture, all kinds of tools, Frigidaires, stoves, washing machines..."

"Did they have toys?" Johnny Ray interrupted.

"You should have seen all the toys, and the most wonderful thing was a television."

"What's a television?" Jeannie asked.

"It's like a radio except it has this window-like thing." She held her hands about a foot apart to indicate the size. "It lets you see the people doing the talking and singing. We saw Roy Acuff and Grandpappy doing their show."

"You mean they was in the store?" Johnny Ray asked.

"No, we could see them in the window on the television."

"I don't believe such a thing," Corie Mae said.

"Mama, it's true," Stuart said. "We read about that last year in our *Weekly Reader*. Mr. Moss told us the waves that carry the pictures through the air bounces off the mountains. He said we probably wouldn't have no television around here for a long time cause we've got so many mountains."

"Well," sniffed Corie Mae, "I won't believe it till I see it."

"Did you buy anything there?"

Betty Lou swallowed the food she'd just put into her mouth. "We had a long list..."

Maggie quickly interrupted and punched Betty Lou with her elbow. "Mrs. Lewis bought her bedspread and curtains there. Mama, you should see them. We picked out pink curtains and a white bedspread. They'll be so pretty in the bedroom with the new wallpaper."

"What else did Mrs. Lewis have on the list?" Johnny Ray persisted.

Maggie answered quickly before Betty Lou could say anything. "Mrs. Lewis had a list of presents to buy. She did a whole lot of shopping."

"And," Betty Lou added, "Mrs. Lewis gave both of us a ten-dollar bill for helping her fix up the bedroom. She said we could spend it however we wished, so I bought three pairs of anklets and a hair barrette." Maggie noticed that Betty Lou didn't mention the tube of lipstick she had bought.

"Did you buy us anything?" Junior asked.

"I bought a sack of balloons. When you finish eating, I'll show you."

Jeannie listened wistfully. "I wish I could have gone with you. Did you go to any other stores?"

"After we finished at the Sears and Roebuck store, Mrs. Lewis drove us downtown. We went through all these streets with red lights—you wouldn't believe how big the city is. We found a place to park in a lot where Mrs. Lewis had to pay to leave the car." Betty Lou took a gulp of her milk. "Then she took us to a place called the S&W Cafeteria to eat our dinner. They had this long counter with all kinds of food. You just walk along and pick out what you want. While we ate, a lady played an electric organ with all kinds of beautiful music." Betty Lou stopped to take another bite.

"Then," Betty Lou continued, "Mrs. Lewis took us to a whole bunch of stores all along the main street. The biggest store was called 'George's.' Mama, you should see the Christmas decorations they had in that store. They had all these big blue, shiny balls about as big as a basketball. They had hung them up on the walls in a bunch with gold ribbons and silver holly leaves. They had this Christmas tree that was as tall as this house with lights and balls all over it. I just couldn't stop looking at everything. It was all so beautiful. I wish you could go see it."

The boys had finished and wanted to see the balloons Betty Lou had brought. After everyone else had gone into the front room, Maggie helped her mother clear the table and dried the dishes. Maggie swept the crumbs from under the table out the back door and off the porch. Corie Mae carried the dish water out to the back porch and poured it into the slop bucket, where they saved food scraps and waste water to feed to the hogs. When Corie Mae came back inside, Maggie handed her the ten-dollar bill Mrs. Lewis had given her. "Here, Mama, maybe this will pay some on the bills. I wish I had some way to make more money, but at least I can do this much."

Corie Mae put the money in her apron pocket and walked into the front room without saying anything. Maggie stared into the darkness outside the kitchen window and listened to the wind whipping through the bare trees. *I thought she'd at least say "thank you."*

* * *

The week before Christmas Maggie used every available minute to study for final exams. Midweek Miss Erickson told Maggie she had made a perfect score on her shorthand test. "I've never had a student who could do shorthand as well as you. I'm really proud of your progress."

JD stopped by the office one day to chat. "Guess what."

"I give up. What?"

"Aunt Lillian's moving out."

"What do you mean? She's going to live somewhere else?"

"She got a job as the cook at City Café here in town. She's going to live in the little furnished apartment above the restaurant. She starts the first of the year."

"She's not going to live at your house no more–uh, anymore?"

"She told Mama it's time she got out on her own. Mama acted like she was glad, but I know she'll miss the rent money Aunt Lillian paid her."

"It's hard to think about her living in town. She's lived at your house as long as I can remember."

JD noticed the big poster advertising the donkey basketball game the Friday after Christmas. "Do you think Aunt Corie Mae'll let you and Betty Lou go to the donkey basketball game with me and Kenny?"

"Wouldn't have the money for admission even if she let us go."

"I'll buy your tickets. Ask her. It's sort of like going to a circus, you know."

"Guess it won't hurt to ask. Thanks for inviting us."

"Better take off. Supposed to be in class. Let me know what Aunt Corie Mae says."

On Friday, Mr. Adkins told Maggie to take down all the Christmas decorations in the office. "I like to get that done before vacation so when we come back we won't have to worry with it. You'll find the boxes in that cupboard. When you get them all boxed up, give them to Mr. Jones to put in the storage room."

"Yes, sir." She opened the cupboard to get the boxes.

"Oh, by the way, Maggie, Mr. Moore told me you are a great basketball player. He'd like to have you on the team. Is there any chance you might do that?"

"I'd really like to, Mr. Adkins, but I'm afraid my parents are against it."

"That's what Mr. Moore told me. Is there anything I could do to help persuade them?"

"If you said anything, it'd just make my mother more upset. But thanks for asking."

Maggie took the boxes and began to take down the Christmas ornaments. She had tied the last of the boxes when Bud Summers walked into the office.

"Hi, Maggie. What's happening?"

She smiled, "Packing up all the Christmas decorations. What're you up to?"

"JD tells me you might come to the donkey basketball game next week. If you come, would you mind if I sat with you?"

"I'd like that, Bud. I hope Mama will let me come."

"Just remember. If she does, we have a date! Anyway, Merry Christmas."

* * *

Maggie and Betty Lou climbed to the top of the bleachers and sat with their backs against the wall. JD had dropped them off outside the gym and then left to pick up Wanda. Kenny sat with his friends on the opposite side of the gym, which was filling up fast.

"Looks like lots of folks wanted to see this game." Maggie took off her coat.

Betty Lou nodded. "I never dreamt Mama would let us come."

"We worked pretty hard helping can all that beef after Daddy and Grandpa butchered Curly. And then after Reverend and Mrs. Lewis brought all those gifts and Mama found out we knew about the secret, she probably felt guilty about saying 'no.'"

"The church ladies were so nice to help us. I never expected Daddy to cry. He couldn't hardly even talk. He just grabbed Reverend Lewis and kept hugging him."

"What surprised me was how they brought presents you and I didn't know about. I really like the sweater set she got you, and this skirt's the nicest one I ever had." Maggie smoothed the blue and red plaid material over her knees.

Soon Maggie's friends joined them. Annie Marie and Ronnie sat on Maggie's right, and Kathy squeezed into the row in front of them. Then some of Betty Lou's friends yelled for her to come sit with them. When

Maggie saw Mary Ann and her father come through the door, she jumped up. "Hold my seat. Going to go get Mary Ann."

As Mary Ann and Maggie made their way through the crowd, someone tapped Maggie's shoulder. "Your mom let you come, I see." Bud smiled at her.

"Wonders never cease."

"Where're you all headed?" When Maggie pointed to the top bleachers where her friends sat, Bud asked, "Is there room for me?"

Maggie grinned. "We have a date. Remember?"

By the time they reached their seats, the buzzer sounded and the handlers began bringing in the donkeys. "They're so cute," Annie Marie said. "Look, they've got leather shoes on."

For the first game, the men faculty played the boys' basketball team. The announcer explained the rules to the players and to the fans. Players can pass or shoot the ball only when seated on a donkey. If the ball gets loose, the player may get off to retrieve the ball, but must get back on the donkey before passing or shooting.

"Look at that cute little donkey Billy Ray's riding." Kathy turned to Bud. "How come you're not playing?"

"I don't much take to the idea of riding on a jackass, I guess."

"Say, Maggie, have you thought about practicing with us?" Kathy asked.

"I told you I can't do that."

"I don't see why not." Mary Ann spoke up. "I talked to Coach about it. He said he'd never ask you because he knew your parents wouldn't approve. But he said if you asked to practice with us, he'd let you. I think you should do it."

"What're you all talking about?" Bud asked.

"Mr. Moore asked Maggie's parents to let her join the team and they said 'no.' We're trying to talk Maggie into practicing with us."

"Sounds like a good idea to me," Bud said. "Why don't you do it, Maggie?"

Maggie shook her head.

The teachers won the coin toss, so they got the ball first. As Mr. Adkins started to pass to Mr. Moore, his donkey began to buck and the ball went wide. Mr. Moore jumped off to get the ball. He tried to hold on to the donkey's bridle, but the donkey began pulling backwards. Mr. Moore turned loose and ran for the ball. When he turned around, his donkey had headed toward the door. The crowd went crazy. "Oh my gosh! I hope I don't get that donkey when the girls play," Mary Ann said.

Mr. Moore finally got his donkey back on the court, mounted up, and threw a long pass to Mr. Lee, but Billy Ray intercepted it. Almost immediately Billy Ray's donkey sat down, and he fell off backwards.

Meanwhile, another of the boys had retrieved the ball and trotted down the floor to make the first score. Billy Ray, still trying to persuade his donkey to get up, finally gave it a swift kick in the rear. The donkey stood, but as soon as Billy Ray got on, it sat down again. The crowd hooted.

"I'm glad I decided not to play," Bud said to Maggie. "I think it's more fun to watch the game up here with you."

A few of the players began to get better control of their steeds, and the game moved along a little faster for the second half. The crowd continued to enjoy the spectacle, hooting, jeering, and laughing. Maggie heard one man say, "I haven't laughed so hard since Aunt Bertha's drawers fell off when she was singing a solo at Grandpa's funeral."

In the second game, the women faculty played the girls' team. Kathy, Mary Ann, and several girls on the team had promised to play, but after seeing how much difficulty the men had controlling the stubborn beasts, some of the girls backed out. Kathy rushed up the bleachers. "Maggie, you've got to help us. We need another player on our team."

"I can't ride a donkey in a skirt."

"We'll have to find you some jeans right quick."

"How're you going to do that?"

Annie Marie stood "I'll give you my jeans, and I'll wear your skirt."

"That's a great idea." Kathy grabbed Maggie's hand and pulled her to her feet. "Come on. Let's go."

Maggie jerked her hand free from Kathy's grasp. "I don't think so."

"Oh, come on, Maggie," Bud said. "Be a good sport. Go show them how it's done."

Maggie reluctantly let herself be led down the bleachers, and soon she had on Annie Marie's jeans, which reached only a few inches below her knees. *If Mama saw me like this, she'd give me the thrashing of my life.* The handler led her toward the only donkey left, the most stubborn one in the whole lot. Maggie balked and tried to back off the court, but the handler persuaded her to let him help her on the donkey.

Strangely enough, Maggie soon had the little jenny going wherever she wanted her to go. Maggie grabbed a rebound under her goal. Her donkey immediately headed in the opposite direction, but Maggie twisted around and put up a hook shot that swished the net. The crowd roared. Maggie, surprised at the applause, ducked her head in embarrassment. When she made the second goal, she enjoyed the approval from the crowd. The spectators came to their feet as her third shot went through the basket, and Maggie grinned and held up two clasped hands.

The cheerleaders yelled, "Two, four, six, eight. Who do we appreciate?" and the crowd replied, "Maggie, Maggie, Maggie." By the end of the game, Maggie's team had scored twenty points more than their opponents.

When the game was over, Bud waited for her. "Hey, girl, you are really a good shot. I can see why Coach Moore wants you on the team."

People she didn't know came by to congratulate her. "Why aren't you on the team?" "You're so good. We need you on the team." Maggie thanked them and smiled. *I really would like to be on the team.*

Bud took her arm. "Let's get out of here."

"I've got to find Annie Marie and change clothes. I can't wear these jeans home."

"Well, I think they're cute."

Maggie saw Annie Marie and Ronnie making their way down the bleachers and waved to them. Annie Marie was so short Maggie's skirt dragged the steps. When they got almost to the bottom, Ronnie stepped on the skirt and ripped it loose from the band. Ronnie was mortified, and Annie Marie could not apologize enough.

"I should never have agreed to do this," Maggie sighed.

"Maggie, I'm so sorry," Annie Marie said. "I'll get you a new skirt."

"It's not the skirt I'm worried about. It's what my mother's going to say when she finds out I did this."

* * *

"No, I will not!" Corie Mae's shrill voice roused Maggie from a light sleep. Wondering what brought that on, Maggie crept down the stairs and sat on the bottom step where she could hear without being seen. *Daddy must have found out about me riding the donkey last night.* She had managed to get into the house without anyone seeing the torn skirt. And although Betty Lou had entertained the family at the breakfast table with the antics of the donkeys, she'd kept quiet about Maggie's participation.

After Corie Mae's outburst, they had modulated their voices so Maggie had to concentrate to hear. "She's always trying to make herself look better'n us," Corie Mae complained. "And you always take her side against me. It looks like you care more about her than me."

"Now, Honey, you know that ain't true." Maggie heard a chair leg scrape the floor, and then a moment of silence. "Reverend Louis explained to me that being on the team helps the girls learn to work together and builds their confidence. Says it helps them learn stuff that'll be good habits when they grow up."

"I don't care what they say. It ain't right for a girl to be playing ball out in public."

"I wanted to talk to you before I said anything to Maggie. I think it'd be good for her to play on the team, but if you're against it, I won't say nothing. She told me this afternoon when she helped me saw firewood she wanted to play on the team, but she didn't want to if you objected. She said she sometimes feels like the town kids look down on her—like she don't belong."

"Good. I don't want her being like them kids."

"But, Corie Mae, it's a terrible feeling to be a outsider. When you said you'd marry me, you made me the happiest man on earth. I wanted to marry you more'n anything. But when I left Harlan and came down here, nobody accepted me. Even your family treated me like a stranger for the longest time. I missed my family and friends so much. I used to take my gun and go to the woods to get us a rabbit or squirrel. When I got out in the woods with nobody around, I'd sit down against a tree and just bawl my eyes out."

Nobody said anything for several minutes. Maggie, shivering from sitting on the cold step in her bare feet and night gown, crept back up the stairs and crawled into bed. She was now wide awake. *Daddy would agree for me to be on the team if Mama wasn't against it, and the preacher is on my side too. If I practiced with the team, Daddy probably wouldn't get mad.* Maggie finally quit shivering and began to feel sleepy.

On Monday morning, she found Mr. Moore. "I can't be on the team, because my mother is still against it, but I think my father wouldn't object if I practiced with the team."

"Then I'll expect you at practice today." Mr. Moore smiled and patted her on the shoulder.

CHAPTER 6

Campbell Holler–March 6, 1887   Damn Harvey. Always
has to be right. Says the man is head of house. When
crossed gets violent. Scared for the children. Caught me
wearing necklace that's been in family for generations.
Jerked it off and broke the chain. Don't know what he did
with it.

(Diary of Mary Louise Campbell)

Spring 1950

Humming softly, Maggie walked along the fence row next to Grandpa's
woods. Here and there purple violets peeked from heart-shaped leaves.
The yellow violets that had first bloomed in February had long ago faded
away as had the little pink flowers Grandma called "pissy beds." Soon the
May apples would make their appearance, and if she were lucky she might
see a jack-in-the-pulpit. Dogwood and redbud trees dotted the ridges with
blobs of white and pink.

Shortly after she got home from school, Corie Mae had said, "Maggie,
before you do the milking, I want you to find us some poke weed so's I can
make poke salat for supper. Be sure to pick only the tender young plants,"
Corie Mae had cautioned, "and don't get none of the root cause it's
poison."

Maggie had picked enough of the shiny green leaves to fill her water
bucket to the halfway mark. The kids had picked along their fences for
several weeks, so Maggie had gone back of Grandpa's house where more
fresh sprouts grew. As she bent to cut some poke shoots, she heard some

movement in the nearby woods. She watched warily while squatting behind the honeysuckle-covered fence. The honeysuckle fragrance contrasted sharply with the strong bitter smell of the poke weed in her bucket.

Then Audie Lee stepped from behind a bush and began lurching toward her. Realizing he had seen her, she stood and watched suspiciously as he waddled closer. *I'm glad he's on the other side of the fence.*

He wore the same old hat as last summer when he had confronted Maggie at the clothesline. His overalls hung loosely on his small frame. Even on this warm day, he wore an old coat, ragged at the cuffs and, as usual, had slung a dirty tow sack over his shoulder. As he came closer, his beady eyes squinting against the afternoon sun, he smiled and held out a handful of poke leaves. Somewhat alarmed, she wondered how long he had watched her. It made her feel a little spooked, but apparently he only intended to help, so she held up her bucket, and he dropped in the poke weeds.

"Thanks, Audie Lee."

"Hunnnn." He pointed to the burlap bag he had removed from his shoulder and held open.

"What?" She took a step back from the fence.

He grunted again and began rummaging around in the bag. After a bit, he pulled out a small tobacco sack and loosened the strings. He poured the contents into his hand and held them out for her to see. Maggie cautiously stepped closer to the fence and leaned forward to look over the odd assortment: a couple of colorful rocks, some buttons, a marble, some nuts and bolts, and even a "vote for FDR" button. She nodded and smiled. "That's nice."

Grunting and gesturing, he held his hand closer to Maggie and pointed to the various items. Obviously from his grunts, he wanted her to do something. She glanced around her feet for a small rock or something to add to his collection. He squinted and frowned, his grunting and gestures growing more insistent. He held the marble out to Maggie.

"Do you want me to take it?" She timidly held out her hand palm up. Audie Lee placed the marble in her hand and grinned, showing his tobacco stained teeth.

Maggie admired the red and green colors. "It's pretty." She held her hand out so he could take back the marble, but he began to put all his trinkets back into the burlap bag. He threw it over his shoulder, and began to stumble away.

"Thank you, Audie Lee." But he never turned around. *Now that was interesting.* She dropped the marble into her bucket.

Once she had picked enough poke, she started toward home, going the shorter way past Grandpa's house where she saw Jeannie and Stuart in Grandpa's barnyard. Grandma and Grandpa had taken a Greyhound bus to Oneida to see Grandma's sister and planned to be gone for several days. Jeannie and Stuart had promised to milk their cow and feed their animals. Jeannie was crying, and Stuart yelled at her. "It's not my fault. You're the one who thought up the stupid idea."

"But what'll we do? We can't let her go like that," Jeannie wailed.

Maggie walked closer. "What's wrong?"

"Oh, Maggie, something awful's happened." Jeannie wiped at her tears with the back of her hand.

"What's that?"

Jeannie and Stuart looked at each other for several seconds. Finally, Stuart hung his head and said in a soft voice, "Grandpa's mare's got a pitchfork in her tail."

"What do you mean?"

"It's tangled up in her tail and when she walks, it punches her and that makes her jump and then it punches her again."

"How'd that happen?"

Jeannie took a deep breath. "When we got to the barn, the horse had got in the feed room."

Stuart jumped into the story. "She had all four feet in the feed room with her head in the feed barrel, and only her rear end sticking out the door. We tried to make her get out, but she wouldn't."

"We threw rocks at her and yelled, but she just stomped her feet and kept eating."

"I even went around back and beat on the wall," Stuart said, "but it didn't do no good."

Maggie knew the big white mare frightened the kids. Actually, Maggie considered her dangerous too. Once the mare had gotten angry with a little goat that grazed in the pasture and stomped it to death. She did not like to pull the wagon, and Grandpa had to pull hard on the reins to keep her from bolting when he hitched her up. She nipped at the kids if they got close enough to her and kicked the dogs if they came around her back feet.

"So, how'd the pitchfork get in her tail?"

"We finally climbed up in the hay loft above the feed room. We leaned over the side, and we could see her rear end sticking out," Stuart explained. "I picked up a pitchfork and poked at her with the handle, but she wouldn't come out. Then Miss Smarty Pants here got the bright idea of twisting the prongs in her tail. She said 'Let's see if we can pull her out by the tail.'" Stuart pointed at Jeannie. "She said we should brace the handle against the edge of the loft and pull down on the handle so's we'd get some leverage. Then she said 'One, two, three' and we pulled down with all our might."

"That brought her out in a hurry." Jeannie flipped her braids over her shoulder. "But she jerked backwards so fast she pulled the pitchfork right out of our hands. The handle plopped down on the ground and she backed out right onto the prongs. And that made her jump, and the pitchfork punched her again, and she jumped again. And there she went right out the barnyard gate leaping every time that pitchfork punched her again." Jeannie moved her hand like the pitchfork poking the horse's rear with every leap.

"Where did she go?" Maggie looked around the barnyard.

"She's clear up at the other end of the pasture. She finally quit running, and she's eating grass, but the pitchfork's still in her tail with the handle dragging on the ground. If Jeannie hadn't said we should pull down on the handle, it wouldn't of happened."

Jeannie made a face at him. "But she'd still be eating the cow feed, wouldn't she? At least it got her out of the feed room."

Maggie smiled as she visualized the mare leaping across the pasture, but she knew they'd have to do something to get the fork loose. She set her bucket of greens in the feed room and latched the door. "Jeannie, go get Grandma's scissors from her sewing box in the bedroom. Stuart, get two or three ears of corn."

Armed with the ears of corn, they warily climbed the ridge toward the big mare. Stuart stood in front of the horse and held out an ear of corn at arm's length. He let her nibble it, being careful to keep his fingers out of her reach, and then began slowly backing up so the horse would follow, reaching for the corn. Maggie stepped behind the mare and gingerly lifted the pitchfork, holding it away from the horse's rear. They formed a strange procession as they slowly snaked their way down the hill to the barn and into a stall.

"Jeannie, put some cow feed in the feedbox so she will eat while I cut this pitchfork loose." Maggie's hands trembled so much she could hardly grasp the scissors. "If she kicks me, it'll probably break my ribs or worse," she said to Stuart and Jeannie who stood at the door looking in. She took a deep breath and began to cut. In a few snips, the pitchfork fell loose, and Maggie released her breath.

Once outside the stall with the pitchfork in hand, Maggie's legs gave away, and she staggered crazily, grabbing at the wall. She slowly slid down the wall and sat in the straw. She took a couple of deep breaths. *I will not faint!*

"Are you okay?" Stuart hovered over her.

Maggie took another deep breath and nodded her head. Then she began to laugh. "I can't believe you thought you could prize that mare out like pulling the cork from the vinegar bottle."

"Well, let's not tell nobody. Okay?" Stuart pulled Maggie to her feet.

* * *

"Giddy up, horse," Johnny Ray commanded. He sat in the little red wagon while Stuart pulled it along. The doctor had recommended he return to school. However, his damaged heart could not pump blood efficiently enough for Johnny Ray to exert much energy. After the smallest activity, his lips turned blue, and he got short of breath, so every morning one of the kids pulled him in the wagon down to the bus stop and pulled him back home each afternoon.

Johnny Ray loved being catered to and took advantage of every opportunity to get special treatment. If he didn't get his way, he would begin to pant and keel over pretending to pass out. Corie Mae always caved in to his demands. In fact, she had wanted him to stay home and not go back to school at all, but when Ray insisted, she finally relented.

Now on the way to the bus stop, Maggie walked along lost in thought. Last night after the kids had gone to bed, she told her parents that Miss Erickson had said the students with the top grades in business courses would go to Cookeville to the East Tennessee Business Education Conference at the end of April. Each student needed to pay thirty dollars to cover transportation and overnight lodging. Corie Mae lividly explained no way could they afford thirty dollars for such a trip, and even if they could, she did not want Maggie going on an overnight trip with a bunch of high school kids. Maggie had asked if she got the money somehow, then could she go? Corie Mae shook her head vigorously. "I already said I didn't want you going on no overnight trip."

Frustrated and angry, Maggie had trudged up the stairs for bed. *It doesn't make sense. It's not like I'm doing something bad.* She lay in the dark staring at the reflection of the moonlight in the small mirror.

This morning Ray had offered to help with the milking. When they were almost to the barnyard, Ray looked at Maggie. "Last night when you wanted to know if you could go on the trip, did you have a notion of how to get the money?"

"No," Maggie had said, "but it doesn't matter, cause Mama won't let me go anyway."

"I don't know about that. I'm just sorry we don't have the money."

Johnny Ray's sudden squeals startled her out of her reverie. Stuart had given the wagon a shove, and now Johnny Ray careened down the hill screaming with delight. The front wheel caught in a rut, turning the wagon over and dumping Johnny Ray onto the ground. Maggie ran to him and helped him back into the wagon. Fortunately, he wasn't hurt–had just gotten his shirt dirty and had torn the cover off a book.

"Stuart, you shouldn't have done that," Maggie scolded. "He could have got hurt."

"He asked me to."

"I'm okay, Maggie," Johnny Ray said. "It was fun."

Maggie gathered up his books and put them into the wagon beside him. "Now, Stuart, be careful."

"You're getting as bad as Mama. Just because he's got a bad heart don't mean he can't never have no fun!"

* * *

Maggie hurried down the street toward the school. As soon as she had come into the office, Mr. Adkins had asked her to take a certified letter to the post office. Now she rushed back to school hoping to have time to look over her English assignment before class. As she passed City Café, she noticed Aunt Lillian sitting in a booth smoking. She decided to take time to say hello.

"I'm sure glad to see you. I told JD to tell you to come and see me."

"I haven't seen JD all week. I think he's cutting classes."

"We're having a big dinner Friday night and another'n Saturday night, and we need some help. Mrs. Jenkins said I could ask you to work for us, and she'd pay you. You could come up here after school on Friday and then spend the nights on my sofa. Maybe JD could pick you up and take you home on Sunday."

"I can't believe I'm hearing this, Aunt Lillian. I need thirty dollars by the end of the month so I can go to Cookeville for a Business Education Conference."

"I doubt she'll pay you that much."

"But it will be a good start. I just hope Mama will let me work. She said she didn't want me to go on the overnight trip, but this morning Daddy talked like if I could get the money I could go."

"Let me know what they say. If you can't work, I need to find someone else."

Maggie gave her a hug. "Thank you so much, Aunt Lillian. I know I can figure out some way to get the rest of the money I need."

Maggie hurried along the sidewalk. She couldn't keep the smile off her face. *Oh, I just can't believe this.* She began whistling and skipped along like a six year old. "Oops." she suddenly realized someone might see her and looked around sheepishly. She remembered Grandma always says "A whistling girl and a crowing hen always come to some bad end" and turned the corner into the schoolyard.

* * *

"Thanks, Maggie, I don't know how we would've managed without your help tonight. " Mrs. Jenkins took off her apron. "I'm assuming you'll help us again tomorrow night?"

"Yes, ma'am."

"That's good. I'd like you to start about five o'clock Now, Lillian, I'm leaving. I'll let you turn out the lights and shut everything up, and I'll see you in the morning."

After Mrs. Jenkins left, Maggie asked, "If I'm not supposed to go to work until five o'clock tomorrow, what'll I do all day?"

"Whatever your little heart desires." They went out the side door and up the stairs to Lillian's apartment. "Have a seat, Maggie." Lillian plopped down and patted the sofa beside her. "If your feet hurt as bad as mine, you need to take a load off." She kicked off her shoes and rested her feet on the rickety coffee table. "Put your feet up. You can't hurt this old table."

Maggie sat on the sofa and kicked off her shoes.

"You did real good tonight." Lillian patted Maggie's shoulder.

Maggie smiled. "Thanks. I was sooo nervous serving all the teachers. I just watched Wanda and tried to do like she did."

"Wanda's worked here almost as long as I have. She's a good waitress."

"If you hadn't told me customers would give me tips, I wouldn't have known what to do. Mr. Adkins gave me a dollar, Mr. Moore and Miss Erickson gave me fifty cents, and some others gave me quarters. I got three dollars and fifty cents."

"Sit still and I'll get us a glass of tea." Lillian stood and walked to the refrigerator in the tiny kitchen.

"After you drink your tea, why don't you get in the bath tub? I feel all hot and sweaty after slaving in that hot kitchen all day. I bet you do, too." Maggie nodded. "While you take your bath, I'll fix your bed."

Maggie lowered herself into the warm water. She had never taken a bath in a tub like this. At home they took baths in a wash tub in the kitchen. She could stretch out her legs and relax. She thought she could lie there and go to sleep. Later she stretched out on the somewhat lumpy sofa and reviewed the events of the week. Corie Mae had protested only a little before agreeing for Maggie to stay with Aunt Lillian and work in the restaurant for two nights. While she wouldn't earn all she needed for the trip to Cookeville, she would surely have more than half of it, especially if she got as many tips tomorrow night as she got tonight. If she could figure out how to get the rest of the money, she believed her father would overrule her mother and let her go. She closed her eyes and sighed with satisfaction.

* * *

The next morning Maggie sat on the little screened-in porch outside Lillian's bedroom and worked on her homework. She had slept later than she could ever remember. She looked out into the tiny back yard where a fuzzy little white dog trotted across the yard carrying a stick in its mouth. Maggie smiled and stretched. She could get used to a life of leisure.

Startled by a knock at the door, she opened it and discovered Wanda waiting on the steps.

"Hey, girl, come on; we're going down to Miller's Falls."

"Who's we?"

"JD and Bud are in the car."

"Let me get my shoes on, and I'll come right down."

Maggie had gone to the falls a few times. Her fifth grade teacher had taken the class there for an all-day picnic, and her church had held baptisms there a time or two. She had forgotten about the roughness of the road. In one place the car dragged on the deep ruts. The unpaved road wound down the steep wooded hillsides and ended at the bottom of a ravine where the creek flowed through a series of rapids and falls. Mountain laurel, pine groves, and ferns covered the hillsides. A few dogwood and redbud trees still bloomed. Maggie sat in the back seat with Bud who had smiled warmly when she got into the car. Now he reached for her hand. "I'm glad you came along."

Maggie smiled and noticed he already had a tan, probably from playing baseball. *He's such a good looking guy.* Not the tallest boy in his class, but he had the best physique, and she loved his wavy blond hair, and his deep blue eyes, his charming smile and those dimples–absolutely adorable. She still couldn't convince herself that he seemed to like her.

JD parked the car, and they walked upstream to a small pool. JD picked up a rock. "Look at that bottle over there on the other side of the creek. I bet you can't hit it."

JD and Bud both threw several times, but neither hit the target. After watching for a few minutes, Maggie picked up a stone and zinged it across the water smashing the bottle to smithereens.

"Show off!" JD yelled and gave Maggie a little shove.

"Hey, quit shoving my girl!" Bud shoved JD.

"Why you knock-kneed, flop-eared, bow-legged, yellow-livered, Nigger loving, Jew baby, Japo, son of a bitch. Push me around, will you?"

Bud laughed so hard, he almost fell over when JD shoved him, but he managed to get his feet under him, and they playfully wrestled around for a few minutes.

When the shoving match slacked off, Wanda tapped JD on the shoulder. "I'll race you to the falls." They jogged out of sight.

Maggie turned to Bud. "What makes you think I'm your girl?"

"I guess I just wished it."

Maggie looked up with a mischievous grin. "You know what my grandma says about wishes?" Bud shook his head. "She says wish in one hand and shit in the other and see which hand fills up quicker."

Bud laughed. "Your grandmother really said that?"

"She amazes me sometimes with some of the stuff she says."

"Trying to tell me it does me no good to wish?"

They had begun to walk slowly along the creek toward the falls. Maggie studied the ground before she answered. She flashed a smile at Bud. "I didn't say I didn't want to be your girl. It's just seems impossible when my mother won't let me go out with anybody. I mean, how can I be your girlfriend if I can't go anywhere with you?"

"I guess we'll just have to see each other at school and any time like this we get the chance until your mother will let you go out."

"That doesn't seem like much fun for you."

"Any time I can be with you is fun for me."

Maggie's heart did a flip-flop. She squeezed Bud's hand. "That's very sweet to say. I enjoy being with you, too."

After walking along in silence past several huge boulders, the water hissing and gurgling as it rushed around the rocks, he led her to a large flat rock extending out into the stream, Bud helped her climb up and sat beside her. He broke a branch from a bush and began pulling off the leaves and throwing them into the water. "Maggie, I've been trying to get up the courage to ask you to go to the Junior-Senior Banquet with me."

Maggie hung her head. When she looked up, she had tears in her eyes. "Oh, Bud, I'd give anything to go, but I can't."

"Don't cry. It's not the end of the world."

"I mean, even if Mama would let me go, which she won't, I don't have anything to wear."

JD and Wanda strolled over and sat on the rock with them. JD took a cigarette for himself and passed the pack to Wanda. When Bud offered one to Maggie, she shook her head. "I better not. It might make me sick, and I have to work tonight."

When the others had lit up, Bud said, "I've been trying to talk Maggie into going to the Junior-Senior Banquet with me."

"Oh, that'd be great. We could all go together." Wanda looked at Maggie, her eyes shining with excitement.

JD leaned back and blew out a series of smoke rings. "I hope you said you'd go, Cuz."

Maggie shook her head. "You know Mama'd never let me go."

"Don't tell her. Just go. It's for sure I ain't telling my mother."

"That's easy for you to say, JD. Aunt Opal doesn't tell you what you can and can't do these days."

"You're right about that, and she sure as hell better not start."

Bud pointed to a hawk sailing around on the updrafts from the falls. He had stretched out his legs and leaned back on one elbow enjoying the warm sun. They watched the graceful bird circling around until it flapped its wings and flew out of sight. The sun glinted on the water as it rushed past the rocks like diamonds or twinkling stars. Maggie filled her lungs with the moist air and thought of fresh clean air right after a summer rain.

"I got an idea," Wanda said. "Maggie could tell her mother Mrs. Jenkins needs her to work in the restaurant again. I'm sure Lillian would agree for her to spend the night, and she wouldn't tell nobody."

"I always wondered why I wanted you for my girl friend," JD teased. "Because you're so smart. That's a perfect idea." He looked at Maggie. "What do you say, Cuz?"

Maggie shrugged her shoulders. "I don't know. I hate lying to my parents."

"Nobody behaves as good as Aunt Corie Mae expects you to. She don't want you to do nothing that's the least bit fun," JD complained. "If you're ever gonna do anything fun, you'll have to do it behind her back."

Maggie swallowed and fought back tears. "She just wants what is best for her kids."

"Why do you take up for her? You know she expects you to work your tail off and never gives you so much as a 'thank you.'"

Bud stood and pulled Maggie to her feet. "Let's go see the falls."

"Meet us at the car in fifteen minutes," JD said. "Wanda has to go to work in an hour."

Holding hands, Maggie and Bud walked in silence to the falls and stood on the bank looking at the water as it cascaded some fifteen feet into a pool about thirty feet across. The water, high from the recent rains, drowned out their voices. Maggie yelled, "Ever dived off the falls?"

Bud put his face close to Maggie's ear. "Lots of times. Us town boys come down here almost every day in the summer. The water's not so fast then, and it's a fun way to cool off. We play water tag and race each other across the pool and all sorts of stuff."

"I don't know how to swim."

"I'm volunteering to teach you."

"Now, my mother would really get upset over that."

Bud led her away from the falls. "Look, Maggie. I respect your feelings about lying to your parents. If you wanted to pretend to work at the café and go to the banquet, I'd be happy to go along with that. But if you feel you can't deceive your folks that way, I understand."

Maggie looked at Bud. "I thought you'd get mad."

"I'll be disappointed if you can't go with me, but I won't get mad."

"Maybe you should ask someone else."

Bud stopped, put his hands on her shoulders and gave her a little shake. "No way. When I said you're my girl. I meant it. I just hope you will agree."

"Okay. I'll ask my parents and see what they say."

Before they reached the car, Maggie turned to Bud. "Thank you for asking me to the banquet. I don't know how it will work out, but I'm delighted to be your girl."

* * *

On Monday, Maggie told Miss Erickson she had twenty dollars toward the money she needed for the trip. Although she admitted her mother hadn't really agreed, she felt pretty sure her father would insist they allow Maggie to go. Later in the day, Miss Erickson told Maggie a couple of the elementary teachers had given tests to their students, and they wanted to pay Maggie to grade the tests.

Maggie decided not to say anything to her parents about going to the banquet with Bud until after her mother agreed for her to go to the Business Education Convention, fearing her mother would not only veto the banquet but also the trip.

On Sunday afternoon, Maggie joined her parents on the porch where they sat in the swing. Her mother's mood had improved somewhat lately, probably because she enjoyed the chance to make garden and plant flowers. "Mama, I noticed the peas you planted have come up, and I think we probably could pull a few green onions any time now." Maggie sat on the top porch step.

Corie Mae smiled. "I think we're going to have a real good garden this year. I just hope we don't have a bad storm like we had last year that washed out lots of the garden."

"What else you aiming to plant?"

"It's too early to plant tomatoes and anything a frost'll kill. So we'll plant beans, corn, taters and stuff like that next week. It's the wrong time of the moon for planting right now."

"Mama, did I tell you the elementary teachers have hired me to grade some special tests?"

Corie Mae shook her head. "When did this happen?"

"Miss Erickson told me about it last week. They're paying me fifty cents an hour."

"I guess that's good. Ever little bit helps."

"I made twenty dollars working at the café last weekend. With the money I make grading the tests, I think I'll have the thirty dollars I need to make the trip to Cookeville."

Corie Mae stopped rocking the swing. "I already told you I don't want you going on no overnight trip with a bunch of students."

"But, Mama, it's only six students. And Miss Erickson and Miss McNeal will go with us. We'll have plenty of supervision."

"I don't care. I don't want you going."

"But, why, Mama? What's wrong with going?"

"I said 'no' once, and I mean 'no,' and that's the end of it." Corie Mae folded her arms across her chest, clamped her lips tightly together and lifted her chin with that I-dare-you-to-defy-me look.

Maggie looked at her father. She couldn't understand why her mother objected so strongly. Ray puffed on his pipe for a few seconds and then took it from his mouth. "Maggie, I'm real proud of how you worked to earn the money. It's not like you waited for something to be gived to you on a silver platter." He put the pipe back in his mouth and took a few more puffs. "I think it'd be good experience for you to make this trip." He smoked some more.

Maggie waited. Her mother slowly shook her head. Ray continued, "You work hard here at home. You do your chores careful. You look out for the littl'ns. We can depend on you. We're proud of you."

"Thank you, Daddy."

Maggie listened to the creaking of the swing and looked across the yard at the beagle puppies rolling in the grass. Stuart would have some good hunting dogs to sell again this summer. Ray knocked his pipe against the porch rail. He turned to look at Corie Mae. "I think Maggie has earned this trip, Corie Mae. We're going to let her go."

"No!" Corie Mae stood up with her hands on her hips.

Ray gently pulled Corie Mae back beside him. He refilled and lit his pipe and rocked quietly for several minutes. "You know, Corie Mae, Maggie's not asking to go do a bunch of foolishness. It's a special honor that she's good enough in her books to be asked to go. She's worked hard for this."

Corie Mae jumped up again. "Ever time you side with her." She wagged her finger in Ray's face. "It don't matter what I think, you always go against me. I'm getting mighty tired of it too. Here lately seems like ever time I make a decision, you cancel it out–'specially if it's got anything to do with what Maggie wants."

Red-faced, Corie Mae shook her fist in Ray's face. "And here you've got me pregnant again. I cook your food, clean your house, raise your kids, and work from daylight to dark. Seems like all you ever want from me is to spread my legs for you so we can make another baby. It don't make no difference what I think about nothing." She turned and slammed the door as she went into the house.

Maggie sat in stunned silence and watched the puppies. Finally she looked at Ray, tears running down her cheeks. "I'm so sorry, Daddy. I didn't mean to make her mad at you." Ray hung his head and sighed. "I didn't know she's pregnant again," Maggie said.

"She just told me a couple of days ago."

She moved to sit in the swing beside her father. "Daddy, do you really think it's okay for me to make the trip? I mean, it makes me sad that Mama gets upset with you because of what I want to do, and now she's expecting and everything."

"Maggie, your mother means well, but sometimes, she sort of gets carried away. I want you to go on the trip. You deserve to go. You've worked hard for it."

"Thank you, Daddy. I promise to do my best. Miss Erickson thinks I can win in shorthand and maybe in typing. It would be an honor to beat out students from all over east Tennessee. It will win honor for the school, too, if I can do it."

"Just do your best, Sunshine. That's all I ask."

* * *

The next Monday evening as Maggie walked back to the house after doing the evening chores, Mrs. Lewis drove up. She had brought Betty Lou home after piano practice. Maggie hurried to get the milk strained into the containers and the milk buckets washed so she could get in on the conversation taking place in the front room.

Betty Lou held up a long white dress made of several layers of a sheer material. Tiny cap sleeves dropped off the shoulders. "That's exactly the kind of dress I need for the banquet," Maggie thought to herself when she walked through the doorway. She noticed her mother shaking her head.

"This is the dress they want Betty Lou to wear for the music program on Friday night," Mrs. Lewis explained "I thought we could dress it up a bit with these tiny pink rosebuds." She held out a package of rosebuds made from folded ribbon.

"I'm not wanting Betty Lou to wear nothing like that," Corie May said. "I just don't think a dress like that is right for a girl her age."

A skillful negotiator, Mrs. Lewis, within half an hour, had not only persuaded Corie Mae to make some needed alterations in the dress and tack on the rosebuds, but she also had gotten Corie Mae to agree to go to the program on Friday night.

"I'll pick you up at six thirty. I hope Ray will go too. He always enjoys hearing Betty Lou play. Jeannie needs to go because her class is singing, so we'll make room for her and Betty Lou in the car." As Mrs. Lewis stood in the doorway preparing to leave, she turned to Maggie. "I hope you'll keep an eye on Junior and Jay while your mother and father are gone."

"I'd be happy to do that." Maggie followed her out the door and down the steps to her car. "Thank you, Mrs. Lewis. I know Mama wouldn't have agreed to go if you hadn't persuaded her."

"I'm sure she will like how well Betty Lou plays the piano. I'm really proud of her myself. I think she has lots of potential as a musician."

"You and Reverend Lewis are so kind to us. I appreciate it very much."

"Maggie, we help out wherever we can. We appreciate how faithful your father is to the church. I always know I'll find him there in his usual place every Sunday." She opened the car door and got in. "I appreciate you, too, Maggie. You help your family so much, and you set a good example for the younger children."

"Thanks, Mrs. Lewis." Maggie waved as the car turned around and started down the road. Climbing the steps to the yard, Maggie smiled. *She's really something!*

* * *

When the kids got off the bus the next afternoon, Joe McPeters pulled his car off the road and Ray got out with a fifty-pound sack of seed potatoes.

"Hi Daddy," Johnny Ray called. "You want to pull your taters in my wagon?"

"Now, that's a good idea, son." Ray put the potatoes in the wagon and lifted Johnny Ray to sit astride the sack. "Hang on tight." Maggie walked beside him as Ray pulled the wagon along the dirt road. "When you get the chores done, Maggie, I want you to help me cut up these taters. I'll hitch up the horses and get the ground ready. We should be able to get them all planted before dark."

"Okay, Daddy." Maggie noticed her father's eyes didn't have the usual twinkle. She guessed Mama was still mad. Corie Mae hadn't spoken to her for the last two days either. Feeling guilty for causing the distance between her parents, she frowned and turned her head toward the woods where she saw Audie Lee. "Daddy, Audie Lee's standing behind those trees over there."

Ray looked toward the trees, raised his hand, and waved. "Hello there, Audie Lee. How're you doing?"

Audie Lee took a couple of steps and returned the wave. Then when Maggie waved, he grinned and began to lope back toward his house. "Sometimes I have the feeling he spies on me."

"Nah, he don't mean no harm. Don't worry about him." Ray gave Maggie a faint smile.

By the time Maggie milked the cows and finished the chores, Ray had the rows laid off for the potatoes. Now he and Maggie sat on the edge of the back porch, cutting the seed potatoes into a bushel basket placed on the ground between them. "Just make sure each piece has at least one good eye," Ray instructed.

"I'll be glad when we get taters big enough to eat," Maggie said. "What's left of the ones we put in the root cellar last year are all shriveled up so they're not much account." When they were almost finished, Maggie said, "Daddy, this boy at school that I like has asked me to go with him to the Junior-Senior Banquet next week."

Ray didn't say anything, but seemed to concentrate really hard on the potato he was cutting into chunks. He reached for another potato and turned to look at Maggie. "What'd you tell him?"

"Told him I'd really like to go but would have to ask you and Mama."

"Humnn." Ray began to chop up the potato. "So what do you think your mother would say?"

"She won't like it. Seems like she's against everything I want to do anymore." Ray didn't respond. Maggie began cutting another potato. "JD tried to get me to say Mrs. Jenkins wanted me to work at the restaurant again and go to the banquet instead. But I decided I couldn't lie to you and Mama like that. When I told Bud, I couldn't do that, he said he respected my decision." Ray continued cutting potatoes without saying anything, so Maggie added, "I thought he'd be mad at me, but he said he wasn't."

"Did you say his name was Bud?"

"Bud Summers. His dad runs the service department at the Ford place. He's one of JD's friends. I think he's a nice fellow. If you all will let me go with him, we'll go with JD and his girl friend."

"What do you think will happen if you ask Corie Mae?"

"She'll get upset. With all that's happened lately, and her being pregnant and all, she'd probably get one of her sick headaches."

"I think you're probably right. So maybe we better not mention this to her." He put his hand on Maggie's back. "Sorry, Maggie, but I think you better not plan on going."

Maggie hung her head. She swallowed back the tears. She wanted to go so much, she had dared to dream her father would tell her she could go. "Okay, Daddy," she mumbled, but she didn't look at him.

Ray took the last potato from the sack. "I'm proud that you didn't try to sneak around and not tell us. It would break my heart to think I couldn't tell when you's lying and when you's telling the truth. I'm sorry to disappoint you, 'specially when you was honest about it." He threw the last pieces of potato in the basket and stood "Let's go get these taters in the ground."

* * *

On Sunday Grandma had invited the family to a birthday dinner for Corie Mae. JD had gone to town to bring Aunt Lillian. "You better enjoy this beef stew. It's the last can of beef we've got. I saved it special for Corie

Mae's birthday," Grandma said. "The last of our carrots, taters and onions, too. I'm glad we've got garden planted so we'll soon have fresh stuff cause all our stuff from last year's 'bout gone."

"I sure do like these leather breeches, Grandma," Junior said.

"I've only got a few messes left, Honey, but I'll make sure you get some the next time I cook up a mess." Grandma looked across the table. "I heard you had a big program at school, Betty Lou. Your mama told me you played the piano for all the kids to sing. She showed me the pretty dress you wore. I wish I could have went to see it."

Betty Lou smiled. "I guess I did okay. Mrs. Lewis helped me learn the pieces."

"I tell you, I was proud of her. She looked so pretty." Ray beamed at Betty Lou. "I never knowed she could play the piano so good."

Perplexed, Maggie marveled that her mother would brag to Grandma after putting up such resistance to letting Betty Lou wear the dress and insisting up to the last minute she didn't want to go hear her play. *I guess I'll never understand her.*

As usual, the women cleaned up the kitchen while the men sat on the front porch and smoked. Almost as soon as Maggie came out onto the porch, JD announced he had to take Aunt Lillian back to town and go to work at the station. When JD and Aunt Lillian got into the car, Kenny got into the back seat.

"Where'd you think you're going?" Aunt Opal yelled.

Kenny just waved and closed the car door.

Aunt Opal jumped off the porch step and ran toward the car. "You come back here. I never said you could go nowhere." But JD backed the car into the road and drove away.

"Them boys don't never do a thing I say." Aunt Opal stepped onto the porch.

"They ain't never had no father to make them mind," Grandpa said. "I told Thomas when he went to Detroit he was deserting his family and someday he'd be sorry."

Maggie smiled to herself. *If only you knew.*

Grandpa relit his pipe and crossed one leg over the other leaning forward with his forearm on his knee. "Ray, I'm starting a new church."

"Oh? Why's that?"

"I been talking to Brother Hicks and some other folks. Seems like that James Lewis down at the Baptist church ain't gonna rule out this new Bible. Lots of folks is saying that church ain't never been spiritual noways. Haskins down here says he'll donate ground right there on the highway." Grandpa took a couple of puffs on his pipe. "Reverend Hicks wants me to be the preacher. Says he's not able to do good preaching no more cause of his bad heart. I guess he's found several people who'll donate timber. They think they'll be ready to start building by summer time. I asked Corie Mae and she said she'd like to join up with us." Grandpa sat back and smiled.

Ray looked around for Corie Mae, but she had gone home to put Jay down for a nap. "We ain't discussed it, but after all the Baptist church has done for us, they's no way we will desert it."

"Not even if they is using this new Bible?"

"I asked Reverend Lewis about that. He explained to me that the Bible was first wrote in old languages, not in English. So nobody could read the Bible in English until King James had it wrote out. But that was nearly four hundred years ago. So this new Bible is just a newer translation from them old languages into more modern English. That don't sound bad to me."

"But they say this new Bible denies the virgin birth. 'Stead of calling Mary a virgin, it says young woman. I don't think it's right to change the scripture that a way."

"Reverend Lewis said that's the word the first languages used. So it's the King James Bible got it wrong. This'un just tried to fix it back right."

"The Bible says not one letter will be changed, so it's a sin to change any of the words."

"But if that's true, then we should still be reading it in those first languages, shouldn't we? It should never been writ in English at all."

"Well, I ain't going to no church that uses this new Bible. The King James is the only true Bible."

Maggie looked at her father with raised eyebrows. She had not known Ray had had such a discussion with Reverend Lewis, and she'd never heard her father dispute anything Grandpa said about religion. But she was impressed with how well Ray could make his point.

"Grandma, that was good birthday cake. Is they any more? I'd sure like another piece." Johnny Ray stood next to Grandma on the porch. He and Junior had been sitting on the back steps throwing rocks at a bucket.

"Honey, I give it to your mama to take home. You'll have to get a piece when you get back to your house."

Ray stood. "Well, kids, I guess we better be getting on home. Thanks for the good dinner, Mama Campbell." Ray hoisted Johnny Ray up on his shoulders, and they walked down the road. Ray turned to Maggie who walked beside him. "This Summers boy, what'd you say his name was?"

"Bud"

"I'd like to meet him. Reckon he'd come out here and sit on the porch with me sometime so's we could get to know each other?"

"Suppose he might. I'll ask him. When would be a good time?"

"See if he can come this Friday night." He winked at Maggie.

At first she was puzzled. Then she squeezed her father's hand. "I'll try to arrange it," she said, "and thanks, Daddy."

* * *

The next Sunday afternoon, Maggie took her homework and walked toward the big rock down by the spring house. As she approached the rock, she saw Jeannie digging in the dirt with a hoe. "What're you doing?"

Jeannie jumped in surprise. "I ain't doing nothing." She clapped her hand over her mouth. "I mean I'm not doing anything. Besides, you're not supposed to know about it."

"About what?"

"You've spoiled it. It won't work now." Jeannie turned angry eyes toward Maggie.

"Sorry, but I don't know what you're talking about." Maggie sat down against the rock and opened her notebook.

Jeannie came and sat beside Maggie. "Did I show you this wart that's come on my finger?"

"Let's see it."

Jeannie held up her hand so Maggie could see the wart. "I asked Grandma what to do to get rid of it, and she told me to steal somebody's dish rag and bury it and don't tell no one–uh, anyone. She said the wart would go away in two weeks."

"So you stole a dish rag?"

Jeannie hung her head. "I took Aunt Opal's when she wasn't looking yesterday. But now you know about it, so it won't work."

"Maybe it'll still work if you bury it somewhere else. I won't look."

"I guess it won't hurt to try."

Jeannie stood and began chopping at some weeds with the hoe. "Maggie, why's Mama so mad at Daddy? She won't look at him and won't hardly even answer him when he asks her a question."

Maggie took a deep breath. "I guess it upsets her when Daddy doesn't agree with her. Once she makes up her mind about something, it's hard for her to change her thinking even when she needs to. I've heard stories about our great-grandpa Campbell who came here from Kentucky and built our house. I guess he was as stubborn as the day is long. Probably Mama inherited some of his ways."

"But what did they disagree about?"

"Lots of stuff, I guess. You know they had a big argument the other day after Grandpa told Daddy Mama wanted to be part of that new church. And then Mama gets all upset when Daddy tells her she's babying Johnny Ray too much."

They didn't used to have arguments. It scares me."

"I wish they could agree on more things. Guess it's partly my fault. I wanted to go on a school trip, and Mama said I couldn't go. Then Daddy said I could go. So Mama got mad when he overruled her."

"So are you going?"

"Yeah. We're leaving on Thursday after school, and we'll stay until Saturday. It's a business education conference where they'll have competitions for business students. Miss Erickson thinks I stand a good chance of winning in shorthand and maybe in typing too."

"Why didn't Mama want you to go? What's wrong with it?"

"She said she didn't think I should stay overnight in some strange place with other students, which doesn't make a lot of sense to me." Maggie threw up her hands. "I don't know what she really doesn't like about it."

"I thought she was mad cause that guy came to visit you on Friday night. He seemed real nice. Is he your boyfriend?"

"He's a friend. Mama says I can't go on dates until I'm sixteen, so I guess for now we are just friends."

"So is he going to come see you again?"

"Oh, I don't know. He didn't say anything about it." Maggie didn't tell her that she and Bud planned to meet when she gets back from Cookeville on Saturday and spend the evening together until JD gets off work and can bring her home.

Jeannie picked up the dish rag. "I'll go find another place to bury this. I just hope it works."

Maggie opened her shorthand book. She wanted to learn as much new vocabulary as possible before the trip. She began making neat transcriptions in her notebook. She smiled when she remembered that Bud had agreed to come to her house on Friday evening instead of going to the Junior-Senior Banquet. Her father had talked with Bud for half an hour on Friday night and then said, "Well, why don't you and Maggie go for a walk."

CHAPTER 7

Campbell Holler–July 15, 1887 Sad Day. Buried our baby boy. Born 3 months early. Lived only a few hours. Harvey made the coffin. Neighbors helped dig grave in cemetery at Freedom Church.
(Diary of Mary Louise Campbell)

Summer 1950

"Here, Jeannie," Betty Lou ordered, "hang these wet dish towels on the back porch." Maggie dried her hands. "Thanks, Aunt Lillian for helping."

"I thought it wasn't fair for Corie Mae to make you wash all the dishes."

"Let's go see what stories Uncle Thomas is telling," Betty Lou said. "I hope we haven't missed a good one." She and Jeannie rushed toward Grandma's front porch where the rest of the family had gathered.

"Are you going to take some time off work while Uncle WC is here this week, Aunt Lillian?" Maggie pushed a chair to the table.

"We're going to go to the Smokies for a few days. Mrs. Jenkins said I could take the whole week."

"It must be hard to see him only a couple of times a year."

"I'm hoping maybe next year I can stay with him in Detroit for a while."

"That'd be great, Aunt Lillian, but I'll miss you." Maggie wondered if Aunt Lillian knew about Thomas's other woman. If she did, she'd never let on. *I'm certainly not going to bring it up.* They each took a chair from the dining room to the porch.

"You kids take those stinking things to the back yard. They make too much noise," Grandma scolded Junior and Johnny Ray, who were playing shootout with the new cap guns Uncle Thomas had brought them.

"But don't be running, Johnny Ray." Corie Mae turned toward Thomas. "He forgets all the time and first thing you know he's ready to fall over."

"He ain't growed much this year, has he? I swan Junior's as tall as he is." Thomas watched the boys go around the corner of the house.

"The doctor says he'll grow more slow now. His blood just don't flow right. I worry about him all the time. Seems like he's always getting a cold or something."

"That's too bad, Sis. But that Junior's sure growing fast," Thomas said. "He brought over a book last night and read it to me. He ain't even started school yet, has he?"

"He'll be in first grade," Betty Lou bragged. "Last year while Johnny Ray stayed home sick, Junior did more of the homework the teacher sent home than Johnny Ray did."

"Junior's not the only one who's done good this year," Aunt Lillian said. "Maggie got first prize for shorthand and second place for typing at the Business Education Convention."

"And don't forget Betty Lou," Grandma chimed in. "She played piano for the elementary music program. And she had the most beautifulest dress you ever seen."

"I guess I'll have to take the whole Martin family out to the drug store for ice cream cones," Thomas said. "Maybe we can do that before we set off the fire crackers tonight."

Maggie looked at her mother, who busied herself with shifting sleeping Jay to a more comfortable position in her lap. She studied Corie Mae's frown. *What would we have to do to make her brag about us?*

Thomas lit a cigarette and passed the pack around to see if anyone else wanted to smoke. He blew smoke out his nostrils. "Papa, do you think we're starting to get in World War III?"

"What you talking about?" Grandma spit ambeer into her can.

"Ain't you heard, Mama? President Truman ordered troops to Korea. They's already fighting there."

"Me and Thomas was saying we probably should dig up our old uniforms in case we get called up," WC rubbed his tummy. "But I know I couldn't fit in mine no more."

"What's this fighting about?" Maggie's brow wrinkled in worry.

"The North Korean army invaded South Korea, and President Truman thinks we should stop it."

"Why would North Korea do that?" Jeannie asked. Where's North Korea, anyway?"

"After World War II, Korea was divided in two parts." Thomas blew smoke toward the ceiling. "The Russians occupied the north, and the U. S. occupied the south They thought after a while the two parts would get back together as one country, but the Russians set up a communist government in the north. We set up a democratic government in the south. So now the North Koreans think they can take over the South and make it all one communist country."

"I knowed it had something to do with them communists," Grandpa nodded his head energetically. "They's gonna take over the whole world if we don't stop them."

"Looks like Harry Truman's going to try to stop them," WC said. "We heard on the radio while we drove down here that lots of U. S. soldiers was already fighting in Korea. I expect they'll start drafting lots more soldiers right soon."

"Will you have to go back to the army?" Jeannie asked Uncle Thomas.

"I don't know, Honey. I think they'll take younger men than me and WC, but I guess if they call us up, we'll have to go."

"I sure hope you don't have to go. War scares me." Betty Lou folded her arms across her chest.

"War's a pretty scary thing. But I guess somebody's got to go."

"Do you reckon they'll start rationing again?" Grandma asked. "I still got some of them ration books in my bureau. Wonder if I could still use them?"

Jeannie turned to Grandma. "What's rationing?"

"During the war they was certain things you couldn't buy unless you had the stamps in the ration books." Aunt Lillian explained.

"Like what?"

"Shoes, sugar, meat, gasoline, all sorts of stuff like that." Grandma said. "When you went to the store, you had to take your ration books, and the store clerk'd take out stamps before you could buy things."

"You mean before you could buy shoes you had to have a stamp?"

"That's right." Corie Mae patted Jay's back. "Ever' year before school started, we'd take all the kids to town to buy shoes. We had a stamp book for ever' one of you."

"I remember doing that," Maggie said.

"Bang! I got you. You're dead!" Johnny Ray yelled.

"No, you missed." Junior came running around the side of the house.

Johnny Ray stumbled around the corner and collapsed on the steps, pale as a bed sheet and gasping for breath. Corie Mae jumped up, put Jay into Ray's lap, and rushed to Johnny Ray. "I told you not to run." She sat down on the steps and took him in her lap. "Breathe slow, now. Come on, I'll count for you. Breathe in ..one ...two ...three ...four. Breathe out ..one ...two ...three ...four. In ..one ...two ...three ...four. Out ..one ...two ...three

...four." Gradually he relaxed, his breathing became easier, and the color came back to his face. He crawled out of Corie Mae's lap and picked up his gun.

"Now, you just sit here awhile longer," Corie Mae put her hand on his shoulder.

"But, Mama, I'm okay now." He twisted away from her. "I won't run no more. I promise." He stepped onto the porch and held out his gun. "Uncle Thomas, my caps is all used up."

"We'll have to fix that." Thomas took down the box of caps he'd put on top of the porch post earlier. He broke off a roll and inserted it into the chamber. "There you go. Now, go kill a bear."

"Come on, Junior. Let's go around back."

The two boys began walking away.

"Remember not to run," Corie Mae called.

"You've got to let the kid have some fun, Corie Mae," Thomas said.

"But it could kill him if he makes his heart work too hard."

"Life ain't worth living if you can't have no fun."

Maggie looked at Thomas. *I wonder what he means by that?*

* * *

About midmorning one day the next week, the church bell tolled for a long time. Corie Mae straightened from stooping in the garden and listened. "Somebody's died." She called to the kids, "Bring what beans you've got picked. We'll go fix dinner right quick so Ray and the boys can go help dig the grave."

"How'd you know they need to dig a grave?" Johnny Ray asked from the shade where he played with little Jay.

"They always ring the bell like that so everybody can come and help when they's a grave to be dug," Jeannie rolled her eyes.

"I just asked! You don't have to treat me like I'm stupid."

Maggie set her bucket of beans in the wagon and placed Jay beside it. "Get in Johnny Ray."

While Corie Mae went to the root cellar to get a can of applesauce and some canned sausage, Maggie stirred up some biscuits, and Betty Lou broke a couple dozen eggs for scrambling. Jeannie set the table. "Our last can of sausage," Corie Mae announced when she came through the back door, "but I guess this is as good a time as any to use it."

Just as they expected, Ray soon came riding in on one of his work horses, leading the other. And Kenny and JD showed up as well. After eating a quick meal, they loaded the trunk of JD's car with shovels, picks, and mattocks. Johnny Ray complained because Stuart got to go and he had to stay home.

After doing the dishes, Maggie walked to the highway to check the mail as she did each day. Johnny Ray begged to go with her so Maggie pulled him in the wagon. "Maggie, it's so hot; let's stop in the shade," Johnny Ray pleaded. They paused in the shade of the beech tree at the top of the hill. Maggie had hoped for a letter from Bud. He had gone to Chattanooga for the summer to work in his uncle's store, and Corie Mae had agreed for Bud and Maggie to write each other.

"Scoot over so I can sit beside you." Maggie squeezed into the wagon.

"I don't see why I couldn't go to the graveyard with the boys," Johnny Ray pouted.

"You'd get tired having to sit there all afternoon in this hot sun."

Johnny Ray got out of the wagon and picked up a stick. "I sure had a good time when Uncle Thomas come home. He always makes us have so much fun. I wish he could live here all the time. Why does he have to live in Michigan? Why can't he live here?"

"Because there're better jobs in Michigan. He and Uncle WC make more money working in the automobile factory than they could make doing farm work."

"Is Bible School next week? I like Bible School."

"Yes, I like Bible School, too. It's the only time all summer I get to see Mary Ann other than Sundays. Since the church has bought a bus, it'll pick us up at our house, and we won't have to walk."

"You mean the bus will come up the holler to our house?"

"Sure will."

"When school starts will the school bus come up to our house too?"

"No, we'll still have to walk to the highway to catch the school bus." Maggie stood. "We better get home. Mama needs me to help can beans."

As they passed the Johnson farm, Maggie noticed Audie Lee standing among the trees. More often now, she saw him at various places. "Hi Audie Lee," she called and waved. He halfway raised his hand before hiding his face and turning away.

"I wish I could ask him for that pretty necklace."

"Maybe if we had something he'd like, we could swap it for the necklace. What do you have that you could give him?"

"Don't know. What do you think he'd like?"

"We'll have to think about it. Maybe we can find something."

Knowing Ray and the boys would be hungry when they got home from working in the cemetery, Corie Mae cooked a large kettle of beans and potatoes for supper. JD and Kenny had eaten meals with either Grandma and Grandpa or with Maggie's family since Aunt Opal had taken another job caring for an elderly woman in Maple Grove. Maggie hadn't seen so much of JD since he started working at the filling station. It was like old times to have him around so much. All eleven of them gathered around the supper table crowding the kitchen to the limit.

"Who died?" Johnny Ray asked as soon as Ray said "Amen."

"Grandma Morrison," Kenny said.

"Who's that?"

"She lived with her daughter Amanda Jones, you know, in that house that's got that big red barn right next to the Joyner's farm?"

"But she's not my grandma."

"No, but everybody called her that cause she was so old."

"How old was she?"

"Almost a hundred," Corie Mae said. "Now quit asking so many questions and eat your supper."

"These are good beans, Aunt Corie Mae, I was hungry." Kenny served himself another helping.

"Did many folks come to help dig the grave?" Jeannie asked.

"Yeah, they's a right smart number showed up."

"Clyde Spangler was the funniest one that showed up." Kenny began laughing so hard he choked and had to leave the table for a few minutes to quit coughing. Maggie noticed that both JD and her father had big grins, and though Stuart had put his head down, she could see his shoulders shaking in silent laughter.

"What's so funny about him?"

"Well," JD explained," he's as drunk as a skunk. We kept pulling him back from the grave so he wouldn't fall in. He couldn't hardly even stand up."

"Then," Kenny said, "the men from the funeral home had trouble with their truck. They'd brought out the tent to cover the grave and that artificial grass they always put over the dirt pile. But the truck was missing and backfiring and throwing a lot a smoke out the tail pipe."

When Kenny stopped to eat a bite, JD took up the story. "Larry Shaddon and Jim Barker had the hood up trying to figure out the problem. Then old Clyde staggered over to take a look. After standing there swaying back and forth and watching, he said, 'I betcha ten dollars I can pee on the spark plugs and kill the motor.'"

"What on earth?" Corie Mae said and everyone started laughing.

JD swallowed. "So Larry said, 'You're too drunk to stand up on the ground. Ain't no way you could stand up on the fender.' So Old Clyde said, 'I betcha ten dollars.' And then Larry said, 'You ain't got no ten dollars.' And Clyde wobbled a few steps backwards and forwards, reached in his pants pocket and pulled out this big roll of money. Looked like maybe a hundred dollars."

Johnny Ray gasped. "How'd he get that much money?"

Kenny said, "Larry asked him, 'Where'd you get that wad of money?' And he said, 'Well, you see, I got this money tree in my back yard. I just whack it with this stick and the money all falls down.'" JD and Stuart laughed.

"You reckon that's true?" Junior asked.

"So what'd he do then?" Jeannie had stopped eating to listen.

Kenny could hardly talk for laughing. "He got on the running board and tried to step up on the fender, but he fell off. So he staggered over to the wheelbarrow somebody'd brought out and rolled it over to the truck. He finally managed to stand up in the wheelbarrow, but that didn't make him tall enough. Jim Barker said, 'If you're determined to do this, I guess we'll have to help you.' So Larry got on one side and Jim got on the other and steadied him till he was standing on the fender looking down into the motor that was sputtering like a John Deer tractor." Then Kenny collapsed in laughter so he couldn't continue.

"So he was weaving back and forth while he tried to unbutton his pants." JD chuckled. "I thought he was going to fall off for sure. Finally he began peeing right on the spark plugs." Everyone was laughing except Corie Mae

"Then what happened?"

Stuart finally stopped laughing enough to help with the story. "This was the funniest part. When that pee hit those hot spark plugs, it sent a bolt of 'lectricity up that stream of water and knocked poor old Clyde backwards. He hit the ground so hard it knocked him out. He just laid there all spraddled out like a dead man "

All three boys were keeling over with laughter. Jeannie, eyes big as doughnuts, was unsure about whether to laugh or not. Betty Lou hid her laughter behind her hand.

"Did it kill him?" Junior asked.

"At first we didn't know. We all ran over and stood there looking down at him. He had wet his pants, and then we smelled a bad smell." Stuart held his nose.

"Jim said, 'Phewee, he's messed hisself!' And then Larry reached down and felt for his pulse and said he could feel his heart beating. About that time he took a breath, so JD poured some water on him, and he opened his eyes."

"Well, I don't think that's a bit funny." Corie Mae stood and began clearing the table.

"What finally happened to him?" Maggie got up to help her mother.

JD stood and pushed his chair in. "Larry and Jim picked him up, sort of tossed him into the back of the old truck like a sack of potatoes. Said they'd take him home." He patted Corie Mae on the back. "Thanks for the supper, Aunt Corie Mae. You're cooking's a heap better 'n Mama's." JD passed Maggie on his way out the door. "I've got to go to work. I promised Joe I'd take the last half of his shift tonight. He's got a date."

Then in a softer voice, "Did you get a letter today?" Maggie shook her head.

"Tomorrow's another day." He pushed the screen door open and went out.

* * *

Each summer the Baptist church held a two-week Vacation Bible School/revival. Reverend Lewis would invite a guest evangelist to assist with the Bible School in the mornings and preach for the revival meetings in the evenings. These two weeks were Maggie's favorite part of summer. She could spend several hours each morning with her friends in Bible School. In the evenings big crowds filled the building and usually guest singers provided special music. People came from miles around to hear the singing and the preaching.

For Bible School each day the children formed two lines that wound down the steps and across the parking lot. As Mrs. Lewis played some lively music, the children marched into the church and took seats by age groups for the opening assembly, where they recited pledges to the flags and the Bible, sang songs, and usually had a little talk from the visiting evangelist. One morning Reverend Dodge, the visiting minister from Morristown, talked to them about how people cannot always make a correct judgment about something or someone based only on appearance.

"We may think someone is ugly, or has bad manners, or is hateful. But God can see what kind of person we are deep down inside. Lots of times when we get to know people better, we find out they are really quite different." To illustrate he held up a muddy colored rock about the size of his fist. "Now children, look at this rock. Does it look pretty?"

"No." The children answered in chorus.

"If I gave it to you, what would you do with it?"

One little boy sitting on the front row said, "I'd throw it at McPeters' old dog." Everyone laughed.

"Anyone else have an idea what you'd do with this rock?"

"You could put it in a rock wall."

"Yes, what else?"

"You could throw it in the creek."

"How many of you would just throw it away if I gave it to you?" Lots of hands went up.

"You see, just like we can't see inside the heart of people, we can't see inside this rock. What if I told you there's something really pretty inside this rock? Would you believe that?" Only a few children raised their hands.

"This is a special kind of rock called a 'geode.' Geodes are hollow rocks, and the inside is lined with pretty crystals." Then he hit the rock with a hammer, breaking it open, and all the kids "oohed" and "aahed" when they saw the beautiful purple crystals inside.

"Like this geode, people may look ugly but once you really get to know them you discover they are really beautiful."

Maggie had always loved everything about Bible School, but the last day, an all-day affair, was her favorite. The mothers brought in food for a picnic lunch. Afterwards Reverend Lewis had the younger children running sack races, three-legged races, and other relays on the church lawn. For the really young kids and for some like Johnny Ray, he had a bubble blowing contest and handed out prizes, usually candy bars, to everyone, winners or not.

For the rest of the afternoon the older kids played softball in the pasture across the road from the church. Parents stood along the sidelines and yelled encouragement and offered advice. Maggie knew Corie Mae objected to girls and boys playing ball together, so she wasn't surprised when her mother took Jay to the other side of the church, where he could lie in the shade.

Finally, the day ended with homemade ice cream. While they waited in line for ice cream, Mary Ann told Maggie she had something to tell her. "What's that?" They had walked away from the crowd to eat their ice cream in the shade of a big sycamore tree.

"Mama's going to join that new church your grandpa's building. She says all us kids have to go there too. Daddy says he'll never go there. He'll keep coming to this church."

Maggie sighed. "That means the only time we'll see each other is at school."

Mary Ann nodded. "But the building's not finished yet, so we won't have to go for a while." Mary Ann licked her spoon. "Mama's talking about going to a revival at Big Mountain next week. Maybe your mother would let you go with us."

"I'll ask. I never know what she'll let me do. Maybe if it's going to church she won't object."

"Let's go ask her."

They first went to talk with Mrs. Collins who agreed to ask Corie Mae for them, and Corie Mae readily agreed. "I'm surprised she agreed so easily," Maggie said on the way to get seconds on the ice cream. The bus drove up to take the first load home. As Maggie got on the bus, she called over her shoulder to Mary Ann, "I'll see you on Tuesday evening."

"Yeah, wear warm clothes cause we'll be riding in the back of the pickup, and it'll be cold coming home."

* * *

"What'd you think of the revival at Big Mountain the other night?" Mary Ann asked.

"It's different. It reminded me of the way JD described the church meeting he took Grandpa to in Kentucky last summer, except for the snake handling." Maggie looked up at the white, fluffy clouds. "Actually, I don't feel comfortable when everybody's jumping and yelling, although I did enjoy the singing. Sometimes I wish Pastor Lewis would allow some guitars and drums in our church. But at least we got to spend some time together. I enjoyed riding in the back of the pickup all huddled together to stay warm."

Taking a break from their bike ride, Maggie and Mary Ann sat on the grass in the shade beside Maple Lane. After Sunday dinner, Mary Ann's father had brought her to Maggie's house with her brother's bike in the back of the pickup. Maggie borrowed Kenny's bike, and the two of them had gone for a ride.

Mary Ann stretched her legs. "Mama says that's the kind of church she likes. She says she can't feel the spirit at the Baptist church. That's why she wants us to go to the new church."

"My mama would like to go to the new church too, but Daddy won't agree. Somehow I can't see Mama jumping up and down, clapping, hollering 'Praise Jesus' and all that stuff. I don't know why she thinks she would enjoy that kind of church except that her daddy is the preacher." Maggie had started picking clover blossoms.

Mary Ann pulled a pack of cigarettes from her pocket. "Want a smoke?"

"Sure." At first, Maggie coughed, but after a bit, she got the hang of it and finished off the cigarette. She felt a little queasy in the stomach and got a headache but didn't complain.

"Oh, I almost forgot. I've got some bad news to tell you," Mary Ann crushed her cigarette butt on the grassy ground. "Kathy's not coming back to school this year."

"Why? What happened?"

"She's expecting."

"Somehow that doesn't surprise me. I thought she let Billy Ray put his hands on her too much. I figured if she let him do stuff like that right out in public, he probably did more when they were alone. And I guess he did, huh?"

"They're getting married next week."

"How'd you find out?"

"I went to town with Daddy yesterday to buy cow feed. I like to go with him so I can pick out the prettiest feed sacks. I saw her walking down the street past the feed store, and we talked a few minutes."

"How's she taking it?"

"She seemed pretty happy except she can't come to school."

Maggie shook her head. "It's too bad. She made good grades, and now she won't get to play basketball any more either."

"We need you to come out for the team now, Maggie. We played bad enough with her as our best forward, but without her we don't stand a chance of ever winning a game. Don't you think maybe you could talk your mother into letting you play?"

"I doubt it. She wouldn't speak to me for weeks after I tried to get her to let me play last year. Now that she's pregnant, she'll say she needs me to help out with the new baby."

"At least practice with us again this year. We got better after you started coming to practice last season. We even won our first game in the county tournament."

As they talked Maggie had started a daisy chain. She formed it into a small circle and put it on her head like a lopsided crown. "I don't know. I guess I can ask again and see what happens. Thing is, she always gets mad at Daddy if he agrees with me. I hate to cause problems between them."

"I don't understand why they won't let married girls come to school. It seems so unfair. I guess Billy Ray will get to come back and graduate next year with his class. At least one of them will finish."

"Where will they live; did she say?"

"With her parents until Billy Ray finishes school and gets a job."

Maggie rested her elbows on her drawn up knees and put her hands over her face. "Darn, this makes me so mad. I really hate to see Kathy stuck with a kid when she's only fifteen."

"How old was your mother when she had you?"

"Seventeen, but she had quit school years before. I know Kathy's in love and all that, but I bet someday she'll be quite upset over this. I know It would upset me."

"Did you get a letter from Bud this week?"

"I got one yesterday. He's getting anxious to come back home. Looking forward to starting football practice."

"Does he sign with 'hugs and kisses'?" Mary Ann grinned when she saw Maggie blush.

"He mostly talks about what he does in his uncle's store."

"Do you think your mother will let you date him when he gets back?"

"She's always said I couldn't date until I'm sixteen, and that won't happen until next spring, so I reckon after that she'll let me, if he asks me."

"Oh, you know he'll ask you. He's written you all summer, and he asked you to the Junior-Senior Banquet."

"He hasn't said anything about dating in his letters, and you know how he always talked to all the girls. He may have written lots of girls this summer for all I know."

"Oh, he'll ask you. I'd bet you money!" Mary Ann stood and picked up her bike. "We better be riding back. Daddy said not to be gone too long."

"You're right. I've got chores to do. Let's hit the road."

* * *

Maggie walked toward home on the dirt road, pulling Johnny Ray along in the wagon. When they got to the beech tree, Maggie stopped in the shade, sat down in the wagon beside Johnny Ray, and began reading the letter from Bud.

"Does he say 'I love you'?" Johnny Ray looked at her with that mischievous grin. He got out of the wagon and started throwing rocks into the woods.

"Just talks about what he's doing in his uncle's store. Says it's pretty boring, and he looks forward to coming home in a few more weeks. He also said his uncle and aunt took him on a trip to see Rock City."

"What's Rock City?"

"It's on top of Lookout Mountain down near Chattanooga where his uncle lives. It's a famous place with lots of big rock formations. Sometimes you see a sign painted on top of somebody's barn that says 'See Rock City.' Mr. Bridgeman over on the main highway has that sign painted on his barn."

"I don't see what's so special about a bunch of rocks."

"Just remember what the preacher told us at Bible School. You can't always tell what something is by just looking at it. Sometimes you don't realize it's something special." She took two pieces of geode from her pocket and showed them to Johnny Ray.

Johnny Ray's eyes opened wide. "How'd you get those? I never knowed you had them."

"Rev. Dodge gave them to me."

Johnny Ray took one of the pieces and studied it. The crystals glittered like diamonds when they caught the sun's rays. "Them's sure pretty. Can I have one?"

"I thought if we get Audie Lee to come close enough, maybe he would swap for the necklace you're always wanting."

"That's a good idea."

Maggie stood and put the folded letter in her skirt pocket. "Climb in the wagon. We need to get home or Mama'll scold us for dilly dallying."

As they approached Johnson's woods, Audie Lee sat on a stump about ten feet from the fence. She left the wagon in the middle of the road and stepped closer to the fence, holding out her hand with the pieces of geode on her palm. Audie Lee stood and edged a little closer. "Come here, Audie

Lee. I want to show you something." Maggie pointed to her outstretched hand.

He picked up his tow sack and shuffled toward her, grinning broadly. He came closer and looked at the rocks with fascination. Maggie held one piece so the light bounced off the crystals.

"Hummmmm." Audie Lee's eyes lit up and he reached for it, but Maggie drew back her hand.

"Show us what you've got in your sack," she said pointing to the bag slung over his shoulder. At first he seemed puzzled. She pointed again. "Let us see what you've got." Finally he grunted, set his bag down, and began to rummage through whatever it held. He drew out a tobacco sack similar to the one he had shown Maggie before. He opened it and after emptying the contents, held out his hand so she could see.

"I see it!" Johnny Ray had come up behind her and peered around her shoulder, standing on tiptoe.

Maggie saw buttons with rhinestone centers, some gold colored buttons, a foreign coin of some kind, a little red plastic ring like comes in Cracker Jacks, and the necklace among some other things she could not identify. Maggie held one of the geode pieces in her outstretched hand and pointed to the necklace. "I'll swap this pretty rock for that piece."

Audie Lee shook his head. He picked up one of the rhinestone buttons and offered it to her. Maggie shook her head and showed Audie Lee she had two pieces of the geode. She offered both of them and pointed again to the necklace. Again, he shook his head and offered her two buttons.

"No, Audie Lee. We want that piece." She pointed at it again.

He got the angry look she had seen before, turned his back while he put his prizes back in the tobacco sack, and grunted as he threw the larger bag over his shoulder and began to walk away. When he had taken about a dozen steps, he turned and shook his fist and grunted loudly.

"He's probably calling us a bunch of bad names," Maggie said. "It may be good we can't understand him."

"I guess he ain't going to give it back, is he?"

"Daddy told us to let him keep it. We should have listened to Daddy. At least we tried." She handed the two geode pieces to Johnny Ray. "Since you didn't get the necklace, you can keep these."

"Thanks, Maggie, but I'd druther have the necklace."

"I know, Buddy, but we don't always get what we want, now, do we?"

* * *

Ray, asked by neighbors to work most every day all summer, had used his evenings and any days off he had to work Mrs. Robinson's farm, often coming home hours after dark. He had planted corn and hay there again on the halves. Having so much work elsewhere meant that Corie Mae and the children did most of the work on their own farm. In addition, they did much of the work on Grandpa's farm since he spent most days down at the highway where construction on the new church had started.

Kenny helped almost every day, and sometimes JD came to help, especially when they needed to use the horses. When Aunt Opal wasn't away nursing some sick person, she helped with the canning and gardening. Grandma spent many hours every day tending her own garden and preserving food. The older children worked as hard as adults every day. Maggie wondered how her mother could work so hard since her pregnancy was past the midpoint.

After a good growing season, they anticipated a good harvest. By midsummer, Ray had cut the hay at Mrs. Robinson's and raked it into windrows with his horse drawn rake. He hired Frank Schmidt to bring his tractor and bale the hay, which he sold to a farmer at Crab Orchard, who raised horses.

Maggie had come into the kitchen for a drink when she heard Johnny Ray, who sat in the porch swing, ask, "What you got in that big box, Daddy? Is it something for me?"

Ray stepped onto the porch. "No, it's for your mama. Where's she at?"

"Her and the girls is in the back yard breaking beans, I think." Johnny Ray jumped from the swing and ran down the steps. "I'll go tell her."

"Don't run! You'll get out of breath," Ray called over his shoulder and came into the house.

"Hi, Daddy," Maggie said. "Did I hear you say that was for Mama?"

Ray set the big box on the kitchen table. "Yeah, go tell Corie Mae to come in here."

All the kids gathered around as Corie Mae opened the box, very excited because Ray did not often bring in a surprise.

"What's that thing?" Johnny Ray wanted to know when Corie Mae lifted a big kettle with a heavy lid from the box.

"It's a pressure canner," Corie Mae exclaimed, "and just in time to can all these beans we've picked today. This is wonderful."

"I don't see what's so wonderful about it," Johnny Ray pouted. "I thought it was going to be something real good."

"It is good. Now when we can beans, we won't have to carry wood and keep the fire going outside for hours. We can just fill this canner with jars of beans, put it on the stove, and it'll be done in no time."

"It's a big one too. It'll hold seven half gallons or fourteen quarts." Maggie had started reading from the instruction booklet. "Daddy, this pressure canner will cut the time it takes to can beans in half."

Corie Mae turned and put her arms around Ray, one of the few times

Maggie had seen her parents embrace. Ray grinned and his eyes twinkled

* * *

Two weeks after Bible School, Johnny Ray came to the breakfast table when most of the family had finished eating. During the summer, Corie Mae let the younger kids sleep as late as they wanted. He raised his shirt. "Look, Mama, I got all these red spots on my tummy."

Corie Mae knelt beside him to get a good look. "Oh lordy, looks like you got the chickenpox."

Maggie nodded. "You know, Mama, Charlie Haskins got chickenpox during Bible School, and Johnny Ray sat by him on the church bus. I guess that's where he got them."

"This explains why you complained of feeling poorly the last couple days. Do you feel like eating some breakfast?"

Johnny Ray nodded and took his usual place on the bench at the back side of the table.

"Now I guess Jay and Junior'll get them too. I'm glad the rest of you kids done had chicken pox. Johnny Ray, after you eat, just stay in the house and play with your trucks or read some of your books. I don't want you playing outside or getting hot."

"Okay, Mama,"

By the next day, Johnny Ray had the red spots on his arms, legs, face, and even inside his mouth. Corie Mae reminded him often that he shouldn't scratch. Grandma told Corie Mae to make a mixture of sulfur and lard to put on the spots if they began to itch. When Johnny Ray protested "It smells like rotten eggs," Corie Mae told him if he promised not to scratch, he wouldn't have to use the mixture.

A couple of days later, Corie Mae and the older children came back to the house after picking sweet corn for canning. They found Johnny Ray digging in the yellow clay bank beside the road. He had taken a spoon from the kitchen to use as a digging tool and had created a series of intersecting tunnels. He pushed little pieces of stick through the tunnels as pretend cars.

Corie Mae scolded him soundly. "I told you not to go outside."

"But, Mama, it's in the shade here. You said not to get hot."

"You know better. Look here, you've got one of my good spoons out here in the dirt. I ought to give you a good whipping. Maggie, get the wash tub and heat some water. We'll have to get this dirt off him. Don't you know if you get dirt in your sores, you could get a bad infection? Land sakes, what'm I gonna do with you?"

"Don't whip me, Mama," Johnny Ray whined. "I promise I won't do it again."

"When we get you cleaned up, I reckon you can just stay in your bed for the rest of the day. And if you step one foot outside the house again, I'll tan your hide good."

* * *

Since Maggie had heard the talk about the war in Korea during Uncle Thomas's visit the week of July 4, she had tried to listen to the news on the radio as often as possible. She often transcribed the news in shorthand to keep her skills sharp. Now almost a month after Uncle Thomas' visit, she hears bad news. It seemed the North Koreans had pushed the Allied soldiers almost off the peninsula. The number of casualties grew larger every day.

"What's going to happen?" Maggie asked her father as they sat on the porch late one evening.

"Don't know, Honey. Guess we didn't have enough troops and equipment when we went in there. If they can hold their position till we get more troops over there, maybe they'll stand a chance."

"JD told me Walter Spinks and Larry Brown joined the Marines after they graduated last year. He thinks they'll be sent to Korea. JD said he wished he could go fight."

"It might seem like a brave thing to do, but war is evil. I don't understand why countries can't find a peaceful way to work out their problems. JD don't have no idea what it's really like. He's better off to finish school and hope he won't get drafted when he graduates."

They sat quietly in the twilight, listening to the frogs, katydids, and even a hooting owl. After a while, Maggie said, "Daddy, I really want to play basketball this year. I wish Mama would change her mind. I talked to Aunt Lillian, and she said I could spend the night with her when we have games. Stuart can do the milking and the chores in my place. Do you think there's any way we could persuade Mama?"

"I don't know, Sunshine. I'll think about it. Maybe we can work something out."

* * *

The next evening, Maggie, Betty Lou, Kenny, Stuart and Jeanie paid a visit to Grandma and Grandpa. "We brought you something," Jeannie announced as she stepped onto the porch.

"What's that?" Grandma spit in her can sitting on the floor beside the porch swing she shared with Grandpa, who smoked his pipe while they gently rocked back and forth.

"Mama made you this apple cobbler. She said you might want to whip up some cream and have a bite of dessert before you go to bed." Betty Lou explained as Jeannie handed the warm pie to Grandma.

"Thank you, Honey. Umm, it smells so good. Would you put it on the kitchen table for me?"

The children stood in a semi-circle around the swing. "What's that you got there? Grandpa pointed to the bundle under Stuart's arm.

Stuart put the bundle wrapped in an old quilt in Grandpa's lap. "Open it up. We want to see if you know what it is."

Grandpa put his pipe on the swing beside him and pulled the quilt back to reveal a stringed instrument.

"Where'd you get this?"

"I found it in our attic," Stuart said. "Daddy had me climb up there to cover a hole the squirrels had made. Found this bundle pushed way back against the roof. All covered with dust like it'd been there for a mighty long time."

"Mama said you'd probably know where it came from," Jeannie had returned to the porch after taking the pie to the kitchen.

Grandpa held the instrument by the neck. It had two broken strings, and the wood seemed a bit moldy. "Law, I never thought I'd ever see this again," Grandpa rubbed his hands over the wood.

"Where'd it come from?"

"It's my mammy's mandolin." Grandpa's voice seemed a little hoarse. "See, my pappy forbid her to play, so I guess she hid it where he'd never find it."

"Why'd he tell her not to play it?"

"Pappy said it's a instrument of the devil. People played mandolins, fiddles, and such for dancing, you know. I remember Mammy'd get this out and play for us when Pappy went off for several days to a camp meeting somewheres. I was just a little tyke then." Grandpa fingered the broken strings. "I hadn't thought about this in years. I guess I thought she'd destroyed it."

"Why'd she do that?"

"Ever time Pappy'd go off to one of them meetings, Johnny and Jimmy, they's my two older brothers, and they'd beg Mammy to get out her mandolin and play. And we'd all jump around like we's dancing. One time we didn't hear Pappy coming, and he walked in right while we's jumping and sanging. He had a awful mighty big temper. He grabbed his horse whip and started hitting Mammy."

Maggie gasped and grabbed Betty Lou's hand as Grandpa continued his story. "Johnny and Jimmy took the whip away from Pappy. Johnny ran out to the chopping block and cut it up in pieces with the ax. They was scared to come back in the house, so they hid out in the woods for days till they saw Pappy hitch up the buggy and start off. Then they come in and told Mammy they's going to leave. She helped pack up their clothes in bundles and fixed some food, and they left. That's the last I ever seen them. Mammy never played the mandolin again. I thought she'd probably burnt it up or something."

"How old was you then?" Jeannie asked.

"I's about six, I guess. Johnny and Jimmy was about fifteen or sixteen. Mammy knowed they needed to leave because Pappy had such a temper, he'd probably killed them. But after that, she never would sing no more."

"That's a really sad story, Grandpa," Maggie said. "Did Grandma ever hear what happened to the boys after they left?"

"They'd send letters addressed to the sheriff. He'd slip them to Mammy when Pappy wasn't nowhere around. They was out in Kansas for a while. The last she heard they was living in Indian Territory out in Oklahoma." Grandpa sat up straighter and rubbed his hands over his thighs. "After that she never knowed what happened to them."

It must have grieved Great-grandma to lose her boys like that. Maggie swallowed her tears. *I can't imagine what it would be like.* After several moments of awkward silence, Stuart asked, "What you going do with that mandolin, Grandpa?"

"Don't know. Ain't got no use for it myself. Don't believe in playing them either."

"Can I have it?" Stuart asked.

"Guess so, but you know them is the instruments of the devil. So just clean it up and hang it on the wall so it won't cause no harm." He carefully wrapped it in the old quilt and handed it to Stuart.

"Thanks, Grandpa. I'll take good care of it."

"Just remember what I told you." Grandpa picked up his pipe and struck a match to relight it.

Maggie stepped closer to the swing. "Grandpa, something else was wrapped up in that quilt." She held out a writing tablet with yellowed and tattered pages.

Grandpa stared at it for several seconds before he reached for the tablet. "What is this?" After carefully turning some pages and reading the entries, he said, "Mammy must of wrote this, but I never saw it before."

"Do you think it's Great grandma's diary?" Maggie hadn't had a chance to read more than a few pages, but she believed Great Grandma had written it.

"Sure looks like it." Grandpa turned to the last pages and read for a few minutes. "My, my, she's talking here about when Johnny and Jimmy left. That's the last thing she wrote. Musta been when she hid the mandolin and this book. Let's see..." He stared at the ceiling in thought. "That woulda been over fifty years ago." Grandpa closed the tablet and lay it tenderly on the swing beside him.

Maggie couldn't tame her desire to read what great grandma Campbell had written. "Grandpa, could I have the diary?"

Grandpa smiled, picked up the book, and hugged it to his chest. "No, Maggie, not now. Someday I will give it to you, but for now I need to keep it."

"Thank you, Grandpa." Maggie bent to lay a kiss on Grandpa's forehead. "Okay kids, it's time we got back home. Mama said not to stay long."

On the way home, Jeannie walked beside Maggie, who strolled with her head down thinking deeply about what secrets that diary might reveal.

"Our great-grandpa had a really bad temper, didn't he?" Jeannie asked when they had passed the old spring house. Maggie sighed. "Maybe that's where Mama and Uncle Thomas got their hot-headedness. "Do you reckon it will come down to any of us?" Jeannie stepped closer to Maggie and whispered. "I don't want to be like that."

"Me either." Maggie pointed to the evening star twinkling just above the top of the ridge. "Let's make a wish on that star to be calm like Daddy." They stood quietly in the middle of the dirt road, soaking up the evening—hearing the songs and croaks of the birds, frogs, and insects and letting the coolness of the evening breeze fill their souls with peace.

* * *

"They's somebody here to see you, Maggie," Junior ran around the corner of the house to the backyard where Corie Mae and the girls sat in a circle peeling apples in the shade of a large maple tree.

"Who is It?" Maggie wiped her hands on the flour sack she had over her lap and stood up.

"It's just me." Maggie turned and saw Bud standing at the corner of the house.

"Well, hello. I see you're back home." Maggie walked toward him.

"Yeah, football practice starts next week, so I came home for that. I thought maybe we could sit on your porch and catch up on how the summer's been, if that's okay with you, Mrs. Martin."

Corie Mae didn't look up from the apple she was working on, but she nodded and said, "Reckon, that's okay."

Bud walked closer to the apple-peeling operation and watched for a few seconds. "Maybe I have a better idea." He pulled his pocket knife from his pocket and handed it to Maggie. "If you'll wash this knife for me, I'll just sit here and help peel apples."

Maggie gave a quick look at her mother who just raised her eye brow and didn't say anything. "I'll run into the kitchen and wash your knife and bring out another chair. Be right back."

Bud took the chair where Maggie had been sitting. "What are you planning to do with all these apples?"

"Today we're fixing apples for drying." Jeannie gave Bud a big grin.

"Oh, by the way," Corie Mae asked, "you had the chickenpox?"

"Yes ma'am. In second grade. Why?"

"Johnny Ray's just had a terrible time with them and now Junior and Jay's got them.

"Is Johnny Ray going to be all right?"

"The doctor says he got some kind of brain fever."

"It's called encephalitis." Maggie came back carrying a chair and a baking sheet.

"I keep forgetting that big word. Anyway, he was real bad sick for a week. We thought we's going to have to put him in the hospital, but finally he started getting better. Seems like he don't want to do nothing but sit in the shade. I hope he gets stronger by the time school starts."

"Here, you can put your apple peels in this pan." Maggie handed the pan and knife to Bud and placed her chair beside him.

"Okay, tell me how to do this."

Maggie explained how to peel, core, and slice the apples for drying. Bud took an apple from the tub of water in the center of the circle. He began to peel the skin in narrow strips. "Now, what do you use dried apples for?"

"What I like best," Betty Lou smiled at Bud, "is to make a stack cake with them."

"What's a stack cake?"

"Mama makes these cake layers that are real thin like big cookies. She cooks the apples into a sauce and flavors it with sugar and spices. Then she stacks them up with a layer of cake and a layer of apples. You let it set for two or three days so the cake soaks up all the moisture. Then you whip up a big bowl of whipped cream and have yourself a real treat."

"Sounds really good. I'll have to try it sometime."

"Mama always makes us a stack cake for Christmas. Maybe you can eat Christmas dinner with us." Jeannie looked to see if her mother agreed. Corie Mae, concentrating on the apple she was peeling had just a hint of a smile.

"Oh, damn, here's a worm!"

"Watch your language, girl"

Jeannie hung her head and her face reddened. "I'm sorry, Mama, but I hate to find a worm."

"Mrs. Martin, did you say both boys have chicken pox? Are they okay?"

"Don't seem to have as many spots as Johnny Ray did, and so far, they haven't been very sick. Most of their spots have started drying up now, so they should be fine in another day or two."

"When we finish here, is it okay if I go in and read them a story?"

"They'd love that. Even little Jay likes to look at books. Then maybe you can stay and eat supper with us."

Maggie looked at Bud with an amused smile. His charm seemed to be working with her mother.

After supper, on the way over to Kenny's house to shoot baskets, Maggie smiled at Bud when he reached for her hand. "I think you're making a hit with my mother."

"I'm really trying to make a hit with you." He squeezed her hand.

"It's working." Maggie squeezed his hand back.

Later, when they got back to the house, Bud asked Corie Mae's permission for Maggie to walk with him to the highway. As they walked along, they talked about school starting soon. Bud told Maggie he'd heard there was a new math teacher and a new history teacher.

Bud stopped and looked at Maggie. "Do you go to church on Sunday nights?"

"Sometimes, especially if the weather's good."

"Can I go to church with you tomorrow night? Do you think your mother would agree?"

"Sure. I think she wouldn't object. If she does, I guess we can just sit on the porch or something." Maggie couldn't help grinning. *Wait until I have a chance to tell Mary Ann.*

When they reached the highway, Bud put his arm around her and gave her a hug. "I'll see you tomorrow then." Maggie had never felt so happy. As she walked back to the house, she felt she floated on air.

* * *

"Did Great-grandpa scare you?" Maggie looked cautiously at her grandmother. They sat on Grandma's back porch breaking beans. Corie Mae had offered to let her mother use the new canner so she didn't have to string up the beans to dry for leather breeches, and Maggie had agreed to help prepare the beans for canning.

"Well, Honey, I tried to stay out of his way. He never threatened me, but I saw lots of times when he'd go to pieces and beat the horses or kick a dog when he got mad about something. I never saw nobody with such a bad temper. And he'd always quote some scripture verse to justify it."

"Why did Great-grandma agree to marry him in the first place?"

"Well, you see, they grew up as neighbors. They's knowed each other all their lives. Granny told me when he came back from the Civil War, he asked her to marry him. She told him she would marry him when he had some property and a house for her."

"I still don't understand why she would want a man with such a temper."

"Oh, he could charm a rattlesnake–so good looking with his distinguished beard and curly hair. He provided well for his family, worked as hard as anyone I ever knew. He was funny, told funny stories, and clowned around with the kids. I reckon Granny must have loved him or she wouldn't have stayed here with him."

"Why did he ever decide to live here in this lonesome holler?"

"This is what Granny told me." Grandma spit into her can and wiped her mouth with a handkerchief. "Harvey fought with the South in the Civil War, but his older brothers all joined the Union army. After the war, they was so much hard feelings between them that Harvey decided to move as far away as possible."

"But why would he choose to live here?"

"I'm not sure how he learned that this land was available. But if he planned to get away a way from Union sympathizers, he made a mistake cause most of the people around here had sided with the Union too."

Maggie worked quietly for a few minutes. "So...Great-grandma left all her family to live in this God forsaken holler with very few neighbors around and a mean husband. I don't see how she could stand to live here with him."

"She was a strong woman in her own way, and she mostly tried not to provoke him. I guess he knew if he pushed her too far, she'd do something drastic, like when she took Helen to Kentucky to live with her mother."

"I always wondered how Aunt Helen came to live in Kentucky when she was born and raised here."

"Of course, this was before I ever knew Doug, and he don't much like to talk about it." Grandma usually called her husband "Papa," so Maggie had to think just a minute to realize who Grandma meant by "Doug." "He was still pretty young hisself when it happened, so he probably didn't know the whole story. But what I know is that all of a sudden one day when Helen was about fourteen or fifteen, Granny packed up the buggy, and they left while Harvey was out in the field. She told Doug to tell his daddy she'd be back in a few weeks."

"So where'd they go?"

"They went to Harlan where Granny growed up. Gone about six weeks, but when she come back she didn't have Helen with her. Helen never saw her daddy again. She lived with her grandparents in Harlan till she got married. She never even come to his funeral."

"Why? What happened?"

"I don't know it all. I guess Helen was a little wild. She would slip out at night, take one of the mules and ride out to a party somewheres. One night Harvey caught her when she was putting the mule back in the barn. I think he probably whipped her. But they was more to it than that. I tried to ask Granny about it one time, but she just said it warn't safe for Helen to be here no more."

"Do you think Great-grandpa, you know, messed with her?" Maggie frowned and looked at her grandmother with one eyebrow raised.

"I suspected it, but no one ever told me for sure. Granny wouldn't talk about it. It broke her heart to be separated from Helen. That's why she went up there and spent the whole summer after Harvey died. I guess he knew Granny might take Doug off somewhere, too, if he mistreated him. So after Helen left, he calmed down a little bit."

"Was Great-grandpa ever mean to your kids?"

Grandma smiled. "He threatened to whip Thomas once, but I told him if he ever laid a hand on one of my kids, I'd kill him. If one of my kids needed a thrashing, he could just tell me, and I'd do it. He knowed I meant it, too. He'd saw me shoot many a rabbit. He knowed I never missed my target."

Maggie swallowed. She'd never heard her grandmother talk this way. They worked quietly for several minutes. Maggie went into the house to get a drink. When she came back, Grandma continued the story. "Sometimes he was as sweet as could be. He'd take the boys fishing, and he taught both of them to hunt, but I always made sure he was never alone with Corie Mae. She loved to sit on his lap while he told her Bible stories, and he whittled little wooden animals for her to play with."

"But if he was such a religious man, what made him get so mean sometimes?"

"You know, he got wounded in the Civil War, and he always walked with a cane. I don't know if his nerves was shot because of the war or if they was something wrong with his mind. It just seemed like sometimes the littlest thing would set him off, and he was like a raging bull. He was really bad if he'd been drinking."

"I didn't know he ever took a drink."

"Actually he even made the stuff. You know that flat place up on the ridge where you kids used to camp out? That's where he had his still. He'd raise corn and make his whiskey. It was easier to sell the whiskey than to sell the corn. I was glad he destroyed his still before Doug and me got married. Granny told me once that Doug really liked to slip up there and help hisself to some of the drippings when his daddy was doing something else."

"So did Grandpa ever drink after you married him?"

"Sometimes. And when he did, he's almost as bad as his daddy. You know your grandpa's got some a that same meanness in him too. I learnt right away not to argue with him. I just listened to him carry on, and then I did whatever I wanted to when he wasn't around."

"I don't think I ever saw Grandpa when he'd been drinking."

"He don't do it much anymore. He knows it makes him mean."

"I'm glad my daddy isn't mean."

"You've got the best daddy I ever saw. When he first come here and wanted to marry Corie Mae, I was against it. She was so young, and I didn't know him from Adam. Granny said he was a very nice boy from a good family. I guess she got to know him that summer in Kentucky. I was so scared that things wouldn't work out for Corie Mae, but he was just wonderful. He moved right in the house with Granny and took care of her like she was his own mother. I've never heard him raise his voice or say a single cuss word. I thank God ever day that He sent Ray to our family. I think it's helped Doug to settle down to have Ray around, too."

"Well, Grandma, looks like we have all these beans broken. While you wash them, I'll go to the well and draw some water so we can wash the canning jars."

"Honey, It's good of you to help me this way."

"I've really enjoyed it, Grandma, especially getting to talk to you and all."

"I guess you better not tell your mama all that I told you. I'm not sure she'd want you to know."

"Okay, Grandma, but thanks for telling me, anyway." As Maggie walked to the well, she thought of all Grandma had told her. *I'll be glad when Grandpa gives me the diary so I can learn more about my family's past.* In many ways Corie Mae reminded Maggie of her great-grandfather—the way she liked to think she obeyed the Bible, the stubborn way she refused to accept someone else's opinion, the way she lost her temper and lashed out at whoever crossed her.

A couple of days later, Maggie dried dishes while Corie Mae washed. "Mama, Grandma told me she used to hunt rabbits. Did you ever see her shoot a gun?"

"I remember lots of times when we 'd run out of meat, and Mommy'd take her gun and go get us a squirrel or two to make a stew. They's one time I won't never forget. I was about six or seven, and I had this cat named Whitey. I loved that cat more'n anything. One day Mommy had just finished a new quilt and put it on her bed. She went in there and Whitey had messed all over her brand new quilt. She got so mad. She grabbed that cat by the scruff of the neck and took her shotgun. She threw the cat out in the backyard and blowed it to pieces. I never seen her so mad before or since. Scared me plum out of my mind. I ran and hid under my bed and didn't come out for hours."

"It doesn't pay to mess with Grandma, huh?"

"I think all us kids was scared to cross her. She never had to take a switch to us or nothing. I never thought about it back then, but I guess she scared Papa too. He would lose his temper and beat up on Thomas and WC. He'd say, 'He that spareth his rod hateth his son,' and beat the boys black and blue. But he never so much as threatened Mommy that I knowed about."

"Did you ever go hunting?"

"I didn't really want to kill anything, but I did shoot a rat one time."

"When was that?"

"I was probably twelve or thirteen, before I come to live with Granny. Something was killing my baby chicks. Finally one evening just about dark, I saw a big rat coming out the hen house. Next evening, I got Papa's shotgun and sat out on the back porch till I saw that rat come sneaking up to the hen house. I'd never shot a gun before, and I didn't know how to hold the gun against my shoulder. I aimed at that rat and pulled the trigger. That shotgun banged against my shoulder so hard it knocked me backwards. Made me black from my waist up to my ear, but I got that old rat!"

Maggie smiled. She seldom heard her mother brag. *My mamma's really got the guts.* She surprised herself with feelings of admiration. "Mama, do you think Johnny Ray'll be able to go to school when it starts next week?"

"Don't know. He really worries me. Just don't have no spunk for nothing. I'm afraid that high fever might did some damage to his brain or something. I guess if he says he feels like going, I'll let him go and see how he does. I'll be depending on you girls to look out for him and for Junior, too. It'll be strange when you all go off to school, and I'll only have Jay here. The house will seem so empty."

"Well, it won't be for long. That little one growing in your tummy will be here before too long."

"I'm thinking this one will be a girl. If it is, I want to name her Helen."

Later Maggie reflected on the summer and how well she and her mother had gotten along. Of course, she hadn't really asked to do anything her mother might object to. But it suddenly occurred to Maggie that her mother missed having Lillian and Opal around. *I reckon she's lonely. That's why she's talked more to me this summer.* Then Maggie thought about Great-grandma, who had come to the holler when she was only twenty, and the nearest house was nearly a mile away. She had left her family in Kentucky and come here to be alone with a husband who was not very companionable to say the least. *I guess I don't know how good I have it.*

CHAPTER 8

Campbell Holler–August 8,1888   New one-room school at the crossroads.   Harvey will let Johnny and Jimmy go until they are 12.   Then they must stay home to work. Never thought he'd agree.

(Diary of Mary Louise Campbell)

Sophomore Year 1950-1951

"JD picking you up?" Maggie and Wanda had finished cleaning up after a big dinner at the café.

"Didn't ask him to." Wanda threw the dirty towels into the laundry basket. "I don't know what's wrong with him, but lately he's about as much fun as a toothache. Not interested in nothing but running around with that bunch of roughnecks that hangs around the filling station. I'm about ready for a new boyfriend."

"Gosh, Wanda, you've been a couple the whole time you've been in high school."

"I know. But JD's not going to stay around when he finishes school. It's probably going to happen anyway, so why not get it over with?"

Maggie sighed. "I wish he'd get some sense. He keeps talking about joining the army."

"I told him if he ever came to pick me up with liquor on his breath again, that'd be the end."

"I heard his mother tell Mama that he came home drunk last week. Aunt Opal said she wished he'd stayed in Detroit last year."

"I hate to see him throw his future away. He's smart, he used to be

135

fun, he could make something of his life. I don't want to have a loser for a boyfriend." Wanda took off her apron and got her jacket from the closet beside the back door. "See you at school Monday."

Maggie locked the door and watched through the glass as Wanda disappeared into the darkness beyond the back fence. She sighed again and turned to Aunt Lillian. "What do we need to do to finish up here?"

"If you'll fix the coffee maker so we just have to turn it on in the morning, that'd be good."

Later Maggie stretched out on Aunt Lillian's couch and tried to sleep but couldn't stop thinking about JD. He seemed headed for trouble, but worrying about it only made her wider awake.

* * *

J"I love this time of year!" Maggie picked up a bright red sweet gum leaf and twirled it with her fingers. "The mountains look like some giant artist has gone crazy with his paint brush."

After Sunday dinner Maggie had suggested that she and JD walk up to the ledge. Their feet rustled the colorful leaves carpeting the ground. On the way up the ridge, they twisted back and forth past huge clumps of mountain ivy and among poplar, pine, locust and sourwood trees, all arrayed in glorious fall colors. As they passed a large hickory, adorned in bright orange and yellow, a squirrel quarreled at them from its perch high on a limb where he hulled the nuts before carrying them to his winter cache.

"I'm surprised that squirrel has found any hickory nuts. Stuart and Kenny have gathered about a bushel. Grandma told them if they would gather the nuts she would pick out the meats to sell and they could have half the money." Maggie dropped her leaf and pulled her skirt close to her legs to avoid a cocklebur bush.

"I should of brought my gun," JD said. "We'd have squirrel dumplings for supper."

"I'll be glad when we kill hogs again. We haven't had any good meat lately. Daddy and Stuart have hunted rabbits and squirrels quite a bit even though the season isn't open yet."

They climbed the last steep incline and stood looking out over the hollow. The ledge, one solid rock thrusting out of the ridge, made a flat area as large as Maggie's front room. Maggie took a deep breath and stretched her arms in a wide gesture. "I love it. Just look at all that color! See those bright red sumac bushes over behind Grandpa's barn. Like flames of fire. And the goldenrod growing along the fence row. I think I'll pick some of that to take home for a bouquet when we go back. And some of that purple iron weed to mix in."

"I don't know if I'd do that. Some people are allergic to goldenrod. With all the trouble Johnny Ray's having, it might not be good for him."

"You're right," Maggie sighed. "I worry about him so much. He's not gone to school for a couple of weeks, and when he does go, Miss Ward says he puts his head down on his desk and doesn't do anything."

They stood without speaking for a few moments as they studied the view. JD pointed to the right. "We should go back the other way and see if we can find any hazel nuts in that grove over by your back pasture."

Maggie nodded and sat down on a large boulder near the back of the ledge. "Grandma told me awhile back that Great-grandpa used to have a still up here. Did you know that?"

"No kidding?" JD sat nearer the front of the ledge and threw rocks at trees down below. Then he turned to look at Maggie. "Wish it was here now. I'd make a bundle selling moonshine. I know lots of people who'd buy it."

"I don't know where he actually had the still. I don't think he'd have kept it out here in plain sight, would he? It must have been back behind that clump of mountain ivy over there." Maggie pointed to the left.

She followed as JD stood and walked toward the tangle of bushes covered with green shiny leaves. They had to crawl on their knees to penetrate the tight thicket, but once inside they found an open space, covered with dried leaves and completely surrounded by the thick growth.

"Wow! Wonder why we never discovered this before?" Maggie looked around the enclosure. "This would be the perfect place to hide a still. He probably used the ledge as a lookout."

"I doubt that, Maggie. He could have hid the jugs of moonshine here, but it takes a fire to make whisky. He wouldn't want a fire in a place so small where the bushes and leaves might catch fire."

"Oh, shows you what I know about how to make moonshine." Maggie noticed some dried leaves mashed down on one side of the small room-like space. "I think something has made a bed here. Look. Here's a gap on this side that's easier to get through." She pulled the limbs back and walked through. A path led from the gap to another clump of bushes.

"I guess he had several places to stash his corn squeezings up here. Reckon we might find a jug of Great-grandpa's white lightening?" Inside the next enclosure, they found a half-gallon jar with some clear liquid in it. JD quickly opened it and took a sniff. "Nope, it ain't moonshine." He carefully tipped the jar to his mouth and took a small taste. "It's just water. Looks like someone's been staying here."

"Maybe it's that bear the sheriff claims someone saw last week. But I don't think a bear'd have a jar of water." Maggie laughed. "I bet it's Audie Lee. He roams around all the time." She ducked out of the enclosure. "Let's follow the path and see where it goes." The path wound around the ridge and led them back to the ledge from the opposite side. They stood once more gazing out over the holler where they had lived all their lives.

"Remember that time we brought the kids up here to camp out?"

JD laughed. "Soon as it got dark, Jeannie started making excuses to go home."

"Yeah, and then Kenny said, 'I smell a skunk,' and everyone began packing up their blankets."

"Me and Kenny have spent the night here lots of times, even this summer. Sometimes it's the only way to get Mama to shut up. We just have to get out of her sight. Seems like she's getting worse about getting on our backs."

"Do you think," Maggie chose her words carefully, "she's just more worried about you?"

JD picked up a couple of small stones and threw them at a dead pine tree. "I guess I do give her a hard time, but she picks at me constantly. She just won't give me no peace. Sometimes I think I can't stand it a minute longer." He threw another rock.

Maggie sat down again. She wanted JD to talk to her, but she knew if she said too much he would clam up. She watched as he kept flinging rocks at the tree, missing every time. Finally she asked, "Do you ever wish you had stayed in Detroit?"

"No." He answered quickly. "Daddy and me would be worse than Mama and me. If I'd stayed up there, him and me would of had it out ever' night. Ain't no way I could of stayed there any longer than I did."

"You know, from what Grandma tells me, our great-grandpa had a terrible temper. I guess he was a madman when something set him off. Sometimes I wonder if that bad temper got passed to later generations. Your daddy and my mama seem to have gotten quite a bit of it." Maggie stood and picked up a small stone. She walked to the front of the ledge. "Do you think Uncle Thomas will ever divorce Aunt Opal and marry Stella?" She hit the tree.

JD looked at her with wide eyes. "How'd you do that?"

"You just have to focus your aim. Think that your hand is following right along with the rock toward the spot you want to hit. That's the way I do it." She sent another one crashing into the tree.

JD picked up a pebble, held it in front of him as he sighted down his arm like a gun and then drew back and threw, missing the dead tree by only a few inches.

"See, that's better. Keep practicing, and you'll get the hang of it." Maggie hit the tree one more time.

"Show off!" JD sat down again, propped his elbows on his knees, and put his head in his hands. "To answer your question. No. Daddy won't divorce Mama. He won't never come home to live with her though because they can't get along. But he won't marry Stella neither. It's her house, and when she gets put out with him, she sends him packing. She did that twice while I lived there. I don't think she'd ever agree to marry him even if he wanted her to."

JD sat up and wiped his arm across his forehead. "I don't know what's wrong with me, Mag. I'm so restless. I hate school. I hate the way Mama treats me. I hate Daddy for treating Mama so bad. I hate myself for the way I've treated Wanda lately." He kicked some rocks off the side of the ledge. "Sometimes I can't stand myself. I think I've got to get away from here." He stood up, picked up a rock, took aim, and hit the pine tree.

Maggie grinned at him. "I told you you'd get better if you focus on your aim."

* * *

The last week in October the weather suddenly turned unusually cold. Johnny Ray had gone to school the last three days. As the children walked home from the school bus, a cold rain began to pelt them mercilessly. Maggie and Jeannie tried to protect Johnny Ray with their jackets. They stopped under the big beech tree hoping the rain would let up, but by that time, the rain had soaked them good. When they reached home and lifted Johnny Ray out of the wagon, his blue lips trembled with cold.

"You should of asked June Wilson if you could stay on her porch till the rain stopped," Corie Mae scolded as she began to strip off his wet clothes. "Now, he'll probably get sick again. Put some water on to get warm. We need a hot bath to warm him up."

After helping the boys change clothes, Maggie got into dry clothes herself and hung all the wet clothes on the back porch. By the time she started to do the chores, everyone was dry and warm. But as she sat beside Old Red squeezing down the milk, she began to cry. *How could I have been so stupid? I should have thought of stopping at Mrs. Wilson's.* She wiped her tears with the back of her hand. "Please, God, don't let Johnny Ray get sick again." she prayed aloud. *I got so preoccupied day dreaming about how to tell Mama and Daddy I'm going to play basketball, I didn't pay attention until too late.*

When they got home from school the next day, Johnny Ray sat in Mama's rocking chair covered with a blanket. He smiled and said he was okay, but Maggie thought he seemed to have even less energy than usual. He ate only a little cornbread and milk for supper and went to bed right away. When Maggie came up to bed hours later after doing dishes and homework, she put her hand on his forehead, but he didn't feel feverish. "Oh God, please let him be okay," she prayed silently as she slipped into her nightgown and climbed into her own bed. Remembering the scorn and accusation in her mother's voice, she began to sob into her pillow.

Betty Lou put her hand on her shoulder. "What's the matter?"

Maggie turned over to face Betty Lou. "I'm so scared Johnny Ray's getting worse again, she whispered into the dark. "It's all because I let him get wet yesterday. It was so stupid."

"He seems a little more tired than usual, but he'll probably be okay. Don't feel bad. I would have done the same thing. We've always walked home in the rain."

"But you should have seen how Mama looked at me. She blames me, and I feel so rotten."

Betty Lou patted her shoulder. "Quit worrying and go to sleep. Everything's going to be all right."

"I wish I could believe that. It seems like everything's going crazy. JD's breaking up with Wanda and talking about leaving. Johnny Ray's getting weaker. Daddy's out of work again, and Mama's going to have that baby any day now."

"Shhhh. Go to sleep. Things will look better tomorrow. You'll see." Betty Lou patted her on the shoulder again and turned over.

Maggie stared into the darkness and listened for Johnny Ray's breathing. *Oh, please, God.*

* * *

Maggie woke when she heard her father's footsteps on the stairs. He spoke softly telling Maggie to fix breakfast and get the kids ready for school. "Your Mama's water broke a little while ago. I guess the baby'll be born today. I'm going to send Stuart to get Grandma, and I'll do the milking. You and Betty Lou better stay home today to help out."

Maggie had helped her daddy when the calves were born and had seen the sows deliver their piglets. But she had never seen a human birth. She felt a little scared as she crept into her mother's bedroom and asked if she could do anything for her.

"Put a couple of old towels in the rocker for me. I want to sit up for a while. And put more coal in the stove so it'll be warm."

Shortly after Jeannie, Stuart, and Junior left for school, Grandma Campbell came panting into the house carrying an armload of feed sack sheets and immediately took charge. "Ray, help Betty Lou take Johnny Ray and Jay to my house. She can watch them there. I built a fire in the stove so the house'll be warm for them. Maggie, we need lots of hot water. Corie Mae, are you having any pains yet?" Grandma explained since neither Aunt Opal nor Aunt Lillian could help, Maggie would assist her.

Maggie hurried to do Grandma's bidding. Soon her mother decided to get up and walk around. When a contraction came, Corie Mae closed her eyes and clinched her fists against her sides.

"Don't hold your breath. Keep breathing," Grandma ordered and massaged Corie Mae's back and shoulders. Maggie watched, kept the fire going under the kettles of water, and, otherwise, felt generally helpless. Obviously the pain was severe, but Maggie never heard a complaint or a whimper. Grandma helped Maggie pull a table close to the stove in the kitchen and gathered blankets, towels and the baby's clothes. "Now when the baby comes, you'll bring it in here and clean it up," Grandma explained.

Eventually, Corie Mae wanted to lie down. Grandma prepared the bed and, once she had Corie Mae situated, sent Maggie and Ray out of the room while she made a visual examination. "I ain't going to touch you with my hands down there cause we don't take no chances on infection, and I put the ax under the bed to cut the pain." Shortly, Maggie heard Grandma say, "It's looking good. Won't be much longer."

Grandma had Ray and Maggie stand on either side of the bed and hold Corie Mae's hands. When a contraction came and Grandma said "Now push," Corie Mae pulled so hard Maggie could hardly keep herself from being dragged into the bed. Finally, Grandma announced, "I can see the top of its head. One more push should do it."

Grandma caught the baby in a small blanket. "It's a girl."

"Thank the Lord," Corie Mae cried and grabbed Ray's hand in both of hers. "I'm so glad it's a girl. We're going to name her Mary Helen, Mary for my Grandmother Mary Louise and Helen for my favorite aunt." Ray leaned down and kissed Corie Mae's sweat covered forehead.

Grandma wiped the baby's face with a cloth dipped in sterilized water, and the baby began to cry. "Maggie, I need your help, here." Grandma laid the baby on Corie Mae's tummy. She picked up a folded newspaper that was burned at the edges. When she opened it up, Maggie saw a pair of scissors and two pieces of string. "I baked these in the oven so they'd be clean. She tied the sterilized string on the cord and used the string to hold the cord up. "Take that other piece of string and tie it close to the baby's belly. But don't touch the cord with your hands." Then Grandma took the scissors and cut the cord about an inch from the baby's abdomen. "Now, take her to the kitchen and clean her up."

"Wait, let me hold her." Corie Mae reached for the baby who stopped crying and nestled close. "Oh, she's so beautiful. Thank you, Lord."

Carefully following Grandma's instructions, Maggie bathed the baby. She talked to her in soothing tones and made sure to keep her covered lest she get a chill. Having cared for so many of her younger siblings, she bathed and dressed her little sister with confidence and efficiency. She put a few drops of alcohol on the bloody cord and tied the belly band tight around the baby to keep the navel from rupturing. She diapered and dressed her in an undershirt and gown.

Ray came into the kitchen to watch. He put his finger into the baby's palm and grinned when she grasped it. "Looks like she's going to have red hair like Elsie Mae." Maggie wrapped her in a blanket and put her in her father's arms. Her eyes filled with tears when she saw how lovingly her father looked at the baby.

Grandma had taken care of the afterbirth, removed the soiled sheets from the bed, and had Corie Mae resting comfortably. Ray carried the baby to her mother who reached for her eagerly. Ray put his arms around Grandma's shoulders. "Thank you, Mama Campbell. Looks like you done a perfect job."

"I helped born ever' one of my grandkids into this world. Ever' one of them was born healthy, thank the Lord."

Maggie stood beside the bed. "Mama, can I get you something? You haven't eaten all day."

"I want a drink of cold water. After I sleep for a while, I want some turnip greens and corn bread."

* * *

Johnny Ray had not gone to school since the day he got wet. Corie Mae insisted that he didn't have to go. He spent much of his time lying on the floor wrapped in a blanket with some toys scattered about him. He never complained of pain, had no fever, and showed no symptoms of a cold or sore throat. But Maggie watched him anxiously. He certainly was not the sassy little boy she remembered helping her pick blackberries.

He only perked up when Bud came and played with him. Bud came almost every Sunday afternoon and went to church with Maggie in the evening. They would ride the church bus home and then he'd hitchhike back to town.

Bud suggested that Maggie should tell her parents she planned to join the basketball team the next Sunday when he was there so he could help persuade them. Maggie had told Coach Moore she would play and had practiced with the team for a month.

Much to their surprise by late Sunday afternoon, all the kids had found something to do so that only Bud and Maggie sat in the front room with Corie Mae and Ray. Bud admired the baby who slept in a cradle near the stove. Corie Mae looked up and smiled.

"Did you get a ride partway today?" Ray asked.

"Yes, sir. Actually, I got a ride all the way from town. I just had to walk from the highway. Good thing too, because it's really cold out there." Bud rubbed his hands together to warm them.

"Are you playing basketball this year?" Ray stood to put more coal in the stove.

Bud and Maggie exchanged surprised glances. "Yes, sir. I'm a starting guard. I think we're going to have a pretty good team this year. We've got two new boys who are really good, and only three graduated last year, so we've got most of our old team back."

Ray took out his handkerchief and blew his nose. "I reckon I just might come to see you play some this year."

"That'd be really great, Mr. Martin."

Ray moved back to his chair. "I was thinking Maggie'd probably like to see you play. Maybe her and me can come to watch you."

Maggie took a deep breath. "You can watch me play too, Daddy. I've decided to play this year."

Maggie saw her mother's head jerk up, and she flinched as the anger in those dark eyes bored into her. She held her breath, and no one said a word for a long minute.

"So when did you decide this? Was you going to at least talk to us about it first?" Ray's voice was soft and Maggie saw a twitch at the corner of his mouth.

"That's what I'm trying to do now, Daddy. I wanted you and Mama to know before our first game."

Corie Mae stood and marched into the kitchen. They could hear her slamming the cabinet door and banging a skillet on the stove.

"Daddy, this is very important to me. I don't want to go against Mama, but I really want to play."

Ray leaned forward with his forearms on his knees and stared at his hands, saying nothing. Bud went into the kitchen. They could her him speaking quietly but couldn't distinguish his words. After a few minutes, he led Corie Mae back to her chair and patted her on the shoulder. "Thank you, Mrs. Martin, for agreeing to listen to me." He pulled his chair closer so that the four of them huddled together. He reached over and squeezed Maggie's hand. "I wondered, Mrs. Martin," he continued in a soft voice, "if you could tell me why you object to Maggie playing on the team."

Corie Mae looked startled. "It...it's just that, you know, it's out in public and everything and the girls wear shorts and...and it...it just ain't right." Her hands fluttered like a bird with a broken wing.

Bud nodded. "What do you think will happen if she plays?"

"I... uh... uh...I don't know. It just ain't right."

"Mrs. Martin, I'll make certain that she's always safe. After the games, if JD can't bring her home, I'll walk her up to her Aunt Lillian's where she can spend the night. You won't have to worry for a minute." Corie Mae stared at the floor but didn't say anything. "Maggie has agonized about this for over a year. She probably could have played without you ever knowing about it, but she was not willing to deceive you that way."

"That's right, Mama. I don't want to do something you think is wrong. But I don't see anything wrong about it."

Bud looked at Ray. "I'm glad you're going to come to some of the games, Mr. Martin. I think you'll be really surprised at how good Maggie is. I know once you see her, you'll be mighty proud." Ray just nodded.

Corie Mae stood. "I've got to get supper started."

Maggie listened for the banging cabinet door, but could hear only normal sounds coming from the kitchen.

Ray stood and patted Maggie on the shoulder. "I'll go do your chores so you and Bud can visit a little."

"Thank you, Daddy." Maggie watched him get his coat and hat and go to the kitchen for the milk buckets.

Bud smiled and squeezed her hand again. "Wow, I never expected it to be that easy. I couldn't believe it when your father brought up the subject. Almost like he knew."

"I don't think I've heard the last of it. Mama'll wait till you leave before she lets loose on me."

"She didn't say you couldn't be on the team."

"Not yet. But the night's not over."

Stuart came through the kitchen into the front room, wearing his heavy coat and cap. He put the shotgun back in the rack above the old fireplace. "Hi Bud." He held out his hands toward the stove. "It's getting real cold out there. Looks like it might even snow."

"You been hunting?" Bud stood to look out the front window.

"Me and Kenny got four squirrels. Kenny's mom didn't want to cook them, so I brought them home with me. Got to go dress them now. Want to help?"

"Sure. I never dressed a squirrel, but I guess I can always learn how." Bud reached for his coat and cap.

Maggie went upstairs to her room to finish her homework. She sat on her bed where the dim light of the cloudy evening came over her shoulder through the small window. As she filled the pages of the stenographer's pad with shorthand characters, she reviewed the way her parents had taken her news. Neither of them had said much. But somehow Maggie felt like a dam about to break. When she heard her father coming in the kitchen with the milk buckets, she closed her books and went to take care of the milk.

Bud and Stuart came inside with the four skinned squirrel carcasses in a dishpan. Corie Mae pointed to the table beside the water bucket. "Just put them there for now. I'll cut them up and put them in salt water to soak after we eat supper. They'll be good with biscuits and gravy for breakfast."

Bud held his hands over the cook stove. "Burr. It's really getting cold. Maggie, I think I better go home now and not go to church tonight. If it storms, it'll be hard to catch a ride." He reached for Maggie's hand and pulled her into the front room. "I'll see you at school tomorrow. Don't worry. Things will be all right."

Maggie closed the door after him and leaned against it, hoping he was right. She went back into the kitchen to take her usual place at the table between Johnny Ray and Jeanie.

Corie Mae put her hand out like a policeman stopping traffic. "Wait a minute. Did you think you could just announce that you're going to disobey me and that would be it?"

Maggie stood still and stared at her mother, her heart fluttering. She swallowed, but didn't say anything. Her mother's angry eyes locked with hers, but she refused to look down.

Corie Mae raised her chin and crossed her arms across her chest. "Let me tell you, young lady. If you think you can disobey me, you're wrong. No child of mine can sit at this table unless you're willing to do as you're told. So until you decide to obey me, you cannot eat at this table with the rest of your family." Corie Mae raised her head even higher, looked down her nose, and pressed her lips firmly together.

Maggie stared at her mother helplessly. She looked at her father who sat at his place with bowed head and realized he would not interfere. The children's faces twisted in confusion and shock.

Corie Mae motioned toward the door. "Go in the front room till we've finished. Then you can come and eat by yourself."

Maggie slowly turned toward the door.

"No, you can't do this!" Betty Lou stood up. "If you won't let Maggie come to the table, I won't sit at the table either."

"Sit down! You'll do what I tell you." Corie Mae shook her finger in Betty Lou's face. "Just because you're learning music, you ain't too good to mind your mama. Now sit down, right now!"

Maggie's cheeks burned and the back of her throat ached. Despite her determination not to cry, tears slowly slid down her cheeks. She climbed the stairs and fell onto her bed, burying her face in the pillow. She had not expected something like this. She couldn't understand her mother's objection to playing basketball or why her mother was so determined to keep her tied down. Maggie heard Mary Helen crying. Usually when the baby woke, Maggie went to her immediately, changed her, and took her to her mother to nurse. Now she pulled the pillow over her head to block out the sound. *She can take care of the baby herself. Maybe if I quit doing all the work I do, she'll see that I really try hard to do my part for this family.* She turned over on her back. She listened to the sleet pinging on the tin roof and hoped Bud had gotten a ride home. She sat up and opened her English book to the assignment. She could understand how JD must feel. *Maybe I should go live with Aunt Lillian. She'd like me to play basketball.* She took her paper and pencil and began answering the questions. After a bit she closed her eyes and recalled how Grandma had taken those scissors and cut Mary Helen loose from her mother. *That's what I need. Some way to cut this cord Mama has tied me down with. But no matter what she does, I'm still going to play basketball.*

* * *

The week of the first basketball game, Johnny Ray became much weaker. On Monday, JD stayed home from school to take him to the doctor, who immediately put him in the hospital, almost twenty miles away. Maggie and Betty Lou took turns staying home from school to go with Ray to the hospital. Either Reverend Lewis or Mrs. Lewis would come to pick them up each morning and bring them home at night. Corie Mae stayed home because she had to nurse Mary Helen, and the hospital would not allow a child younger than twelve in hospital rooms.

On Thursday afternoon. Maggie listened as the doctor called her father into the hallway and explained that Johnny Ray needed to spend most of his time lying down since his heart had become so weak it could sustain very little activity. He told Ray they should let Johnny Ray do whatever he felt like doing. They were to give him vitamins and iron because of his anemia. Maggie explained to the doctor how several weeks earlier she had allowed Johnny Ray to get wet and cold.

"The heart is a muscle, and like any muscle, it gets tired." The doctor spoke in reassuring tones. "The rheumatic fever has weakened it, and that makes it tire more easily. Getting wet didn't make it weaker. It has been slowly getting weaker since he had encephalitis last summer."

Maggie, relieved to know she hadn't caused it, heard the implication that the weakening would continue. She started back into the room to help Johnny Ray get dressed to go home when she heard her father ask how much longer he could live in this condition. Without turning around, she paused in the doorway to hear the doctor's reply.

"It's hard to say. His heart could continue to beat for a long time. It's possible it could even get stronger, or it could just suddenly quit."

At school the next morning, Maggie found Miss Erickson and asked if she had some time to talk. They agreed to meet in the library at noon. When Maggie explained to Miss Erickson how her mother refused to let her sit at the table with the family for meals and how she had not spoken a word to her for over a week, Miss Erickson asked, "Are you getting enough to eat?"

"Mama doesn't try to keep me from eating, she just won't let me eat at the table with the family."

"Do you think playing basketball is worth the price you're paying?"

Maggie rubbed her hand across her forehead. "I'm trying to decide. My sisters tell me not to back down. Jeannie thinks she would like to play basketball, too, when she gets in high school. They say if I don't back down now, Mama will have to allow them to participate in various activities later." Maggie caught her breath in a sob. "But what hurts most is that she doesn't even speak to me. She doesn't even look at me, like I'm invisible."

"Do you think it might help if I talked with her?"

"No. It would make it worse. But thank you for offering." Maggie struggled to control her tears, without success. "On top of that, I think my little brother's going to die." Maggie put her head down on the table and sobbed.

Miss Erickson reached across the table and took Maggie's hand quietly waiting until she stopped crying. "Maggie, I'm really sorry about your little brother. I know it's hard to think about anything else right now." She paused and squeezed Maggie's hand. "What does your father say about your playing basketball?"

"Nothing much. In the past when Mama opposed my doing something, like going to the Business Education Convention last spring, he overruled her. She doesn't like it, but he always has the last word." Maggie sighed "But this time he said me and Mama would have to work it out."

"I can't advise you to disobey your parents. Personally, I don't think playing basketball is wrong. But deliberately doing what your mother had forbidden you to do is another matter." Maggie nodded. "On the other hand, I've seen you practicing with the team, and I know they are depending on you. So I don't feel comfortable advising you to give it up either." She smiled a crooked smile. "I guess I'm not much help, am I?"

"Actually, it helps a lot to have someone listen to me, someone who understands. I guess what it boils down to is that I'll have to give it a try and see if I can hold out. I just hope I can play well tonight with all this on my mind."

"Looks to me like you just decided to stay on the team. I think it is a bold decision. I support you, but you will not lose my respect if you decide later to change your mind. During the game tonight, you'll have to focus and concentrate to keep your worries out of your mind. I'll be up in the bleachers yelling for you."

"Thanks, Miss Erickson. You've been a big help."

* * *

Maggie had perfected an unusual hook shot. Starting near the foul shot line, she would take a quick dribble away from the goal to her right and fling the ball over her head toward the backboard. Because of her height and the high arc of the ball, guards hardly ever blocked the shot, and it swished the net for a goal most of the time. They had won their first two games. The praise Maggie got from her teammates, fellow students, and even strangers gave her the courage to bear the ostracism her mother continued to impose at home.

Maggie diligently did her chores and helped out every way she could. Betty Lou and Jeannie kept urging her to hold out against Mama. It helped to have allies, but the atmosphere at home remained tense. Johnny Ray's slowly worsening condition, and the burden of yet another hospital bill weighed heavily on Maggie. As usual, Ray had little work during the winter months, and she approached December with little hope for a festive celebration at Christmas time.

Early in December after a spell of dry weather, their father asked Maggie and Betty Lou to stay home from school for a few days to help pick corn. Earlier, Ray and Stuart had cut the stalks and formed shocks. Even though the weather had moderated slightly, their hands became so cold they could hardly feel the ears of corn when they tore them from the stalks and tossed them into the wagon. By noon they had filled the wagon, and Old Maude, Maggie's favorite mare, had pulled it to the barn. After lunch they returned to the field of shocks to pick another load. Despite the cold, it was a pleasant time. Ray joked with the girls and told them stories of his youth back in Kentucky.

Bud continued to make his Sunday afternoon visits. He always asked Corie Mae for permission to take Maggie to church. Corie Mae would look at him and shrug her shoulders, and they took her gesture as assent. With Bud's encouragement and the enthusiasm of her friends for her performance on the basketball court, Maggie gained the courage to continue to defy her mother. But she noticed that her skirt bands were looser, and Miss Erickson, with obvious concern, commented on the dark circles under her eyes.

The third Friday in December, Maggie's team had to play Nemo, which was unbeaten for the season and had won every game against Maggie's school for the last four years. JD offered to take Ray to the game, and Maggie was excited that her daddy would finally see her play. At the end of the first half, Maggie's team led by ten points. Nemo's coach switched their tall center, Peggy Smith, to guard Maggie. She was taller than Maggie and very aggressive. While she could not block Maggie's hook shot, she often intercepted passes or tied up the ball. Maggie's team suffered several turnovers, and Nemo tied up the score.

As the fourth quarter started, Mary Ann took the ball at center court and passed to Maggie, who got in her special shot for a score. The referee turned to take the ball back to center court, and Smith gave Maggie a shove. Mary Ann heard her call Maggie a "Bitch."

"Ignore her," Mary Ann yelled, but Maggie was angry. She had done nothing to this girl. Why was she being so rude? As the quarter moved along, the aggression continued. Maggie made a foul shot putting her team ahead, and as soon as the referee turned his back, Smith tripped Maggie making her fall. Some in the crowd began to yell at Smith, who only grinned and shook her fist at them. She moved close to Maggie and said, "If you make another shot, me and my team will catch you after the game and beat you to a pulp." The next time Maggie got off a successful hook shot, Smith spit in Maggie's face.

Without thinking Maggie swung her fist, and blood spurted from Smith's nose. When Smith began to scream, the referee called time out and threw Maggie out of the game. The crowd roared in protest while she walked back to the bench hanging her head. Coach Moore stood to face her. "Go to the dressing room right now!"

She sat alone on the bench beside the showers with tears streaming down her face. She had let the team down, she had let Coach Moore down, but most of all she had let her father down. He was watching her play for the first time, and she had gotten herself thrown out of the game for bad sportsmanship. She imagined how disappointed he must feel.

She heard the final buzzer and could tell by the sparse cheering that her team had lost. Her teammates began streaming into the dressing room, and gave her hugs. "Good for you, Maggie." "You gave that creep what she had coming." "I hope you broke her nose." "She's the one who should have been thrown out of the game." "If I'd been there, I'd hit her myself."

But her teammates protested loudly on Monday when Coach Moore told Maggie she would not play in the next two games. "But that girl was pushing Maggie, calling her 'Bitch,' tripping her and even spit in her face."

"I know that, " Coach Moore explained. "But my players do not let the opponent get them rattled. Getting Maggie thrown out of the game was exactly what she wanted, and Maggie fell for it. All of you need to understand that I will not tolerate any unsportsman-like conduct. Maggie can practice with the team, but she will sit on the bench for the next two games." He blew the whistle to start practice. "Some things are more important than winning."

Later he talked with Maggie privately. "I understand how she provoked you, and I need you to understand that I'm not angry with you. But I feel I must penalize you as a matter of principle. My players need to know I will not allow retaliation no matter how provoked they are." But his words did little to ease Maggie's disappointment and humiliation. She would have quit the team except that when she had joined her father in the bleachers that night, he had put his arm around her and said, "I'm sorry you lost your temper, Sunshine, but if you was going to hit her, I'm glad you done a good job of it."

* * *

On the Friday night after Christmas, Maggie and Wanda helped Aunt Lillian close up the restaurant. They had served the local Angus Breeders Association for their annual meeting. Wanda had joked about what a bunch of bull they were. A knock at the door caught them by surprise.

"It's JD." Aunt Lillian opened the door. "What are you doing here this time of night?"

JD stepped through the door and looked around. He had such dark circles under his eyes that Maggie thought he'd been in a fight. "I need to talk to you and Maggie." JD turned to Wanda. "You can listen in, too, if you want."

"Thanks, but if it's family business, I'll grab my coat and go on home."

"Wait." JD turned to Aunt Lillian. "Is it okay if I drive Wanda home and then come back to talk to you two?"

"You don't need to take me home. I can walk. I do it all the time."

"I know, but I'd like to take you home tonight. Please."

Wanda shrugged and nodded. Maggie locked the front door behind them and watched as JD held the door for Wanda to get into his car. "Did Wanda tell you that she broke up with JD?"

Aunt Lillian turned out the lights. "Yes. She's been sort of weepy all week. But I admire her for sticking to her guns. When he showed up on Christmas Day half drunk, she wouldn't let him in the house and told him never to come back."

"That's what Wanda told me." Maggie walked through the apartment door while Aunt Lillian held it open. She had helped at the café off and on for several months. She also spent the night with Aunt Lillian when she had no way to get home after a basketball game. She no longer felt like a guest, even had some extra clothes stashed in the closet. Maggie hung up her jacket, kicked off her shoes, and sat on the sofa.

Aunt Lillian took some milk out of the refrigerator. "Think I'll make some hot chocolate. That's one of JD's favorites."

"I'm surprised he showed up tonight. This morning Kenny told me he hadn't been home since Christmas morning. I don't know where he's been. He didn't look very good, did he?"

"I'm afraid to guess where he's been. I really worry about him." Aunt Lillian motioned to the pan on the stove. "Will you stir this cocoa while I find that bag of marshmallows I bought the other day?"

Maggie and Aunt Lillian had each drunk a cup of hot chocolate and washed their cups by the time JD came. He rubbed his red eyes and sighed as he removed his coat and threw it over the back of the sofa. He sat quietly on the sofa staring at the floor until Aunt Lillian handed him his hot chocolate with three marshmallows floating on the top.

Maggie sat beside him. "Are you okay? You look like you've been run over by a dump truck."

"You might say I have." He blew on the chocolate and took a sip.

"Except I guess I drove the truck over myself."

"What do you mean?" Aunt Lillian brought a chair from the kitchen table.

JD took a deep breath and slowly let it out as a sigh. "Aunt Lillian, you do know about Stella, don't you?"

Aunt Lillian nodded. "Yes, I even met her when I visited WC last summer. Why?"

JD took another swallow of chocolate and hung his head for several seconds. "I guess I've made a bad mistake, several mistakes, to tell the truth." He stared down at the marshmallows that had melted into a sweet white syrup. "I told Mama." He took a quick breath almost like a sob. "I knowed I shouldn't of done it. But she made me so mad. Before I knowed what was happening I had wrestled her to the floor. And I was sitting on top of her, holding her arms to the floor to keep her from slapping me again. And I just blurted it out." He wiped his eyes with the back of his hand.

With a pounding heart, Maggie released the breath she had been holding and finally found her voice. "I'm so sorry, JD. Why did she attack you?"

Another deep sigh. "It's a long story. I guess it started Christmas night. I've been thinking I should break up with Wanda. I just ain't been treating her right, standing her up, ignoring her, arguing with her. She deserves much better'n that." He quickly emptied his cup and set it on the coffee table. "I decided I should just go ahead and do it on Christmas night. She had told me if I ever come there drinking she would break up with me. So being too chicken to say the words myself, I drunk half a bottle of wine so she would have to say 'It's over.' I was a coward, and I apologized to her tonight. Like I say, she deserves better'n me." He stood up and took his cup to the kitchen sink. He rinsed it out, filled it with water, and drank it down in noisy gulps.

He stared out the kitchen window. "When I left her house on Christmas night, I was so mad at myself and ashamed of my behavior I didn't know what to do. I drove around awhile, but being Christmas night, nothing was open. Finally, I drove down to Miller's Falls and drank the rest of the wine and cried my eyes out. I don't know if I passed out or just fell asleep." He turned around and took a few steps toward Maggie and Aunt Lillian and put his hands in his hip pockets. "The next thing I knowed it was 12:30 Tuesday afternoon. I was supposed to start work at 10:00 that morning." He sighed and flopped down on the sofa. "I went down to the creek and washed my face. That icy water woke me up real fast. When I got to the station, Mr. Sexton handed me my pay check and said I was fired. I can't blame him. I ain't done him right lately neither. That was the third time I'd been late in the last week."

Maggie put her hand on his shoulder. "What's happened to make you like this?"

"I don't know. It's just like I don't give a hoot about nothing." He stood up again and began pacing. "Anyway I drove down to Deer Creek Camp and spent the rest of the day drinking and playing pool at Joe's Bar." He stopped beside Aunt Lillian's chair. "Okay if I smoke?"

Aunt Lillian nodded and slid an ash tray across the coffee table toward him. He lit a cigarette and blew out a cloud of smoke. "Along about midnight this guy named Marvin Black come in with a woman. They sat at the bar drinking, and after a while they got into an argument. He begun slapping her around and made her nose bleed." JD took another drag on his cigarette. "You know me. When he hit her again, I told him to leave her alone. He said, 'And just what would a little squirt like you do about it?' So I picked up a heavy ash tray and threw it. It hit him in the head and knocked him off his bar stool. He staggered to his feet and made a lunge for me. Pretty soon we had broken glasses, turned over tables, and hit each other with our fists, bottles, chairs, and anything else we could get our hands on. We made a real mess of the place. Joe called the sheriff. He took both of us to jail."

Aunt Lillian gasped. "He locked you up in jail?"

"Yeah, for three days." JD put out his cigarette in the ashtray and sat down again. "I guess the sheriff went out to see if Mama would put up my bail, but he told me she said 'I hope he rots in there.'"

"So how'd you get out?" Maggie pulled her feet up under her. In spite of the warm room, she shivered.

"I guess the owner of the bar came to the sheriff's office, and told him he had decided to drop charges if we would sign a statement saying we'd never come back there again. So about ten o'clock this morning, the sheriff opened the door and let us out. I hitchhiked down to Deer Creek Camp to get my car and went home."

"And that's when the fireworks began, I guess." Aunt Lillian rubbed her hands over her face.

"And how. I hadn't even got through the door till Mama made a lunge at me knocking me back out on the porch. I finally got into the house, but she was all over me, calling me all sorts of names and slapping me. That's when I snapped and threw her to the floor. I straddled her holding her arms down on the floor, and she spit in my face." JD got to his feet, felt in his pocket for his cigarettes, and lit up again.

Maggie swiveled her feet back onto the floor and sat up straight. "So exactly what did you tell her?" She twisted her hands together.

JD blew out smoke. "Everything. I told her Daddy had a woman in Detroit. She called me a liar. So I told her about Meeka and that Stella was a black woman. Then she spit on me again. Finally I said if she didn't believe me she should get on a Greyhound Bus and go see for herself."

Aunt Lillian stood and put her arms around JD. "I'm sorry. I guess it had to come out someday, but I'm sorry you're the one to tell her. She'll be mad when she finds out I've known all this time and didn't tell her."

Maggie came and stood with them. "What do you plan to do now?"

"I have to leave. Daddy'll kill me when he finds out I told."

"Where'll you go? And what about school?"

"I don't care about school. I've probably already failed too many classes to graduate. And I don't know where I'm going; I've just got to get out of here. I've saved up some money. I'll go somewhere and get a job. I'll write you when I get settled somewhere. I thought I'd start out tonight, I've got all my stuff in the car, but I wanted to see you before I left."

Aunt Lillian released him and took a step back. "Why don't you stay here tonight?"

"You're too tired and upset to be driving this late," Maggie argued, "and besides, you don't even know where you're going."

JD nodded. "Okay, I'll stay, but I'm leaving tomorrow for sure."

"Maggie, get the extra blankets out of the trunk at the foot of my bed. We'll make him a pallet here on the kitchen floor. I'll go talk to Opal tomorrow, and if she wants to go to Detroit, I'll go with her."

"Thanks, Aunt Lillian. You've always been good to me, like another mother." JD gave her a hug.

Maggie lay in the dark trying to sort out her feelings. On the one hand, she understood that JD couldn't stay, but she didn't want him to leave. He had only a few months till graduation. If he leaves now, he'll never graduate. Where can he go? And how could she stand to lose him? *That's one cord I don't want broken.*

* * *

31 February, 1951

Dear Maggie,

Guess what? I'm in the army here at Fort Jackson, South Carolina. Don't tell Mama. Don't want her or Daddy to know where I'm at. Maybe I'll surprise her & show up in my uniform when boot camp is over.

I hate my Sgt. I think I could actually kill him. Sometimes when he gets in my face & yells at me, it takes all my strength to keep from hitting him. He made me do 100 push-ups yesterday because he found a wrinkle in my bed. Tomorrow we are going on a 10 mile march. It makes my feet hurt just to think about it. But the chow is good & I've met some fun guys.

When I left, I went to Knoxville & got a room at the YMCA. Got a job washing dishes at a restaurant til I found out how to enlist. Sold my car. I'm sending you a money order for you to use for yourself. You've always stood by me & been my best friend. I want you to know how much I appreciate you.

Write & tell me what happened when Mama went to Detroit. How is Wanda doing? I do miss her, but don't tell her. How is Johnny Ray? Is Kenny doing ok?

I got to go now. Write soon. I miss you.

Your Cuz, JD

Maggie read the letter again and handed it to Aunt Lillian. "You should read it, too. I'm not surprised he ended up in the army." She looked at the money order. "I can't believe he sent me a hundred dollars. What should I do with it?" She folded the money order and put it in her pocket. "I'll give at least half of it to Daddy to pay on the hospital bill."

"I think JD meant for you to spend it on yourself."

"I'll still have enough to go to the Business Education Convention and buy my dress to wear to the Junior-Senior Banquet. Daddy wouldn't let me go last year, but I think I'll get to go this year, especially since Bud's a senior, and this might be the last year I get to go with him."

"Do you think Corie Mae will start speaking to you when basketball season is over?"

"I don't know. It's hard to believe she hasn't spoken to me a single time in over two months. I'm sort of getting used to it. At least I don't keep expecting it."

Aunt Lillian handed the letter back to Maggie. "Tell him I'm glad he's okay. I've been so worried about him since we hadn't heard nothing all this time."

"I better get back to school. Mr. Adkins sent me to the bank, and I just stopped in to see if you'd heard anything from JD. I'll see you again Friday when we have a game at Central City. It'll be really late when we get home because it's a long ways over there."

"Be sure Bud walks you up here. Just knock on the door. I'll be expecting you. And good luck. I hope you beat them good."

"Thanks, Aunt Lillian." Maggie gave her a hug. "I'll do my best."

* * *

Dear JD,

I was so relieved to get your letter. Aunt Lillian and I have been worried to death about you. When will boot camp be over? Will you get to come home for a furlough? I can't wait to see you in your uniform.

Thanks for the money order. I know you said for me to spend it on myself, but I gave Daddy $50 to pay on the hospital bill. He gave me a hug and he had tears in his eyes. That made me feel good.

I haven't seen Aunt Opal since she got back from Detroit. She won't come to our family dinner on Sundays. Kenny says, she's not keeping the house clean and spends most of her time in bed. He eats supper at our house most nights. I don't think Kenny knows about Stella, so he's not sure what's making your mother so depressed. Aunt Lillian went to Detroit with your mother, and she said Uncle Thomas wouldn't even talk to Aunt Opal. He would only talk to Aunt Lillian. He said if your mother would agree not to tell anyone about Stella, he would not ask her for a divorce. He would still live in Detroit and she would still live here. He would continue to send money as he has done in the past, so nothing's really changed except now your mother knows. She told Aunt Lillian she would accept these terms until Kenny graduates from high school.

I know you don't want her to know where you are, but she is really worried. Your leaving and finding out about your Daddy's other life were two big blows that fell on her all at once. It would help her if you would write to her. I told Kenny to tell her I had gotten a letter from you and you were all right. But I didn't tell him where you were.

Johnny Ray stays in his bed almost all the time now. Daddy set up his bed in the front room again where it's warm. Sometimes he goes to the table to eat and sometimes Mama brings his food to him in bed. I don't know how much longer he can hold on. I dread the day when his heart gives out.

The rest of us are doing all right. Little Mary Helen is so cute. She is almost 5 months old now. Junior loves to make her laugh and almost anything he does causes her to cackle.

We have lost only 2 games so far. We have only two more games of the regular season. Then we'll start the county tournament. Mary Ann and Connie have worked out a good play to get the ball to me so I can do my hook shot. My picture was in the county paper last week as the player with the most points in one season. I got a copy of the paper and brought it home. I saw Mama pick it up and look at it, but she still doesn't talk to me or let me come to the table to eat. Mr. Collins has given Daddy a ride to games two or three times. He doesn't say much to me about it, but I'm glad he wants to go.

It's time for me to do the chores. Be careful. Take care of yourself. Don't' let that Sgt. get under your skin. Hope we'll see you soon.

Your cuz, Maggie

* * *

A day or two later, Maggie went to the barn to do the chores but could not find the cows. She called for them as she walked through the pasture, but didn't hear the bell that hung around Big Red's neck. She walked along the back fence hoping to find where they had broken through. Finally, she saw the post lying on the ground and the fence wire mashed down. She followed the tracks up the hill and into the woods. She had walked some distance up the ridge when she heard Big Red's bell. She began to call to the cows, and soon she saw them coming toward her. "What are you doing out here? Trying to run away?"

The cows followed Maggie back down the hill toward the gap in the fence. Suddenly Audie Lee stepped from behind a bush and took a few stumbling steps toward her. "Hi Audie Lee. I haven't seen you for a long time. Where have you been hiding? Up on the ledge?" She watched as he waddled closer and took the tow sack off his shoulder. After searching through it, he opened one of his tobacco sacks and picked out Johnny Ray's necklace and offered it to Maggie.

When Maggie reached for it, he pulled it back and made motions. She didn't understand at first, but finally realized he wanted her to swap something for the necklace. She put her hands in her pockets, but found only a large safety pin. He angrily shook his head. Frantic lest she lose this chance to get the necklace for Johnny Ray, she looked at Big Red who stood nearby. She pointed to the cow bell and looked at Audie Lee with raised eyebrows. At first he grinned and stepped a little closer to look. But then he shook his head and put the necklace back into his pouch. Maggie watched him throw the burlap bag over his shoulder and lurch back into the bushes. She wished she still had the geode pieces in her pocket.

Later that night when she was reading to Johnny Ray, she told him about her encounter with Audie Lee. "I think if I had had the geode pieces he would have traded with me. Do you know where they are?"

Johnny Ray's eyes brightened. "Yes, Maggie. If you look beside the bed upstairs where I used to sleep, there's a little hole in the wall. I put them in there." Maggie found the geode pieces and began carrying them with her hoping she would run into Audie Lee again. But the days slipped by and Audie Lee never showed.

The last week in February the rain fell in torrents, washing gullies in the hillsides and turning the dirt roads into rivers of mud. The superintendent cancelled school when many creeks flooded and water rose over the bridges. Grandpa Campbell said he could never remember such a rain coming in February. Maggie hoped the county tournament scheduled to start in three days would not be cancelled as well. By Wednesday the creeks had receded enough that busses could get through, and school resumed. With the tournament only one day away, Coach Moore pushed the girls hard during the practice, but announced, "I think you are ready to win this tournament."

When Maggie and the kids got off the bus that afternoon, Reverend Lewis waited to give them a ride home. He said he didn't want them to have to walk in the mud. But as they approached, Maggie saw the doctor's car parked in front of the house. She looked at her pastor. "It's Johnny Ray, isn't it?"

He nodded. "Yes, I'm afraid he left us about two this afternoon. The doctor is here for your mother. She's taking this pretty hard. She needs you now, Maggie."

Maggie looked at Reverend Lewis with wild eyes. "Johnny Ray's dead?"

When the realization hit Jeannie in the back seat, she began screaming. Even though he didn't understand what had happened, Junior began crying, too. Maggie opened the door and pulled Junior into her arms. "Shhhh." she whispered into his ear. "You're okay. Maggie's not going to let anything happen to you."

Reverend Lewis helped Jeannie out of the car and held her while she sobbed. "He was a brave little boy," he said and patted Jeannie's back.

"But I didn't get to tell him good bye." Jeannie pushed away and ran down the muddy road.

"Here." Maggie handed Junior over to Reverend Lewis and ran after Jeannie slipping and sliding in the muddy ruts. When she caught up with her, Maggie pulled her toward the barn where they climbed to the hay loft and fell into the hay. Holding each other, they cried until exhausted.

"I never thought he'd just go away like this." Jeannie sat up and wiped her eyes with the back of her hand. "When I left this morning he said, 'Bye,

Jeannie. See you later.'" She began crying again.

Maggie searched through her coat pockets for a handkerchief, but came up with the two pieces of geode. She looked at them, and fresh tears ran down her cheeks. "When I told him good bye this morning, he said, 'Maggie, maybe today you'll get the necklace from Audie Lee.'" Her shoulders shook as she sobbed. "He wanted it so much. Now it's too late."

* * *

Toward the end of April on a bright Sunday afternoon, Maggie climbed to the ledge to work on the oral report she had to make in her world history class. She wanted to find a place where she could practice in private. She stood looking over the hollow and spoke confidently to the audience of freshly leaved trees interspersed with bright spots of redbud and dogwood. After going through her report for the third time, she sat down on a rock and let her mind wander. Memories of the last several weeks flashed through her mind like pictures in an album.

She saw her father, Grandpa Campbell, Stuart and Kenny returning from digging the grave. They were covered in mud from head to toe as the recent rains had left the ground soaked. That in turn prompted her memory of the casket being lowered and hearing the splash as it sank into the water standing in the grave. She still had bad dreams about that. Sometimes she waked suddenly hearing the splats as the men shoveled the mud onto the casket.

She closed her eyes to erase that picture and saw her teammates hugging her and expressing their sympathy. She shuddered as she recalled how, though they hadn't said it was her fault they had lost the tournament, she thought she saw the blame in their faces and struggled with her guilt for letting down the team, and indeed, the school. In the trauma of Johnny Ray's death, she had completely forgotten about the tournament. The kindness of Coach Moore, when he had come to the house to reassure her and express his sympathy to her parents, helped moderate her reaction to their imagined reproof.

She shifted her gaze to the dirt road she could see here and there between the trees and recalled how cars had worn deep ruts bringing friends, church women, even relatives from Kentucky. They came in droves carrying food, expressing their sympathy, standing quietly beside the casket set up on the funeral bier in the downstairs bedroom. Thanks to Aunt Opal, who dragged herself out of her own stupor to help, the house was cleaned, the kitchen scoured, and the children bathed in preparation for the wake. Maggie smiled remembering that Aunt Opal had recently accepted another job caring for an elderly woman, apparently putting her disappointments behind her. The fact that JD had come home after boot camp and made some overtures of reconciliation apparently had encouraged Aunt Opal to get her life back together.

Maggie stood, picked up a rock, and hit the dead pine tree down below the ledge. She smiled as she remembered how she and JD had stood here last fall flinging stones at the old tree. Her smile faded as her fears that JD would be sent to Korea surfaced. After his furlough he had reported to Fort Meade, Maryland, where he was being trained as a medic. She sighed, picked up her papers, and turned to go back down the trail.

A scene that brought both joy and pain filled the screen of her mind. During the night of the wake for Johnny Ray, Maggie had come downstairs to see if people still kept watch. Her father slept, sitting in a folding chair furnished by the funeral home, his head leaning against the wall. Hearing voices in the kitchen, Maggie had found her father's two sisters from Kentucky, Aunt Dar and Aunt Cindy, talking with Grandma Campbell. She had found her mother standing beside the casket in the bedroom. Quietly stepping beside her, Maggie put her arm around her mother's waist. Corie Mae had turned to look at her, then enfolded Maggie in her arms, and the two of them swayed back and forth weeping hot tears of grief and regret. When the tears had stopped, Corie Mae held Maggie at arm's length. "I don't understand why God lets a sweet little boy die. But He knows best. We just have to accept His will."

Maggie tripped over a root, almost turning a somersault, before getting herself upright on the path again. She wiped the tears from her eyes. In those moments that she and her mother had held each other, she had hoped all was forgiven and forgotten. Once she had wanted to be cut free of her mother, but now she wasn't sure. She wondered how many other cords would be broken. *Johnny Ray and Elsie Mae are gone. Who knows what JD is headed for? With Bud graduating, will that cord be cut too?*

Thinking of Bud reminded her how he had come to her side as soon as he heard about Johnny Ray's death. He had skipped school and spent the day helping. He washed dishes, carried in wood and coal to keep the fires going, and even persuaded Corie Mae to eat. He had stood with Maggie beside the casket and held her as she wept.

Maggie noticed the shadows growing longer and quickened her pace, remembering Bud planned to go to church with her tonight. After graduation, he expected to work in his uncle's store in Chattanooga again until he started classes at Tennessee Tech in the fall. Maggie wanted to spend as much time with him as possible before he graduated.. She had bought a formal dress to wear to the Junior-Senior banquet in a few weeks. Although Corie Mae had agreed for her to go with Bud to the banquet, Maggie hadn't shown her the dress, which she had left at Aunt Lillian's. Remembering the way her mother had objected to the dress Betty Lou wore for the music program last year, she didn't want to take a chance that Corie Mae would veto her plans. As she came around the curve past JD and Kenny's house, she saw Bud coming down the hill toward her. He ran to her, threw his arms around her and swung her around in a circle before setting her down on the steps to the house.

CHAPTER 9

Campbell Holler–November 12, 1888   Disappointment.
Had plan to go to Harlan for Thanksgiving. Harvey got
typhoid fever. Almost died. Now too weak to travel.
Haven't seen my family for 15 years.
(Diary of Mary Louise Campbell)

Junior year 1951-1952

Maggie had mixed feelings about school at the beginning of her junior year.
The summer had been long and boring–and sad. It seemed that every day
brought some reminder of Johnny Ray.   Several times she had found her
mother holding a favorite toy of Johnny Ray's and wiping tears from her
eyes. Her father's eyes seldom twinkled with humor. They all missed him,
but everyone seemed afraid to talk about it. Some days when she felt
particularly low, Maggie wandered up to the ridge and pelted the old dead
pine.

Slowly over the summer Corie Mae ended her silent treatment and had
begun to talk to Maggie, but always with the pursed lips and a disapproving
tone. Shortly after the funeral, Maggie had matter-of-factly taken her old
place at the table with no repercussions. Maggie understood that taking
care of Mary Helen, who was now ten months old, and the usual hard
summer work had kept Corie Mae busy and preoccupied, but she had
hopes the relationship would improve even more.

JD had finished his medic training and had been shipped to a base in
Japan. Maggie continued to hope he would not be sent to Korea, but that
possibility seemed always in the back of her mind. She missed him. School

was not the same. Not only was JD not around anymore, but she missed Bud as well. For two years she had seen Bud every day at school. Now she found herself searching the faces in the crowded hallways hoping to see his quick smile, gorgeous dimples, and meaningful wink. She had seen him only a few days when he came home after working all summer for his uncle in Chattanooga before he moved into the dorm at Tennessee Tech in Cookeville. He promised to write often, but Maggie suspected his idea of often did not match her own–that certainly had seemed the case during the summer.

At least she could see her school friends every day. She and Mary Ann had three classes together and sometimes managed to persuade their parents they needed to study together on weekends. But her classes no longer inspired her and she often felt restless and at loose ends.

Each year the junior class presented a play in the gap between football and basketball seasons. Maggie had agreed to be the prompter, a demanding job. While the other cast members goofed off backstage having fun, she had to keep her attention glued to the script. By the time of the dress rehearsal, she had memorized the entire play–a good thing as it turned out. When she arrived at school on the morning of the performance, Miss McNeal, the play director, met her at the door. "Oh Maggie, we've got a problem!"

"What's the matter, Miss McNeal?"

"Darlene was rushed to the hospital last night for an emergency appendectomy. Do you think you can take her place?"

"Oh no. She has the lead role. I can't do that. She's on the stage almost all the time."

"You know all her lines and also know all the stage directions. I know you can do it."

"But, Miss McNeal, I haven't ever practiced it. What if I forget?"

"I'll be prompting, so if you forget I can give you your lines, but I'm sure you won't forget." She took Maggie's arm. "It's the only solution. Otherwise, we'll have to call off the play."

Maggie reluctantly agreed and spent every free moment until time for the action to begin with her nose in the script trying to make sure she knew every line. In the end, it wasn't Maggie who messed up. At one point in the script, Ronnie was supposed to say "The get-away car was a station wagon." Instead he said "The get-away car was a stagon wation." Realizing his mistake, he began to laugh and couldn't stop. He stood on stage with his shoulders shaking, put his hands over his face and turned his back to the audience, his hysterical laughter finally turning to sobs. Miss McNeal, a genuine fussbudget, was beside herself, flapping her arms like a drowning person to get Ronnie's attention while she hissed, "Stop it! Stop it this minute!"

Some audience members began to applaud and cheer, calling out "Bravo!" "Way to go Ronnie!"—exactly the tension-breaker that was called for. Members of the cast crowded around Ronnie, patting him on the back and encouraging him. Finally, Ronnie turned toward the audience and gave an exaggerated bow, which instigated another round of enthusiastic whistling and applauding. The players returned to their places. Miss McNeal, in a loud stage whisper, gave the next line, and the action resumed where it had left off. Everyone thought it was the best play the school had given in years.

When time for basketball practice rolled around, Maggie assumed that since she had played last year, she would be allowed to play again. She didn't bother to ask her parents. A couple of freshman who came out for the team turned out to be strong players. One of them, Eleanor, filled the spot under the goal where her height was needed for rebounding. Coach Moore felt the team had the best prospects for a winning season yet. Maggie's father had managed to buy an old pick-up truck so he could come to watch her play and then give her a ride home.

All in all the year seemed to be going along well enough under the circumstances, but Maggie dreaded Christmas. It would seem so bleak without Johnny Ray and JD. At least, Bud would be home for a couple of weeks and that would brighten up her life considerably.

***

Dressed in her nightgown and robe, Aunt Lillian opened the door and stepped back for Maggie to come in. "So, how did the game go?"

Maggie unwound her neck scarf and took off her gloves. "We won, finally. It went into overtime, and Mary Ann fouled out. I thought sure we'd lose, but fortunately, one of their guards fouled Eleanor, and she made both shots. We still have a perfect record for the season."

Aunt Lillian locked the door. "Are you froze to death? Did you walk from School?"

"Billy Ray and Kathy gave me a ride. I'm not cold at all." Maggie hung her coat in the closet.

Aunt Lillian pointed to the coffee table. "Guess what? You finally got a letter from JD. While you read it, I'll make us some hot chocolate."

13 January 1952

Dear Maggie,
I've been stationed here at Camp Shinodayama near Osaka, Japan, since last October. Sorry I haven't written.

I got your letters and it's good to hear from home. Keep those letters coming. How is your team doing this season? Winning every game, I hope.

I'm being trained as part of a MASH unit. We'll be shipping out to Korea within the next few days or weeks. I would not brag to my buddies, but I'm pretty darn good at getting an IV line started and last week I even assisted Major Andrews in surgery. Maybe when I get back home, I'll study medicine. Ha! Ha!

The MASH units near the front stabilize the wounded and then ship them here to this hospital to be treated. We see all kinds of injuries and medical problems. A few weeks ago, we got a fellow with a busted leg. The medics had used a carbine as a splint. He had traveled by ambulance, plane, boat, and ship to reach our hospital. When we unwrapped his leg, the carbine was loaded and cocked!

Winter is not so bad here in Japan, but the guys coming here from Korea talk a lot about how cold it is there. We see lots of frostbite. One medic told me it got so cold their medicines froze and they had to warm the plasma for a hour before they could use it. I guess I'll get used to it if I have to.

Don't worry about me. I'm doing great. Tell Kenny I think about him a lot and hope he's doing good in school. Are you still going out with Bud? Tell him hi for me. Write when you can.

Your cuz, JD

Maggie tossed the letter back on the coffee table. "I hoped he'd stay in Japan, but looks like he's going to Korea. Probably there already." She kicked off her shoes. "I hate this war. I don't know why we have to go halfway around the world to fight people who have done nothing to us." Her voice was hoarse with anguish.

Aunt Lillian set two mugs of hot cocoa on the coffee table and sat beside Maggie on the sofa. Maggie handed the letter to Aunt Lillian. "Here, you should read it too." Maggie sipped her chocolate.

After reading the letter, Aunt Lillian folded it and replaced it in the envelope. "At least, he seems to like what he's doing. I'd never thought he'd be interested in being a medic."

"Yeah, wouldn't it be something if he becomes a doctor when he gets out?"

Aunt Lillian sipped her hot chocolate. "I think you should let Opal read this. He probably won't write her, but she deserves to know where he's at and what he's doing. Maybe she would be proud of her son for doing something worthwhile."

"Okay, I'll take it to her when I go home tomorrow night. Daddy's supposed to pick me up after he finishes working over at Maple Grove. He's got a lot of good out of that old pick-up he bought. He's been hauling coal for people and delivered a load of hay to a guy in Hamby last week. Now he has a way to jobs when he hears about them. He's made more money this winter than any other year. I heard him tell Mama he'd paid all the hospital bill. Now they only have to pay for the funeral."

"It's been hard for him and Corie Mae, having to pinch pennies so much. I really don't see how they've done it. I know you've helped out when you've had some money. Which reminds me, we can use your help tomorrow afternoon if you're going to be around."

Maggie nodded and absently picked up the county paper lying on the coffee table. She turned to the sports reports to see if her team had made the news. After browsing through the back pages, she turned the paper to the front and gasped when she saw the picture below the headline: CO. BOY KILLED IN KOREA. "Oh, no. This is Walter Spinks! I used to hate him, but I didn't want him to get killed. It says his body will be brought home for burial next week." Maggie sighed and folded the paper. "Aunt Lillian, I'm so scared for JD. I don't know what I'll do if he gets killed." Tears filled her eyes and slowly rolled down her cheeks.

Aunt Lillian put her hand on Maggie's shoulder. "Well, Honey, let's not think about it. No sense worrying over something that ain't even happened."

Maggie wiped her eyes and finished the cocoa "I guess you're right, but I can't help worrying. I guess I'm closer to JD than anyone else in the world–even closer than to Bud. If something happens to him, I know I'll just die."

"I know." Aunt Lillian patted her on the shoulder. "You must be tired. Get ready for bed. I'll fix the sofa for you." They both stood and Aunt Lillian put her arms around Maggie and held her for a long time.

* * *

When Ray picked her up the next day shortly before dark, Maggie blinked in surprise when she saw Kenny in the truck. She squeezed herself into the front seat and slammed the door. When her father headed the truck in the opposite direction from home, she asked, "Where're we going?"

"I have to pick up something. Kenny come to help load it."

Soon they arrived at an old building that looked like it might have been a church. Ray backed the truck toward the steps where a man dressed in a long overcoat sat, a knit cap pulled down low on his forehead. He rose when they got out of the truck and stuck out his hand. "Howdy, Mr. Martin. I begun to think you wasn't coming. It's about to get too dark for us to see inside. There ain't no electricity here."

"Told you I'd be here. This here's my nephew Kenny and my daughter Maggie. They can help us load it."

"Glad to make your acquaintance. Name's Harry Brock." He led the way inside the building. In the dim light Maggie could see a few rough benches on either side of a big potbellied stove. A rickety-looking pulpit stood in front of a window with cardboard covering a broken pane. Harry Brock walked to the front and pulled a tarpaulin from an old upright piano.

"My wife took good care of this piano as long as she lived. She kept it covered to keep out the dust and she kept it tuned even after they quit having services here. It's in good shape even if it's old. She'd be glad to see somebody get some good out of it."

Maggie, still puzzled, watched with fascination as her father pulled a roll of money from his overalls and slowly counted out one hundred dollars, much of it in ones. Even in the near darkness, Maggie could see the twinkle in his eyes when he looked at her and grinned. "I've looked for a piano I could buy for my daughter for years. I'm much obliged to you, Mr. Brock, for letting us have this. We'll take good care of it. My daughter plays so pretty. Maybe you can come to our church sometime and hear her play."

"I'd like that." Mr. Brock went to the back side of the piano. "I think we can just roll her to the door. Then we'll have to lift her down the steps and into the truck."

They shoved some of the benches aside to get the piano past the old stove. When they reached the door, each took a corner and with much huffing and puffing managed to get the piano into the truck. Ray covered it with a tarp and tied it to the wooden side boards.

Once they moved slowly down the dirt road to the highway, Maggie leaned around Kenny. "Daddy, does Betty Lou know about this?"

"No, I didn't tell nobody except Kenny. I wanted to surprise her."

"You mean you didn't even tell Mama?"

"If she'd knowed I had this much money, she'd wanted to pay the funeral bill." Ray steered carefully around a curve so the piano wouldn't shift. "Ever since I knew Betty Lou could play so good, I told Mrs. Lewis I wanted her to have a piano of her own. I been saving a little here and a little there for over two years. I kept it hid in the smokehouse. Mrs. Lewis told me a month ago about Mr. Brock wanting to sell the piano in that old church building. I finally got the last of the money yesterday."

Maggie leaned forward so she could see her father's face in the lights of the dashboard. "But, Daddy, where'll we put it? There's no room in our house."

"We'll have to move some stuff out, I guess."

"Mama'll have a fit."

"Well, we'll figure out something."

Maggie stared out into the darkness. She knew the piano would please and surprise Betty Lou, but she couldn't help thinking that no one had ever peeled off one hundred dollars for her.

When they got home, Ray had Maggie open the barnyard gate and carefully maneuvered the truck through the pasture to the back of the house. "It's too heavy to carry up all those steps."

Hearing the motor and seeing the truck lights at the back brought everyone outdoors with choruses of "What's that you got there?" "What are you doing?" "What's in the truck?"

Ray led Betty Lou to the back of the truck and let down the tailgate. "Climb up there and untie that rope." He put the beam of a flashlight on the knots so she could see to get them undone. "Now, throw off the tarp."

"It's a piano!" Everyone began talking at once. Betty Lou stared at the piano. She gently rubbed the wood on the front and turned toward Ray. "Is this for us?"

"It's for you, Betty Lou. It's your own piano." Ray grinned.

"Oh, Daddy!" Betty Lou took one step to the back of the truck and threw herself into Ray's arms, almost knocking him off his feet.

Corie Mae, carrying Mary Helen on her hip, moved to the back of the truck to get a better view of the piano. She looked at Ray. "Where did this come from?" Ray just pointed at the piano, but didn't say anything. "Well, it ain't coming in my house. We ain't got no room for it. And besides, I ain't having all that racket going on with kids banging on it all day." She carried Mary Helen to the back porch. "All you kids get back inside. It's too cold out here."

Ray sighed and patted Betty Lou's back. "Don't worry, Honey. We'll figure out something." He gave Stuart a little nudge. "Climb up there and cover it back up. We'll let her set here till morning when we can see better."

As it turned out, Kenny suggested moving the piano into his house. Most of the time, he lived alone since Aunt Opal was often away nursing sick people. "Aunt Lillian's room is empty, and Betty Lou can come over and practice when she wants." Then Stuart got the idea of moving in with Kenny so Jay could have his bed upstairs. Aunt Opal agreed to both plans. She said since Kenny ate so many meals at Corie Mae's table, it was only fair that they do something in return, but she did have some rules. They could not use the front room, and they had to clean the whole house at least once each week.

Soon Opal's empty bedroom where they moved the piano became a place of escape for all the older children. Stuart had taught himself to play Great-grandma Campbell's mandolin. JD had sent Kenny a guitar for Christmas. Betty Lou began teaching Jeannie to play the piano. By the time of the annual talent show at school, they could play and sing "Tennessee Waltz" and "Goodnight Irene." When they weren't making music, they listened to the radio and read Kenny's comic books, which Corie Mae would not allow in her house.

Working around Corie Mae's prohibitions and objections became easier for all the children as they had become more skilled at devious manipulations. After Ray got the old truck, they would first persuade him to take them to an activity and then would simply tell Corie Mae, "Daddy's taking us to the play at school," or whatever the event was.

* * *

Maggie's skill as a basketball player and the team's ability to work together had improved considerably. Her team had won a slot in the regional tournament the last week in February. Bud planned to come from college to take in the tournament games. Maggie's father agreed to take all the children to see Maggie play. At first, Corie Mae objected, but finally allowed all the children to go except four-year-old Jay and little Mary Helen.

The last game of the tournament, Maggie's team played for the championship. When the team came out for warm up, Maggie searched the gym until she spotted her family sitting high in the bleachers and waved to them. Junior stood up and, placing his hands around his mouth like a megaphone yelled, "Yeah Maggie!" Maggie also located Bud who blew her a kiss.

Their opponent was Nemo, but the aggressive center who had caused Maggie to be thrown out of the game a year ago had graduated along with four others of their best players. Coach Moore took Maggie out of the game during the last quarter to allow some of the other girls to play, and they still won by eight points. Maggie stood proudly with her teammates as they received the trophy.

After the game, Bud and Maggie drove around for a little while, but because it was so late, Bud soon took her home. He opened the car door for her and pulled her into a close embrace. His kiss was short because they both knew Corie Mae probably watched them from her bedroom window. In the bright moonlight, they could see their breath freezing in front of their faces. Maggie shivered.

"Better get you inside before you freeze. I'll pick you up for church in the morning and take you to the café for lunch." He hugged her to him as they climbed the steps to the porch.

"Thank you for coming to see the games. Seems like it's been a long time since you were home for Christmas break." Maggie pinched him lightly on the cheek. "I thought maybe you had forgotten about me."

Bud grinned. "Not a chance." He gave her another quick peck on the lips. "Get in the house before you freeze your behind off. I'll see you tomorrow."

After lunch the next day, Bud drove Maggie to Miller's Falls. They walked along the creek talking of various things. Bud comforted her when she got teary speaking of her fear for JD's safety. She turned to him then, gave him a kiss and asked, "Will you be my date for the Junior-Senior Banquet this year?"

"Now that's a date you can count on, Baby. I'll knock the stuffing out of anyone else who tries to be your date!" Maggie laughed. Maggie began to shiver from the cold, and Bud led her back to the car. He started the motor and turned on the heater.

After a few more minutes of hugs and kisses, Maggie pulled away and looked at Bud. "I've noticed your letters don't come as often as they did last quarter."

The muscles in Bud's jaw contracted. "You're right. I've gotten busy with stuff and neglected to write. I'm sorry."

Maggie held his eyes with hers. "Should you be telling me what's keeping you so busy?"

Bud finally looked down at his hands and drew a long breath. "Maggie, you're my best friend. I want that for always." He switched off the motor. The silence of the woods surrounding them seemed ominous. A bright cardinal flew into a tree beside the car, cocked his head, and looked at them with his black eye.

Bud took Maggie's hand and looked into her eyes. "You're right. I do need to tell you something. In fact, that's why I wanted to take you to lunch and find a place where we could talk in privacy." He took another deep breath. "Maggie, I hope someday we can be more than best friends." He brushed her cheek with the back of his hand. "But I think we're both young and need to have other relationships before we make any lasting promises." He paused and looked away. "I have dated a couple of girls on the campus. They can't hold a candle to you, but seeing them has made me realize I want to date other girls. I think you should date some other guys too." He squeezed her hand. "I will be very jealous of them, though."

Maggie pulled her hand away, opened the car door and got out. She began to run down the path beside the creek toward the falls. She had not been willing to admit it, but she noticed Bud had been less attentive to her during his Christmas break. Now she could pretend no more. *He wants to date other girls, but he will be jealous of any boys I date. Doesn't seem fair.* Standing by the falls, feeling the mist spraying her face, she remembered how last year she had wondered if this cord might be broken. She mused that ties she wished she could sever held fast, while those ties she wanted to hold on to kept breaking. Deep down she agreed with Bud–they were both young, but at the same time she felt like someone had slammed a door in her face. She heard the crunching of leaves as Bud walked toward her.

He stood beside her for a time watching the water rush over the falls. Finally, he tugged her to him and looked into her eyes. "Maggie, I don't mean to hurt you. I respect you more than I can say. I do want us to always be friends."

"I understand." Maggie picked some lint off his coat collar. "I just feel at the moment that I've lost the best trophy I ever won. But I will always be proud that I was your girl for a while." She tried to smile, and in spite of herself a tear slipped down her cheek.

Bud wiped the tear away with his gloved finger. "If you ever need a friend, I'll be there. I do want to be your date for the Junior-Senior Banquet. But if you decide you want to ask someone else, I'll understand." He pulled her toward him and held her.

Maggie swallowed and opened her eyes wide to stop the tears, then slipping from his embrace began to run. "I'll race you to the car."

* * *

Mary Ann had been very sympathetic when she learned that Bud was dating others. Maggie felt the depressing effects of the cold and darkness of winter more keenly than in other years, and she knew it was not altogether due to the weather. However, by mid-April, spring had come to the holler again, and Maggie's spirits lifted.

Bud still wrote an occasional letter, and she looked forward to going to the Junior-Senior Banquet with him in a couple of weeks. She had received no more letters from JD, but she wrote him every week anyway. On this day as she walked home from the school bus stop, she felt like skipping. Junior said, "Maggie, what's the big hurry? Don't go so fast, I can't keep up."

"Sorry, Little Brother. This gorgeous weather just makes me feel like dancing."

"You better not be dancing. Mama says it's the Devil in people that makes them dance."

Betty Lou, walking beside Kenny, said, "We're learning to square dance in gym class. I think it's fun. I don't think it has anything to do with the Devil. But, Junior, you better not tell Mama."

"Okay. I won't."

After Maggie changed her clothes, preparing to do the evening chores, she heard a car. She ran to the front porch to see, and clutched her throat when she saw a khaki sedan with U. S. Army painted on it going past. That could mean only one thing. She jumped off the porch and ran down the steps to the road. She raced into the yard, as a soldier knocked on the door. Aunt Opal opened the door and came onto the porch. She looked at the soldier and sank into the porch swing. "No. Don't tell me. Please, not my JD."

The soldier stood ramrod straight in front of her. "Mrs. Campbell, I am Sergeant Jones. It is my duty to deliver this message to you from the Department of Defense." He handed her an envelope which she threw on the ground.

"I don't want to hear it." She bent forward and hid her face in her skirt.

Maggie picked up the envelope. "Aunt Opal, let me read it for you." When she didn't object, Maggie opened the envelope, unfolded the paper and read in a shaky voice. "This is to inform you that CPL James Douglas Campbell was killed in action in Korea 25 March 1952."

Opal didn't raise her head, but began to wail. Maggie tossed the paper onto the swing beside Aunt Opal and then screamed, "I knew this would happen!" She began to run toward the ridge. Arriving breathless and holding her side in pain, she sat on the big boulder at the back of the ledge and let the tears fall. She slowly slid to the ground and lay face down sobbing into her folded arms. After a while she got up, picked up a handful of rocks and began to fling them at the old dead pine tree that somehow still managed to be standing. She threw with all her might as if she would knock the tree down with a stone.

"Why did it have to happen?" She screamed to the sky that had turned pink with the setting sun. "He was good. He didn't deserve to die." She shook her fist. "I hate you, God!" She sank down and lay on the big rock crying the bitterest tears of her whole life. Shadows began to fill up the holler, and she roused herself. She had chores to do. When she started down the path, Audie Lee stepped out of the clump of mountain laurel and lurched toward her. He held out his hand displaying the necklace on his palm. He grunted and gently placed the necklace in her hand. He looked into her eyes while he closed her fingers around the necklace, then turned and staggered around the clump of laurel disappearing into the woods.

Maggie stared at the necklace. The years of being jostled around in his tobacco sacks had polished it to a brilliance that surprised her. Seeing the beautiful thing that Johnny Ray had wanted so badly caused her to begin weeping again with silent tears for all the broken cords: Elsie Mae, Johnny Ray, Bud, and now JD. She began to descend the ridge with slow steps and a heavy heart.

* * *

Dear Bud,

JD was killed in Korea and his body is being shipped home. His funeral will be Saturday, April 26. I need a friend.

Maggie.

She had forgotten when she wrote the letter that the funeral coincided with the Junior-Senior Banquet. She moved through the next few days like a zombie. Some days she went to school, but sat dazed in class forgetting to prepare assignments. Some days she stayed home to help Aunt Opal clean house and prepare the front room for the viewing. Uncle Thomas and Uncle WC came home, neighbors brought in food, relatives came from Kentucky.

On the evening of the wake, Maggie slipped away and climbed the ridge. It had been a beautiful day, unseasonably warm with clear skies. She stood on the ledge looking down the holler at the cars making their way to JD's house until the yard had filled up. Men stood in the yard among the cars smoking and talking quietly. The women, many carrying a dish of food, went inside. Maggie had watched earlier in the afternoon as the hearse arrived, and members of the local American Legion dressed in their uniforms had carried the flag-draped coffin into the front room. Reverend Lewis had spoken a few words of comfort, read the 23rd Psalm, and offered a prayer. Maggie watched it all with a heavy heart but dry eyes. She thought she had shed all the tears she had.

Now standing near the front of the ledge, she got a glimpse of someone on the path below. Soon the person moved into a clear spot, and Maggie saw Bud. She flew down the path and jumped into his arms. As he held her close, the tears she thought had dried up began to flow again.

Bud stayed beside her until late that evening, holding her hand, letting her cry on his shoulder, even sometimes shedding tears of his own. He came the next day and took her to the church for the funeral. He sat with his arm around her during the service and stood close for the ceremony at the grave. When the American Legion members gave the three gun salute, she flinched with each crack of the rifles, but Bud steadied her. The sad wail of "Taps," played by a boy from the high school band, sent a knife through her heart, and she turned to walk away. Bud led her to his car, took her home, and stayed close by her until late that night.

He came the next day to say goodbye, and they walked up to the ledge, where they stood looking out over the holler, where the fresh greens of spring had covered the hillsides. Maggie loved this view at all times of the year, but spring was her favorite. She turned a sad smile toward Bud. "Thank you for coming."

"I'll always be here if you need me."

Maggie picked up a rock. "I bet you can't hit that dead tree down there." Bud took the stone from her and threw it toward the tree, but it fell short by a yard. Maggie picked up another and as always her aim was true. It bounced off the tree and fell to the ground.

"Bull's eye!" Bud yelled. "Do you remember that time at the falls when JD kept trying to hit that bottle on the other side of the creek and you zinged it with the first try?"

"Yeah. That was the day you said you wanted me to be your girl."

Bud looked at her intently. She hoped he was going to change his mind and say he still wanted her to be his girl. But he shoved his fists into his pockets and took several steps away. He stopped and turned to face her. "Hey, I'm sorry our date to the Junior-Senior Banquet got messed up."

"Me too. I had really looked forward to it. But I didn't feel right to try to go to the banquet on the day of JD's funeral."

Bud walked back toward her a few steps. "I didn't want to go under those circumstances either." Then he grinned and those dimples Maggie loved punctuated his cheeks. "I was just thinking maybe I could be your date for next year."

Maggie moved closer to him. "You've got a date, for certain! Let's just hope nothing like this happens next year."

Bud leaned toward her, and she thought maybe he would kiss her, but he kept his hands in his pockets and slowly drew himself up to his full height. "What do you have planned for the summer?"

"I'm not sure. Miss Erickson has arranged for me to have an interview with Gilbert Carson who has a law office in town. She says he wants someone to do office work about three days a week. I'm supposed to go to his office at 11:00 Monday morning."

"That sounds great. Have you talked with your folks about it?"

"No, I thought I'd wait until I see how the interview goes. I know Mama will say no. I just hope Daddy will think it's a good idea." Maggie kicked a rock off the cliff and watched it drop to the ground below. "What about you? What are you doing this summer?"

"I'm going to work for my uncle again. He wants me to change my major to Business and take over the store when I graduate. They have only one daughter and she's not interested in the retail business. She's getting married in June and plans to move to New York with her husband who has some big job in finance. My folks think it's a good opportunity for me."

"In your letters last summer you seemed rather bored with it. Do you really think you'll like it?"

"Well, last summer I did the grunt work. Being manager will be a whole different ball game. Yeah, I think I'll like it."

"Good. I hope you turn it into a million dollar enterprise!" She put her hand on his arm.

He took his hands out of his pockets and covered her hand with his own. "Maggie, I have to drive all the way to Cookeville tonight, and I also need to study for a test in Economics tomorrow. I'm sorry, but I'm going to have to say goodbye." He put pressure on her hand. "Thank you for needing me this weekend. I hope I can always come when you say you need a friend." He took her hand in his and led her to the path. Once they reached her house, he didn't come inside, but rather quickly got into his car and drove away.

Maggie watched the car until it rounded the curve. She slowly climbed the steps to the porch where her father stood just outside the door. He put his arm around her shoulder and pulled her close. "Sometimes life hurts, Sunshine."

* * *

As Maggie had predicted, her mother strongly opposed her taking a job in the lawyer's office. "You can't never tell who all might come into a law office. What if some drunk comes in when Mr. Carson is out somewhere? Besides, I need you here to help us like always."

Fortunately, Maggie had already talked with her father who had asked several questions and finally agreed that it was a good opportunity for her. Maggie supposed her mother had realized the decision had already been made because she stopped protesting, but announced, "Nothing good will come of this. Just wait and see!"

Mr. Carson's office was above the Five and Ten a few doors away from the café. Beginning in June, Maggie's father took her to work on Wednesday mornings and picked her up on Friday evenings. She stayed at Aunt Lillian's at night and had free time in the evenings to be with her friends. Mary Ann had gotten her driver's license and often drove her father's pickup into town in the evening. They would visit other friends, hang out at the drug store, sometimes go to a movie. Maggie enjoyed more freedom than ever before.

The work challenged her, but she found it interesting. Mr. Carson had quite a backlog of filing and reports. Almost every day he had Maggie take dictation for a letter or a legal document. The legal terms sometimes baffled her, but he patiently helped her learn. After a couple of weeks, he told her he had increased the amount of her paycheck to match the quality of her work.

One Wednesday in mid-July after she had worked for six weeks, she opened the door to her office and saw a young man sitting at her desk. He grinned at her. "Oh, is this your desk?" He stood. "I'm sorry." He stepped away and made room for Maggie to pass with a flourishing gesture of his arm. "Be my guest, Miss...er?"

"Maggie Martin. Who are you?"

"Jack Carson, at your service, Ma'am." He pretended to doff a hat and bowed deeply.

"I'm sorry? I don't understand."

Just then Mr. Carson walked through the door. "Good morning, Maggie. Did you meet my nephew? He's a second-year law student at the University of Kentucky and will serve an internship with me this summer. I asked him to work on that Burton case. I hope you'll be able to do the secretarial work for both of us. If it is more than you can do in three days, we may have to hire you for another day."

"Sure, Mr. Carson. I'll do my best."

Mr. Carson nodded and smiled at her. He motioned to Jack. "Come with me. I've got some people you need to meet. We should be back before noon, Maggie. Is there anything you need before we go?"

"No, thank you, sir. I need to finish typing the briefs you gave me on Friday."

Maggie watched as Jack followed his uncle out the door. Before moving out of sight, Jack turned, waved, and gave her an exaggerated wink. "Toodleloo."

Not knowing what to make of this guy, Maggie tried to put him out of her mind as she started her work. She did not understand why, but he made her feel uncomfortable. Pretty good looking, though. Wavy blond hair and blue eyes. She scolded herself for continuing to think about him when she wanted to concentrate on her work.

After work that day, Maggie and Mary Ann went to the drug store to get a root beer float. They sat at the soda fountain when Jack walked in. "Well, who do we have here? My secretary and her friend. Won't you introduce me, Maggie?"

Maggie turned to face Mary Ann. "Mary Ann, I'd like you to meet Jack Carson. He's Mr. Carson's nephew who will work in our office for a few weeks. Jack, meet my best friend, Mary Ann Collins."

"Ah, nice to meet you, Mary Ann." He took a stool beside her. "So, tell me, Mary Ann, what does a fellow do for fun in this town?"

"Not much, I'm afraid."

Maggie made a production of noisily slurping up the last of her float. "Well, that's the end of that. Are you finished too, Mary Ann?" Maggie gave her arm an urgent pull.

Mary Ann quickly hopped off her stool and as they headed for the door, looked over her shoulder. "Bye, Jack. Nice to meet you." Once outside, Mary Ann said, "Wow! What was that?"

"I don't know what it is about him, but I get nervous when he's around. He only started working this morning. Mr. Carson kept him busy most of the day, and I didn't see much of him, thank goodness."

"Well, I think he's a good looking guy." Mary Ann rolled her eyes and grinned.

Maggie ignored Mary Ann's comment. "I heard a bunch of town kids are getting up a softball game in the school yard. Want to go down there?"

On Friday morning, Jack came in to Maggie's office and sat on the corner of her desk. "How's Miss Maggie this morning?"

"I'm fine, Jack. Did you have some work you need me to do?"

"Well, yes, I do, but I forgot to bring it with me. I came in to see if you would go to the movies with me tonight."

Maggie tried to keep the shock off her face and out of her voice. "Thanks, Jack. It's kind of you to ask, but my family has plans for me when I get home tonight. I'm sorry." She picked up her stenographer's pad. "Did you need me to take a letter, or was it something else?"

Jack sighed. "It's just some envelopes I need you to address. I'll go get them."

Maggie worried all weekend about what she could do to discourage Jack's attention. She thought about talking to Aunt Lillian, but didn't get a good opportunity. She knew she shouldn't mention Jack to her mother. Corie Mae would make her quit at once. Mary Ann thought she should not worry. So what if Jack flirted with her. He would only be in town a few more weeks. What harm could he cause in such a short time?

About noon the next Wednesday, Mr. Carson asked Maggie to come into his office and take some dictation. When he had finished dictating four letters, he stood. "Oh, by the way, Maggie. I meant to tell you earlier. I'm going to Nashville tomorrow. I'll be gone the rest of the week. I'd like you to try to get that stack of filing caught up while I'm gone. You've really made lots of headway with that. I don't know what we would have done without you this summer. You've been a God-send."

"Thank you, sir. I'll do my best to get it completed in the next two days."

Jack didn't come into the office at all that day. Mr. Carson said he was doing some research over at the courthouse. Later that night when she mentioned to Mary Ann that Mr. Carson would be gone the rest of the week, Mary Ann raised her eyebrows and gave Maggie her wide-eyed look. "Oh my! That means you and Jack will be all alone." Maggie sucked in a quick breath and frowned. "Oh, Maggie, don't worry. He won't do nothing. I don't know why you're so afraid of him. I just wish he'd ask me to go out with him."

Maggie dreaded going to work the next morning. When she unlocked the door and went into her office, she saw a dozen red roses in a vase in the middle of her desk. She walked around and sat in her desk chair. Maggie noticed a card clipped to the ribbon. "We appreciate all the work you do for us." There was no name. Mr. Carson must have put them there before he left town. She smiled. She leaned over and took in the light fragrance. She smiled again.

Jack came into the office only a few minutes before quitting time. He carried an armload of papers. "Hey, Maggie. Wow! What pretty roses."

Maggie smiled. "Yes, they are pretty. I appreciate them very much."

"Well, I'm pooped. I had to stand all day searching through files trying to find all the information for Uncle Gilbert. I'm leaving early. See you tomorrow." And he left.

Maggie opened the mail that had come that day and placed it on Mr. Carson's desk, just as he had trained her to do. She saw two checks, which she entered in the ledger, and clipped together with a deposit slip. When she went back to her office and saw the roses, she smiled again. She took her purse from the bottom drawer, turned out the lights and locked the door.

Maggie worked feverishly the next day filing the documents. She fully expected to get the "to file" bin empty before quitting time. About four o'clock she stood in front of the bank of file cabinets when Jack came in. He had taken off his tie and unbuttoned his shirt collar. He held his coat slung over his shoulder with one finger. His blond hair had slipped down over his left eye, and his smile showed a mouth full of very white teeth. In spite of herself, Maggie was struck by his good looks. She forced a smile. "Hi, Jack. Did you have another busy day over at the courthouse?"

"Nah. I guess you could say I played hooky today. 'When the cat's away, the mice will play.'" He hung his coat on the coat rack behind the door and came over to the files. "Say, did you really like the roses?"

"Yes, they're beautiful. I'll take them home tonight so my family can see them."

"I thought you'd like them. That's why I got them for you."

Maggie held a document in midair and stared at Jack. "I thought your uncle left the roses for me."

"No, my cute little secretary, I'm the one." He moved a little closer to her. "I came by to see if you wanted to give me a proper 'thank you.'"

Maggie put the paper into the file and pushed the drawer closed. "I do appreciate them. No one ever gave me roses before. Thank you, very much." She picked up the next paper to be filed.

"Oh, I was looking for more thanks than that." He stood behind her and put his hand on her right shoulder. "I think I deserve a little kiss." He turned her around to face him, and that's when Maggie realized he was drunk. She twisted out of his grasp and stepped away from him.

"Jack, I don't mean to be rude, but I don't want to kiss you. Now, if you will take your coat and leave, I can get this filing finished before quitting time." She moved to the last file cabinet and opened the drawer.

Jack stuck out his lower lip the way Johnny Ray used to when he did not get his way. "Maggie, you've really hurt my feelings. I was trying to be nice to you. Why don't you like me?" He moved behind her again and put his arms around her waist.

Maggie tried to break out of his embrace, but he held her tight. She stomped his foot, and he yelled, but didn't turn her loose. His hands moved up to her breasts. She butted his nose with the back of her head. When he screamed and turned her loose, she pushed him backwards and started for the door, but he made a lunge for her, grabbing the back of her blouse. She jerked to get loose, popping all buttons off, and leaving her blouse in Jack's grip, ran for the door, down the steps and into the street. Hugging herself to hide her bra, and with tears streaming down her face, she raced as hard as she could to the café straight through to the kitchen where Aunt Lillian stood at the stove stirring a pot of soup.

"Why, Maggie, what on earth has happened?" Aunt Lillian wrapped a clean towel around her and led her upstairs to the apartment where Maggie explained everything. Ray heard the story when he came to pick Maggie up and immediately went to the sheriff's office. The sheriff accompanied Ray and Maggie to Mr. Carson's office where they found the door standing ajar. The office stood empty, but someone had smashed the vase of roses against the wall and scattered the unfiled documents about the room. Maggie wanted to clean up the mess, but the sheriff told her to lock up and leave everything just like it was.

The next Monday, Mr. Carson came to Maggie's house and apologized profusely explaining that Jack had left town and he had been unable to contact him. He begged Maggie to come back to work, but Corie Mae would not hear of it. "I was against it from the start. I said nothing good would come of this, and I was right. An office with only men is no place for a young girl to work."

Maggie had mixed feelings when she heard Ray tell Mr. Carson, "I agree with my wife. Maggie won't be coming back to work." While she could see her mother's point, especially after what had happened, she had enjoyed her job and was sorry to have to give it up. Finally Mr. Carson persuaded Ray to let Maggie accept a check for the wages she would have received if she had worked the rest of the summer. A few weeks later, Ray told Maggie he had checked with the sheriff's office, and a judge had issued a warrant for Jack's arrest.

CHAPTER 10

Harlan, Kentucky–June 25, 1892...Finally got to go to Harlan. Mama and Papa delighted to meet the 4 grandchildren. Johnny 12, Jimmy10, Helen 6. Little Doug 2 is the prettiest child I ever saw.
(Diary of Mary Louise Campbell)

Senior Year 1952-53

"Hey, Maggie! Hurry! Got some exciting news," Mary Ann jiggled her hands impatiently as Maggie climbed the school steps where Mary Ann waited. "Gosh, that's a pretty dress." She rubbed the fabric of Maggie's sleeve between her thumb and index finger. "Did your mom make it?"

"No. Bought it with money I made this summer." Maggie grinned and the girls moved along with the crowd into the hallway. "Now, what's this big news?"

"Oh, wait until you see him."

"See who? What are you talking about?"

"The new coach. He's sooooo good looking."

Maggie stopped and stared at Mary Ann with squinted eyes and a worried frown. "We have a new coach? What happened to Mr. Moore?"

"I guess he went to a bigger school over near Nashville. Least that's what I heard. But this new guy–oh Lordy, he's the best looking man I've seen in a long time."

Maggie slowly walked down the hallway, head down, shoulders drooping. "I've had it with good looking men. I can't believe Coach Moore would leave our senior year–especially after our good season.."

"Hello girls." Eddie Jones, classmate since first grade, opened the locker next to Maggie and Mary Ann.

"Hi, Eddie. You going to have the locker next to ours?" Maggie and Mary Ann began stacking their books into the locker they shared.

"Looks that way. Hey Maggie, what's with the sad face?"

"Mary Ann just told me Coach Moore has gone to another school."

"Yeah, it's true. I met the new coach at football practice last week."

Mary Ann tapped Eddie on the shoulder. "I saw him getting out of his car a few minutes ago. He looks like a movie star."

Eddie slammed his locker door. "Let's just hope he knows a lot about football and basketball." Eddie tucked his notebook under his arm. "I'm going to English first period. Where're you all headed?"

"We have English, too." Mary Ann started toward the restroom. "Save me a seat. I'll be there in a minute."

Eddie and Maggie walked into the classroom where classmates greeted one another in a hullabaloo of excited voices. When the bell rang, Miss Margaret closed the door and welcomed the senior class. Maggie opened her notebook and sighed. *Losing Coach Moore doesn't seem like a very good start to this year.*

* * *

Later at lunch, Maggie and Mary Ann sat at a table with several girls on the basketball team. When the new coach walked into the room, Mary Ann waved. "Coach Matthews." Everyone in the cafeteria turned to watch. Maggie focused on the slender, well-muscled man as he walked toward their table, gleaming white teeth dominating his smile. He was good looking, Maggie had to admit. His brown eyes and curly black hair reminded her of JD.

Mary Ann made a sweeping motion with her arm toward everyone at the table. "We're all on the basketball team."

"Well, I'm glad to meet all you all. I understand you had an undefeated season last year. I'm expecting another good year."

"We can't wait until time to start basketball practice." Mary Ann batted her eyes as she looked up at the coach who stood behind her chair. "This is Maggie Martin. She holds the record for the highest number of points scored in one season in the history of the school." Mr. Matthews smiled at Maggie and nodded. "I'm Mary Ann Collins, a forward." She then introduced all the other girls and told their playing positions.

"I'm mighty glad to know I have such a good looking team. Enjoy your lunch." He beamed his white teeth again and walked away.

Mary Ann sighed loudly and placed her hands on her chest. "I think my heart's going to jump out of my body."

"You sound like a love-sick puppy. He's the coach, for goodness sakes!" Ulla Dean scolded.

Maggie shook her head. She had never seen Mary Ann so goo-goo-eyed over a member of the opposite sex–even worse than last summer when she met Jack Carson. Later back at their locker, Maggie asked Eddie what he thought of the new coach.

"Don't know. It takes a little bit to get used to someone new. But from what I've seen so far, I reckon he's okay." Eddie waved and walked away. "See you later."

* * *

Maggie had agreed to work at the café on Monday, Wednesday, and Friday evenings and all day on Saturday. "Just until basketball season starts," Maggie had explained to Mrs. Jenkins, who agreed that they could negotiate new hours when the time came. Maggie had asked Jeannie and Stuart to take over the chores of milking and feeding the livestock when she stayed in town. At first her mother protested, but when Maggie began giving each of them two dollars each week from her tips, Cora Mae quit complaining.

The following Saturday, Mr. Matthews showed up at the café for lunch. Maggie directed him to a booth and handed him a menu. "Welcome to City Cafe, Mr. Matthews."

"Let's see. You're Maggie, right?"

Maggie nodded. "I'll get you a glass of ice water while you look over the menu." When Maggie set the glass in front of him, Mr. Matthews covered her hand with his and held on.

"So, you're the basketball star?"

"I do my best, Coach." Maggie tugged gently on her hand, but he held fast.

"If we're going to make a good team, you and I must get to know each other really well."

Maggie jerked her hand loose. "I'll try my best on the basketball court, and I think that's all that's needed." Maggie marched into the kitchen and asked Carolyn, the other waitress, to take Mr. Matthews' order.

The next week, when Maggie met Mr. Matthews in the hallway at school, she avoided his eyes, though she said "Good Morning, Coach" when he spoke to her. Mary Ann, on the other hand, turned to walk down the hallway with him, chatting about how good she thought the football team had shaped up. Maggie suggested to Mary Ann that she was being too forward, but Mary Ann sniffed, threw back her head, and did not speak to Maggie the rest of the day. Over the next few weeks, Mary Ann spent less and less time with Maggie, but used every opportunity to flirt with Coach Matthews.

We've been best friends since first grade. I can't believe she would break up our friendship. But Maggie had little time to fret over the rift between them. With putting in so many hours at the café and working in the school office one hour each day, she felt pushed to get all her assignments prepared. Since Mary Ann no longer dogged her steps, Maggie noticed she often walked to class with Eddie. One day he asked Maggie if she had seen his car.

"No. I didn't know you had a car."

"I bought it with money I made last summer working on construction for Mr. Williams. I'd like to give you a ride sometime."

"Sure. I'd like that. Maybe next week when we're out of school for the Teachers' Institute."

As they reached the history classroom, Mary Ann came rushing up. "Hi, Eddie. Hi Maggie. You all ready for this quiz?" Mary Ann didn't wait for an answer, but chose a seat two rows away from Maggie. *At least she spoke.*
\

* * *

After school one day in late fall, Maggie gathered her books and prepared to walk to the café.

"Maggie, you got a minute?" Miss Erickson called from her desk as Maggie passed by the door.

"Sure, Miss Erickson." Maggie came into the room and sat at a desk in the front row.

Miss Erickson smiled. "I've been wondering, Maggie, if you've given thought to the kind of job you'd like to have after graduation."

Maggie stared at the floor as she considered her answer. She looked up then and smiled. "I really enjoyed working for Mr. Carson last summer. I think I'd like to work in a law office."

"I'm glad you said that because I think you would do well as a legal secretary. However, if you really want to get a job in a larger law firm, you need to learn more about the workings of an attorney's office. Maybe you and I could work together after school on a legal secretarial course."

"But Miss Erickson, won't that make you late going home?"

"Don't worry about that, Maggie. I have a good friend who teaches the legal secretarial courses at Knox Business College. I'll contact her to send us some materials. We'll start as soon as I hear from her."

"Thank you, Miss Erickson. I don't know what to say. I certainly don't expect you to go to this trouble for me."

"Miss Erickson smiled. "Maggie, I've never had a student who worked as hard and achieved as much as you. It pleases me to think I may have a small part in preparing you for a good job when you graduate. All the thanks I need is for you to do your very best." After only a week of study, Maggie realized that the way Mr. Carson had operated his law office was a far cry from the practices she was learning.

* * *

One day when they met at their locker, Mary Ann handed Maggie a post card she had received from Coach Matthews when he went to Knoxville for the teachers institute. It simply said "This is a good conference. See you next week. Love, Ken Matthews."

"Did you see how he signed it?" Mary Ann took the card from Maggie and hugged it to her chest. "Isn't that really great?"

"You don't want to know my opinion." Maggie took her American history book from the locker. Mary Ann pursed her lips, grabbed her notebook, and marched down the hall ahead of Maggie. A few days later, Ulla Dean told Maggie she had seen Mary Ann riding in Coach Matthews' car on Saturday.

"I don't understand her at all lately. We used to be such good friends, but now she hardly speaks to me. All she can talk about is Coach Matthews." Maggie 's voice cracked and she fought back tears.

"I don't like him. My brother's in his world history class and he says they don't do anything except play games. Jim says he has favorites that he gives good grades to and everyone else gets bad grades. I wonder where they found such an excuse for a teacher."

"I guess he did okay with the football team. They've won more than half their games. I just hope he knows something about girls' basketball." Maggie's smile was grim.

For the first few days after basketball practice started in November, Coach Matthews had them doing drills and running laps around the gym to build stamina. Once they started doing some scrimmaging, he watched them play for a few minutes, and then called Maggie to the sideline.

"Maggie, don't dribble away from the goal when you shoot."

"Why?"

"Because when you're moving away from the goal, you aren't in a position to rebound."

That made some sense to Maggie. She nodded her head. "Okay Coach, I'll try to remember that."

At the end of practice, Maggie approached the coach. "When I dribble toward the goal, I'm not in position to make my shot."

"So?"

"That's the shot that has earned our team a winning season. If it works, I don't understand why I should change it."

"But you aren't the coach, are you? If you want to be on this team, you'll have to do as the coach says." Burning with anger, Maggie turned and walked toward the dressing room.

For the next week, the coach taught them new plays. Maggie noticed that the new plays put Mary Ann in position to do most of the shooting. One day after practice, Mary Ann bragged, "He's going to make me the star player this year."

For their first game, they played Lawndale. Maggie tried hard to follow the new plays, but every time Mary Ann got the ball, she threw up a shot, which she missed more often than not. Aggressively rebounding, Maggie managed to prevent several turnovers, but the team play they had developed under Coach Moore's direction had disappeared. Realizing they were about to lose in the last quarter, Maggie reverted to her old pattern and started throwing up her famous hook shot every time she got the ball. She also made two foul shots to put them ahead.

The wild crowd started yelling "Go, Maggie, Go!" When Lawndale called a time out with only a minute left, Coach Matthews took Maggie out of the game. Noticing Maggie was not on the floor, the crowd began to yell, "We want Maggie! We want Maggie!" Lawndale tied the score with only seconds left, but fortunately, Mary Ann made a foul shot winning the game by one point.

In the locker room, Maggie stood silently beside her locker as Mary Ann boasted about winning the game. Ulla Dean gave Maggie a hug and whispered, "Don't listen to her. You're the one who won the game."

As Maggie hurried to leave the dressing room to catch the beginning of the boys' game, she heard Mary Ann tell one of the other players that Ken was going to take her home after the boys' game. Maggie knew Mr. and Mrs. Collins would not approve of Mary Ann's getting involved with the coach. But Mary Ann had been her best friend since first grade. She could not bring herself to betray her even though they had recently grown apart. *Maybe if I told Miss Erickson, Mary Ann wouldn't know I had blown the whistle.* She even thought about speaking to her own parents, but she knew if her mother found out what sort of person Mr. Matthews was, she would make Maggie quit the team. So she kept her concerns to herself.

In practice the next day, Coach Matthews stopped the warmup exercises and singled out Maggie. "I thought I would make you a team player. But, no, you had to hog the ball and show off with your fancy shots. On Friday night, Sandy will start in your place." Maggie eyes widened in disbelief, but she said nothing.

Ulla Dean moved to Maggie's side. "But Coach, if Maggie hadn't made those shots, we would've lost the game."

Coach Matthews scowled at her. "Well, if you can't accept my judgment, you can sit on the bench too. Now, let's get back to practice." Mary Ann laughed, but the other team members, dispirited and listless, resumed practice like a bunch of robots, all mechanical, no enthusiasm.

After the next game, which they lost, the coach singled out Maggie again, blaming her for their loss. Maggie could hold her anger no longer. "It's not my fault we lost. In a few weeks you have turned a championship team into a bunch of losers." Maggie's face was red and her voice became louder. "If you were a real coach, you would know how to help us get better instead of tearing down everything we've learned from Coach Moore. You've spent all your time trying to make your favorites look good." Maggie swallowed and wiped her forehead with the back of her hand. "If you're thinking you'll kick me off the team, you can forget it, because I'm quitting right now. I'll turn in my uniform tomorrow." She turned on her heel and headed for the dressing room.

Ulla Dean started after her. "Wait for me. I'm quitting too."

* * *

On Monday when Maggie came to work as the office assistant, the principal called her into his private area. "Maggie, I understand you quit the basketball team."

Maggie took a deep breath and shifted her weight from one foot to the other. "Yes, Mr. Adkins, I did quit the team."

"May I ask what brought that on?"

Maggie took another deep breath. "I guess Mr. Matthews and I just can't get along. He thinks I can't accept his coaching. He said it was my fault we lost the game Friday night."

"But you played only half the game. How could it be your fault?"

"I guess you'll have to ask him, Mr. Adkins. I thought it best for me to quit since we haven't been able to get along from the beginning."

"If he's willing, would you consider coming back on the team?"

"Thanks, Mr. Adkins, but I don't think so. I'm so angry at him I don't think we can ever work together."

Later that day, Eddie told Maggie the students in world history class had hatched a plot to set a trap for Mr. Matthews. "He gave them a question to answer for their assignment. The whole class agreed to copy word for word the same paragraph from the textbook as their answer. Then they will compare the grades he gives them." Eddie grinned. "I heard some parents are in on the plot too. They may just cook his goose!"

"Does he show favoritism to some of the boys on your team?"

"Yeah, but it's not as bad as he's treated you. I don't blame you for quitting, but I hear it's upset the Booster Club. They want you back on the team." Eddie leaned against Maggie's open locker door with his right hand resting on top of the door.

Maggie looked up at Eddie. "Wow, I didn't know anyone cared."

"Would you come back?"

"Not as long as he's the coach."

"That's too bad. Have you told your folks you quit?"

"I just told them I thought it was more important for me to work at the café. Mama seemed glad, but Daddy said he wished I hadn't quit. He's always lectured me about finishing what I start. But when I told him I had trouble keeping my grades up with all I had to do, he seemed satisfied."

Eddie stood up straight and put his hands in his hip pockets. "Hey, Maggie, how about going to the movies with me sometime?"

"Sure, Eddie. That would be fun. We'll have to find a time when I'm not working and you aren't playing ball."

"How about Sunday night. We could go to the drive-in over on the Clinton Highway."

Maggie hesitated. She knew her mother would not approve of her going to the movies at all and certainly not on a church night, but she didn't want to hurt Eddie's feelings. "I tell you what. You go to church with me on Sunday morning, and I'll go with you to the movies on Sunday night." *I just won't tell Mama where we are going.*

* * *

During the Christmas vacation, Maggie worked at the café every day except Christmas Day. Two days before Christmas she was surprised when Ray came into the café and ordered a hamburger. He asked Maggie if she had a minute. When he had taken a large bite, he looked at Maggie who sat in the booth opposite him drinking a Coke. He put his sandwich down, wiped his mouth with the back of his hand and swallowed. The way his large Adam's apple bobbed when he swallowed had always fascinated Maggie. Before he spoke, he took a drink of iced tea and his Adam's apple bobbed again. Maggie couldn't help smiling. Finally, he said, "Maggie, Larry Collins come to see me this morning. I guess Mary Ann didn't come home last night. She told her folks she planned to spend the night with you. Do you know anything about this?"

Maggie frowned. "No, Daddy. I haven't seen Mary Ann since last Friday. She hasn't told me anything." Maggie busied herself wiping the moisture off her glass with a napkin.

Ray took another bite. Then he reached across the table and took Maggie's hand. "Is there something else you should tell me?"

Maggie sighed. She looked at her father, then looked away before she began wiping at the moisture on her glass again. "I really don't know anything, Daddy. We haven't been very close since I quit the team." She paused and took a deep breath. "But I heard she's been going out with the basketball coach. Maybe she went somewhere with him."

186

"You mean the teacher? Why would she go out with him?"

Maggie pressed her lips together in a grimace. "Daddy, I don't know why. She just sort of went crazy about him from the first time she saw him. She flirted with him so much it embarrassed me, and when I tried to tell her it was not appropriate, she got mad at me."

Ray pushed his empty plate out of the way. "But you're sure you don't know where she spent last night?"

"I'm sure." Maggie looked directly at her father. "Daddy, I'm telling you the truth."

"Okay, Maggie. I wish I didn't have to go tell this to Larry. He's liable to go after this guy with his shotgun."

Maggie hadn't thought of that. She frowned in thought. "Daddy, maybe some of her other friends might know where she is. What if she wasn't with Mr. Matthews after all? Maybe before you tell Mr. Collins about the coach, we should ask some of her other friends."

"Who could we ask?"

"Sandy lives here in town. She and Mary Ann have been running around together lately. Maybe she knows something."

"Are you real busy? Could you take some time off to go with me?"

Maggie looked at the clock on the wall behind Ray. "Actually, I have to take a break from two o'clock to seven. I could go with you in half an hour."

When Maggie and her father pulled into Sandy's driveway, Mary Ann came to the door. "Are you looking for me?" She had pulled a blanket around her to cover her pajamas. Two other girls on the team peeped around her to see who was at the door. "We all spent the night here at Sandy's house."

Maggie pulled the screen door open wider and stepped closer. "When your parents found out you did not stay at my house last night, they got really worried."

Ray walked up the steps to the porch. "Why don't you let me take you home?"

Mary Ann frowned. "Just tell them I'm here at Sandy's and I'll be home later tonight." Then she stepped back into the room and closed the door.

Ray stood still with his mouth open for several seconds. Then he turned, walked down the steps, and opened the door to the truck. "Guess I'll go tell Larry where she's at, and if he wants to, he can come get her hisself."

Maggie got into the truck. "You going to tell him about the coach?"

Ray seemed to be mulling that thought as he backed the truck out into the street. "Maybe I'll wait till she has a chance to explain what she's doing. But I will tell him later."

When he dropped Maggie off back at the café, he patted her shoulder. "Thanks, Honey. I knew you would tell me the truth. I'm sorry you and Mary Ann have had a falling out."

"Thanks, Daddy. I'm sorry too." She smiled at him. "Don't forget to pick me up on Christmas Eve. We're closing the café at two o'clock. I want to be home for Christmas Day. I have presents for everyone."

"I'll be here, Sunshine."

The next day Maggie raised her eyebrows in surprise when Bud came into the café with a girl. They took a seat in Maggie's section. She gave them menus. "Hi, Bud. You're home for the holidays, I guess."

"Yes." He turned to the girl. "This is my best friend, Maggie Martin. I especially wanted you to meet her." Then he touched Maggie's hand. "Maggie, I'd like you to meet Donna Thornton."

Maggie smiled. "Any friend of Bud's is a friend of mine. I'm pleased to meet you." Maggie turned to see another table filling up. "I'll let you look over the menu and I'll be back shortly to take your order." Maggie felt quite awkward. She could think of nothing to say to Bud or his friend. Fortunately, several other customers came in, keeping her very busy.

Bud came to the cash register to pay the bill. "Maggie, may I come out to your house on Christmas afternoon to visit with your family? I'd like to see everyone."

"Sure, Bud. Junior and Jay would love to see you. You won't believe how much Mary Helen has grown."

"I'll see you then."

"Merry Christmas," Maggie called as they went out the door.

* * *

Maggie never knew for sure whether or not Mary Ann had spent the night with Ken Matthews and used her friends as an alibi. But the first day back at school after Christmas vacation, as Maggie worked in the office, Mr. Collins came in and asked to meet with the principal. Maggie could hear their muffled voices through the closed door and marveled that Mr. Collins seemed calm enough to keep his voice low.

When they came into the outer office, Mr. Adkins thanked Mr. Collins for coming in. "I'll certainly keep you informed as our investigation moves forward. I understand your concern." He held out his hand.

Mr. Collins gripped the offered hand. "Thank you, Mr. Adkins." Then, holding his hat with both hands, he turned to Maggie. "How're you doing, Maggie? We haven't seen much of you lately."

"I'm fine, Mr. Collins. It's good to see you. Tell Mrs. Collins hello for me. Maybe I'll see you at church next Sunday."

"Probably so." Mr. Collins put on his hat as he walked out.

Mr. Adkins turned back toward his office mumbling to himself.

Maggie watched curiously during the next several days as teachers came and went from Mr. Adkins' office. Eddie, who always seemed to know what was going on, said the principal wanted to find out what the teachers knew about Mr. Matthews' classroom procedures and his supposed involvement with Mary Ann.

The semester would be over by the end of the week. Maggie had final exams in most of her classes. On Thursday morning, she got to school early and went to the library to study her notes for the English exam. After a few minutes, Eddie sat down in the seat beside her.

"Hey, what you doing? Cramming for English?"

Maggie smiled at him. He was a sweet guy, and she could not resent him too much for interrupting her study. "You guessed it! Are you ready?"

"As ready as I'll ever be. English and I don't go together very well. I'll be satisfied if I come out with a C for the semester."

"I hope you do better than that."

"Thanks, Maggie. Say, didn't I see you riding around with Bud Summers on Christmas Day? Are you two still seeing each other?"

"No, Eddie. We're just friends. Actually, he told me he has decided to ask his girlfriend to marry him."

"Oh." Eddie thumbed the pages of his English text. "Uh...Maggie? Are you okay with that?"

Maggie gave one of her famous sighs. "I guess so, Eddie. I can't do anything about it, so I may as well be okay."

"You cared about him a lot, I guess."

"Yes, Eddie, I did. But it's obvious that we're going in different directions, so it wouldn't have worked. I hope he'll be happy with Donna. She seems like a very nice person."

The five-minute bell rang. They stood, gathered their notebooks and materials, and shoved their chairs to the table. Eddie touched Maggie's shoulder. "Maggie, it may be too soon to ask, but would you be my date for the Junior-Senior Banquet?"

"Sure, Eddie. I'd be delighted to go with you."

* * *

The students in the world history class learned when they came to class on the first day of the second semester that Mr. Adkins would be their new teacher. The girls' basketball team showed up for practice to find that Miss Fisher, the physical education teacher, was their new coach. And Mr. Beasley, the science teacher, finished out the season as the boys' basketball coach. Obviously, Mr. Matthews had disappeared, but no one made an official explanation. Someone asked Mary Ann what had happened and she snapped, "How should I know?"

The week after Easter, Miss Erickson asked Maggie to stop by her office after school. When Maggie came into the room, She noticed a distinguished-looking man sitting at Miss Erickson's desk. The gentleman, dressed in a dark grey suit, stood when Miss Erickson took Maggie's arm and led her toward him.

"Maggie, I'd like you to meet Edward Erickson, my favorite uncle. Uncle Ed, this is the student I have been telling you about, Maggie Martin."

Mr. Erickson held out his hand. "I'm pleased to meet you, Maggie.

Maggie shook his hand. "It's my pleasure, sir."

Miss Erickson drew up a couple of student desks and motioned for Maggie to sit in one while she took the other. "Maggie, Uncle Ed is a partner in a large law firm in Cincinnati. He wants to talk with you about coming to work for him after you graduate."

Maggie froze. *Cincinnati. That's so far away. How would I get there? Where would I stay? I don't know anybody there.* She could think of nothing to say, so she smiled weakly and nodded.

"I know this is a surprise for you, Maggie, but I've been talking to Uncle Ed about you for a couple of years, hoping he could find a place for you in his firm. He had to go to Knoxville for a conference and thought this was a good time to meet you. You don't have to agree to anything today. He just wants to get to know you a little and give you some time to be thinking about his offer."

"That's right, Maggie." Mr. Erickson smoothed back his hair. "Diane has bragged about her star pupil for years. I was willing to hire you sight unseen, but since I was making this trip, I thought stopping here would not only give me a chance to actually meet you, but I'd get to visit with my favorite niece as well." He smiled at Miss Erickson.

After a moment of awkward silence, Maggie realized they were waiting for a response from her. "This is such a surprise, I don't know what to say. I wouldn't have been able to do so well except for Miss Erickson. She has given me so much extra help and encouragement." Maggie turned toward Miss Erickson. "Thank you so much."

Miss Erickson patted Maggie's arm. "I know you probably have a thousand questions, such as housing, transportation, learning to get around in a big city, to name a few. But don't worry about any of that. I'll go with you to Cincinnati, help you find a place to stay, and get you situated. You probably want to talk this over with your family, too."

Maggie sighed, dreading that ordeal. "Yes, of course."

Mr. Erickson began asking her questions about school, her family, her work at the café, and soon they chatted comfortably. Finally, after nearly an hour, Mr. Erickson looked at his watch and turned to his niece. "Diane, I hate to end this pleasant interview, but we must be on our way if we're going to get that steak dinner tonight."

"You're right." Miss Erickson stood up. "Maggie, thanks for stopping by. You don't need to give us an answer today. We can talk some more next week. If you want me to, I'll talk with your parents. I think this would be a perfect opportunity for you. I hope you will decide to accept."

"Thanks, Miss Erickson. I appreciate your making this opportunity for me." Maggie shook hands with Mr. Erickson again. "Thank you, sir, for the offer. I certainly will give it serious thought."

They gathered their belongings and all walked down the hall together. "Can we drop you off?" Mr. Erickson offered. "Looks like it might rain." When they stopped at the café, Mr. Erickson got out and held the door for her. Maggie stepped from the shiny new Cadillac like some celebrity.

* * *

A few weeks later, Miss Erickson came to visit Maggie's parents on a Sunday afternoon. Just as Maggie had predicted, Corie Mae sat straight in her chair with her lips pursed. When Miss Erickson finished her explanation of the job offer in Cincinnati, Corie Mae stood up.

"Thanks for coming, Miss. But Maggie ain't going nowhere to work for another lawyer. You know what happened to her last summer. She ain't going to have that happen again." She started to walk toward the kitchen.

Ray went to her and gently took her arm. "Now wait a minute, Corie Mae. Let's talk about this some more."

"I ain't got nothing else to say. She ain't going. That's it." But she let herself be led back to her chair. Maggie had found out on Christmas Day that her mother was expecting again. *She's always more cantankerous when she's pregnant.* As Corie Mae listened without saying anything while Miss Erickson explained how she would personally escort Maggie to Cincinnati and help her find a place to live, her nose lifted higher and her glare became more vicious. "She ain't going."

No amount of persuasion could crack her defiant objections. Maggie noticed her father had not said anything. *He's going to let me handle this battle on my own.* Finally, Maggie rose from her chair and stood about three feet in front of her mother. "Mama, I'm eighteen years old. I can make my own decision. I'd hoped you would be proud that I had worked so hard to deserve this once-in-a-lifetime opportunity. I'd like to go with your blessing, but I am going and you can't stop me."

Corie Mae stood up and raised her hand as if she would slap Maggie, but glanced at Miss Erickson and lowered her hand. "Okay, Miss Smarty, maybe I can't stop you from going, but I can tell you not to come back." She took a step closer to Maggie. "I've knowed you was going to leave ever since you got in high school and got them highfaluting ideas in your head. So just go off up there and learn them big city ways, but don't never come back here." She marched into the kitchen.

Maggie turned to her father. "Daddy, I hope you're glad I can do this." Ray stood up and put his arms around her.

"I've always been proud of you, Sunshine. I will miss you, and I'm a little worried about you being in that big city without any friends or family around. But I think you've made the right decision. I'll be glad to see you any time you can come back."

Still holding Maggie, he turned to face Miss Erickson, who had tears in her eyes. "Ma'am, I can't thank you enough for all you've done for my daughter. It makes it easier to let her go when we know you'll help her get there and get settled in. We will always be beholden to you for...for everything."

Miss Erickson took a handkerchief from her pocket and wiped her eyes. "Mr. Martin, I think you have to give yourself some credit. You've given Maggie lots of encouragement. She has so much respect for you. I think if you had objected, she might not have made this decision."

Ray gave Maggie's shoulder a squeeze and then shook hands with Miss Erickson. "Thanks for coming."

Maggie walked Miss Erickson down the steps to her car and watched as she turned around and headed back toward the highway. Sadie, who was now an old beagle, came and licked her hand. "Thanks, Sadie, I needed that."

* * *

The last weeks of the senior year went by swiftly. Maggie did not go to Washington, D.C, with the Senior Class. She had enough money in her savings account to pay for the trip, but she thought she needed to save her money to help get a place to live in Cincinnati. She enjoyed the Junior-Senior banquet. She wore the dress she had planned to wear the year before but didn't because of JD's funeral. Eddie was a real gentleman, dressed in a new suit he had bought to wear to graduation. He brought her a corsage, and they laughed as he tried to pin it to her light blue gown.

It pleased Maggie when Mary Ann's date asked Eddie if they could double with them to go to the banquet. Afterwards, they all piled into Eddie's car and drove to Oak Ridge to get dessert. As they sat at the table, Mary Ann apologized to Maggie for breaking up their friendship. "I just don't know what got into me. I lost my head. You were right to tell me I was out of line. So I'm hoping we can be friends again."

Maggie nodded. "I have missed doing stuff with you lately. Maybe next week we can get together after school for some catching up."

About three weeks before graduation, Mr. Adkins called Maggie into his office. "I'm proud to tell you that you are the Valedictorian of the class. So you need to start working on your speech."

"My speech?"

"Yes, the Valedictorian always gives an address on behalf of the class."

"Oh, my. I'll be so nervous I won't be able to say anything."

"It's not so hard. Miss Margaret will help you write it and then help you practice."

"Oh, no. Can't someone else make the speech?"

"That's your job, Maggie, and I know you will do it well. Why don't you go talk with Miss Margaret now?"

For the next two weeks, Maggie spent every free minute working on the speech. She rewrote it many times. Each time she would take it to Miss Margaret, who would make some suggestions, and Maggie would go back to the typing room to revise it again. Finally, Miss Margaret announced, "It's perfect!"

The next Sunday when the family gathered for dinner at Grandma Campbell's table, Maggie announced that she was giving the graduation speech. "I want all of you to be there—Grandma, Grandpa, and all my family." Maggie looked around the table at her parents, her brothers and sisters, and her aunts.

"Why, congratulations, Maggie." Aunt Lillian began clapping her hands and everyone else joined in, except Corie Mae. "Hooray for Maggie!"

"Graduation is May 22 at seven o'clock in the school gym. That's Thursday of next week. Reverend and Mrs. Lewis have offered to give rides so all of you can go." Maggie looked pointedly at her mother who immediately shifted her eyes and began clearing the dirty dishes from the table. "I need all of you to be there so I won't be so scared."

Grandma walked around the table and stood behind Maggie. She gave her a kiss on the cheek. "You're the first one in our family to graduate from high school, Maggie. We're all very proud, and you can count on us being there."

Corie Mae picked up a stack of plates. "I ain't going." She turned her back and marched into the kitchen. Maggie hung her head.

Aunt Lillian picked up a stack of plates and followed Corie Mae into the kitchen. Maggie could hear them arguing. "You should be proud of her. Why don't you go?"

"Maggie ain't interested in what I think She don't care nothing about this family. If she did she'd not be aiming to leave as soon as school's out."

"Maggie has told me how much she wishes you would come. I know it would please her so much if you would change your mind."

"I ain't going. So just stop talking about It."

Dear Bud,

I need a friend. Will you come to Graduation on May 22. I'm giving the Valedictorian speech. Need your moral support.

Maggie

On the last day of classes, Betty Lou, who was finishing her sophomore year, met Maggie in the hallway. "This package came for you yesterday. It's from Bud. I thought you'd want to have it right away." She handed Maggie a small package. "Hurry. Open it. I want to see what it is."

While Maggie read the note, Betty Lou opened the jeweler's box. "Oh my gosh! It's a gold watch! Just look at it." She put it on and held her arm up in front of her eyes. "Oooh I like it."

"Okay, sister, give it up. Let me see it." While Maggie admired the watch, Betty Lou grabbed the note and read. "Oh, wow! He says he will come to your graduation. Do you think he's broke up with that girl?"

"No, Silly, he is coming as a good friend."

Betty Lou grabbed Maggie's arm and admired the watch some more. "I wish I had a good friend like that."

"If you do, you will be a lucky girl." The bell rang and the girls hurried off in opposite directions.

The big night finally arrived. Maggie sat on the platform with the various dignitaries and participants staring out into the filled-to-capacity gym. Her blue graduation gown covered her new yellow dotted Swiss dress. She wore nylon stockings and the first pair of high heels she had ever owned.

The crowd had filled all the chairs on the gym floor and many people sat in the bleachers. Maggie searched the crowd hoping to find her family. Finally, she saw her Grandpa Campbell about halfway back. Grandma sat beside him and the rest of the family sat in the row behind them. Hoping against hope that Corie Mae had changed her mind at the last minute, Maggie squinted against the bright lights and looked carefully, but she was not there. *I know Bud is here somewhere*, but she could not find him in the crowd either.

The band played a couple of numbers and three of the classmates sang a song. Mr. Deerman, the school superintendent, made a few remarks, and finally Mr. Adkins introduced her. She rose to walk to the podium and was startled by the roar of applause. Her classmates all stood cheering for her. *I simply cannot start crying.*

Her knees felt weak and her voice came out in a little squeak. She had to clear her throat and start over again. "Mr. Deerman, Mr. Adkins, members of the faculty, graduating seniors, families of the graduates and friends." Fortunately, she had memorized the speech, because her tear-filled eyes could not read the words. She swallowed. "Thank you for coming tonight to honor us as we finish this important phase of our growing up. We give special thanks to our parents, family members and friends who have supported us, encouraged us, and without whose help we would not be here." Maggie looked up from her script, but caught her breath in a sob when she remembered her mother had not come.

She looked down at her script, but couldn't find her place, and she couldn't remember what came next. On the verge of panic, she happened to look toward the bleachers on her right and suddenly her eyes focused on Bud. *He's here!* She swallowed again and gave her head a little shake, which caused her mortar board to slide down over her eyes. Her classmates began to laugh and applaud. Instantly, her panic passed. She straightened her hat, stood straighter, and resumed her remarks.

The rest of the evening passed in a blur. Somehow she had marched across the stage to shake hands with Mr. Deerman and receive her diploma. When the graduates marched out for the recessional, Bud waited for her at the back of the gym.

"Ah, Maggie. What an excellent speech. I'm proud of you." He gave her a hug. "I thought you were about to lose it for a minute, but you handled it like a pro."

"Thanks, Bud. Thank you for coming. I'll never forget what a great friend you are." She held up her left arm so the sleeve of her gown fell back to reveal her watch. "Thanks for the gift. I will treasure it always." Her voice choked up, but the tears didn't overflow.

"I hope every time you check the time you'll think of old Bud, your best friend forever."

Bud walked with her to turn in her graduation garb. Maggie exchanged lots of hugs and best wished with classmates–even shed a few tears. Then they met Maggie's family in the parking lot.

Junior, dressed in a new white shirt, grabbed Bud's hand. "Hi, Bud. I didn't know you'd be here." Maggie noticed that all the boys had on new white shirts. *Mama must care a little bit if she made sure the boys had new shirts.*

Bud shook hands with Grandpa and Ray and greeted all the family members. "It's good to see all of you. Didn't Maggie do a great job?"

Reverend and Mrs. Lewis came and added their congratulations and the family began getting into the various cars to go home. Bud held Maggie's hand and walked over to the truck where Ray helped the children load up. "Mr. Martin, if it's okay with you, I'll bring Maggie home."

"That's fine. Just take good care of her. She's the first graduate in this family, and we don't want nothing to happen to her!" Ray winked at Maggie and she saw that twinkle in his eyes.

* * *

Maggie spent the next few days moving all her clothes and odds and ends from Aunt Lillian's apartment, sorting through all her belongings, deciding what to give to her sisters and what to take with her. Aunt Opal came over on Sunday afternoon with two large boxes. Uncle Thomas had sent money and told her exactly what to buy for Maggie's graduation present. The younger children crowded around and exclaimed when Maggie opened the boxes to reveal two pieces of matching luggage.

"Thank you, Aunt Opal." Maggie gave her a hug. "I thought I would take my clothes to Cincinnati in boxes. Now I can go in style. We'll leave early Wednesday morning. I hope everyone will come to see me off." Corie Mae watched from the kitchen door, but said nothing.

The day arrived. Miss Erickson drove up in her Chevrolet with Miss Margaret. "I thought we'd like some company on the trip." They loaded Maggie's bags into the trunk. All the family gathered around. Maggie hugged each of her brothers and sisters. She hugged Ray, who held her for a long moment. "I love you, Sunshine. Don't stay away too long."

Maggie looked around. "Where's Mama? Isn't she even going to tell me goodbye?"

"Nah, she's hoeing in the garden," Stuart said as he handed Maggie a little wooden whistle he had made. "If you get lonesome, play this and think about us."

After saying goodbye to Grandma and Grandpa, Aunt Opal and Kenny, Maggie finally opened the door to the back seat. "Well, I guess it's time to go." Maggie turned in the seat so she could see out the back window as they pulled away. Tears rolled down her face. She watched as her family stood in the middle of the road waving. In the instant before the trees hid the house, Maggie saw her mother standing on the front porch, fanning herself with her straw hat. *It almost looks like she's waving.*

Maggie wiped the tears from her eyes and slid down into the seat facing forward. She reached into her pocket and withdrew the heart-shaped necklace. The early morning sun, peeping through the trees, momentarily touched the stones, flashing a bright reflection throughout the car.

ABOUT THE AUTHOR

Mary Jane Salyers grew up in East Tennessee during the 1940s and 1950s, the period covered by this novel. She taught in secondary schools and colleges during her teaching career. She has three daughters, and now lives in North Carolina with her husband Bill Salyers.

You can visit her web page at
http://wwwmjsalyers.wordpress.com/

Made in the USA
Monee, IL
27 November 2020